A Classic
Christmas Crime

EDITED BY
TIM HEALD

BERKLEY PRIME CRIME, NEW YORK

A CLASSIC CHRISTMAS CRIME

A Berkley Prime Crime Book / published by arrangement with
Pavilion Books Limited
26 Upper Ground, London SE1 9PD

PRINTING HISTORY
Pavilion Books hardcover edition / 1995
Berkley Prime Crime hardcover edition / November 1998
Berkley Prime Crime mass-market edition / October 1999

The Penguin Putnam Inc. World Wide Web site address is
http://www.penguinputnam.com

ISBN: 0-425-17151-5

Berkley Prime Crime Books are published
by The Berkley Publishing Group,
a division of Penguin Putnam Inc.,
375 Hudson Street, New York, New York 10014.
The name BERKLEY PRIME CRIME and the BERKLEY PRIME CRIME
design are trademarks belonging to Penguin Putnam Inc.

PRINTED IN THE UNITED STATES OF AMERICA

10 9 8 7 6 5 4 3 2 1

Acknowledgments

————— ◆ —————

Mugs © Margaret Yorke 1995
And Broke His Crown © David Williams 1995
Bearing Gifts © Nicole Swengley 1995
Season of Goodwill © Mike Seabrook 1995
More than Flesh & Blood © Susan Moody 1995
The Proof of the Pudding © Peter Lovesey 1995
Charades, Anybody? © H. R. F. Keating
The Mistletoe Murder © P. D. James
Operation Christmas © Tim Heald 1995
A Card or a Kitten © Liza Cody 1995
Political Corrections © Simon Brett 1995
Boxing Unclever © Robert Barnard 1995
Gold, Frankincense and Murder © Catherine Aird 1995

Contents

— ◆ —

Introduction

◆

The first "Classic" Crime anthology celebrated Agatha Christie's centenary. Because Christie was so quintessentially English the book was entitled *A Classic English Crime* and the authors were all drawn from the ranks of the British Crime Writers Association of which Agatha herself was once an enthusiatic member. For that first volume I simply asked writers to give me a murder set in the classic cosy English "Golden Age" between the two World Wars. Otherwise I was open-minded. "Butlers," I advised my contributors, "libraries and small Belgian detectives will be left to the discretion of the writers."

The book worked. In fact it worked so well that I was reluctant to attempt a sequel. Imitations may be a sincere form of flattery but they can go off at half-cock. It seemed a pity to risk failure after success. However "Christmas" was as inviting as "Christie" and most of my team were keen to have another go. Christmas suggested rural manors cut off in blizzards and full of houseguests and servants with all too plausible motives for doing one another in. It was also far—in reality—from the season of goodwill. In fact, it is at Christmas that many of us are at our most lethal. Family feeling can turn sour, fuelled by all that food and drink and unwonted togetherness. So this is a celebration of an unseasonable lack of the traditional Christmas spirit.

Three of my original contributors do not appear in this second Classic. Julian Symons, one of the finest British crime writers and a leading authority on the genre, died, sadly, before I could ask him. Two others, Paula Gosling and Celia Dale, were unable to accept but the rest of the cast agreed to take a second bow. All are members of the British Crime Writers Association and well established upholders of a tradition of which their country is justifiably proud. Our numbers have been augmented by three new additions to the team. P. D. James is hardly a ''newcomer'' in any other sense for she has inherited the mantle of Dame Agatha herself, as the best known British crime writer of her times. Mike Seabrook and Nicole Swengley, though both experienced professional writers, are tyros when it comes to fictional crime though Mike was no stranger to it in real life. He trained as a lawyer and was a London policeman before becoming a full time writer. Tragically, since writing this debut tale, he died just a few days short of his forty-eighth birthday.

Anthologies such as this are inevitably hybrids if not curate's eggs. All that this one has in common is that every story celebrates crime at Christmas. They take place in Florida and India as well as the classic English village. Murders are committed in hospital and prison as well as around the homely hearth. Some of the tales are light, almost facetious; others are bleak, bordering on the disturbing. Taken together they represent a novel approach to Christmas. I like to think that at least they will save thousands of Boxing Days from the sated anti-climax and murderous indigestion prompted by the over-indulgence of the day before.

Read and rejoice!

Tim Heald

Mugs

— ◆ —

MARGARET YORKE

He was such a nice young man.

Mildred Cox had been instructed by Tricia, her daughter, never to let anyone she didn't know into her house, but Mr. Bryan—Nick, as later he asked her to call him—was different. He wasn't "anyone." For one thing, he wore a suit, a dark grey one like her son-in-law wore to the office. His tie was prettily floral—so modern, just like those of some newscasters on television and not at all gaudy.

She didn't tell Tricia about Nick's visits, not even when Tricia noticed the small green Worcester bowl had gone from the top of the tallboy, nor that she no longer used her Georgian teaspoons which had been a wedding present.

The first time he came, she thought he must be someone she ought to recognize—a childhood friend of her son's, perhaps, or someone who'd been with him on his last trek from which he never returned. She'd welcomed him in that spirit, sitting him down with a cup of tea, hoping a clue to his identity would be revealed without her asking. They'd discussed the weather, which was not very good that day, raw and windy, and he'd said how nice it was to see a real coal fire. She'd asked where he'd come from and he mentioned Brighton. That was a long way. It must have taken him several hours, she'd remarked.

"Only two," he'd said, smiling. He had a charming smile. "The M25, you know."

She'd not been on it herself, but she knew about it. Choked with traffic it was, every day. You saw that on television.

"You must be tired, then," she'd said.

He said he was glad of the tea. Two sugars, he took. She used her good Crown Derby cups and saucers, and he admired them.

"You don't often see such fine porcelain being used these days," he said.

"No," she agreed. "It's all mugs, isn't it? But I like to get my better things out now and then."

"I expect you've got a lot of china you've had a long time," he suggested, and as soon as he had finished his tea she was showing him her Coalport plates and an engraved spoon that was even older than her teaspoons. He said it might be worth quite a bit. "Even a tenner," he said, handing it back. "I know someone who might like it—a friend of mine's just had a daughter and I'm her godfather. It would make a perfect christening present." He picked it up again and turned it over, his admiration obvious.

"Take it," said Mildred, and if he was a friend of Jack's he could have it for nothing.

But he disclaimed Jack. He'd found it didn't do to pretend acquaintance unless you were sure of your facts, and he didn't know who Jack was.

"I do a bit of collecting myself," he confided. "It's my hobby. Sometimes I buy in things I like and sell them onto other collectors, so that I can build up my own special interest—that's porcelain," he explained. "But I can place anything good."

"What a nice hobby," said Mildred, and poured him out more tea.

By the time he left she had sold him the Worcester bowl

and two Staffordshire plates, as well as the spoon, and had received £35 which she put in a Toby jug on the dresser. He'd admired that, too; it bore the face of Sir Winston Churchill, and he said people built up collections, acquiring as many varieties as they could. She'd use the money for something special.

He left, promising to come back if he was in the area again, and he did, several times.

Mildred never discovered exactly what brought him to the locality, since he hadn't come specifically to visit her. She still felt he must somehow be connected with Jack. Maybe he'd tell her eventually.

In December she went to town on the bus. It was a pleasant ride—twenty minutes if the traffic was not too bad. She stepped aboard behind a young man in his early twenties— a nice-looking fellow with well cut fair hair, spotless jeans and a fresh face. He had only a £20 note for his fare and the driver hadn't got enough change. How lucky he was to have plenty of ready cash, thought Mildred.

"How much is your fare?" she asked, and was told it was £1.60.

"I'll pay," she said, smiling. If she had a grandson—if Jack had had a son—he might be like this young man.

"I travel free," she added, showing the driver her pass.

"Are you sure?" The young man was astonished. "It's very good of you. Thanks."

"It's your lucky day," she said.

"It certainly is," he replied. He couldn't believe it.

"You'll do the same for someone else one day, won't you?" she said, and he nodded.

"Yes—yes, I will," he agreed, and repeated, "Thanks," then swiftly ran up the stairs to the upper floor of the bus.

Mildred sat near the front, watching the road. What a delightful young man. They weren't all yobbos and louts or car thieves and drug addicts. Of course, in terms of charity there were many more deserving cases, but it lay in his power to aid one of them and she hoped he would.

She had come into town to do her Christmas shopping. She had a list with Tricia's name at the top, followed by that of Susie, Tricia's daughter. There were other gifts to buy: presents for friends at the day centre where Mildred, though seventy-nine, was a helper, and the kind librarian who always mentioned it when the latest Maeve Binchey or Rosamund Pilcher was on the returns trolley. They were such good writers, Mildred thought, with characters you would like to meet, unlike those in some of the other novels she had tried. Tricia was easy: a new book about birds, for she was a keen bird-watcher, never happier than when out with binoculars on some bleak hill. Mildred had once given her a beautiful silk blouse in a shade of peacock blue, which would set off her glowing auburn hair and pink-and-white skin, but Tricia seldom wore it; she went to few dressy occasions, preferring to be in tracksuit and trainers. Tricia worked for a building society where, by day, she wore their uniform; personal clothes didn't interest her. Mildred always gave Gerry, her son-in-law, a bottle of whiskey; it was an annual joke as he opened it on Christmas Day and poured her the first tot. Mildred always stayed with them for Christmas, just overnight; they lived only ten miles away.

The problem present was Susie's. When she was younger it hadn't been difficult, and even recently she'd wanted tapes for her stereo. She wore it plugged into her ears as she cycled to work in the mornings—a dangerous habit, her father said, as she couldn't then hear traffic coming up from behind. Susie said that, in the rush hour, she knew it was there anyway. Mildred wished she had a car. Perhaps, when Nick came again, she could discuss with him the possibility of raising enough money to buy her one. It needn't be new, after all. Nick might even know of a reliable one that was for sale.

Thinking of Susie, Mildred sighed. She had fond parents and a secure home, and a job with prospects in the council offices where she spent her days before a computer. When she had reached five foot, Susie stopped growing upwards but continued to expand sideways, despite Tricia's efforts to feed her on salads and fruit. She got hungry riding her bike; and no one could say she lacked exercise. Chocolates and cake were what she most enjoyed eating.

Susie sometimes came over on her own to see Mildred, and even occasionally stayed the night. In summer she cycled the distance but usually she travelled on the bus, and, rarely, borrowed her mother's car. She was always cheerful and would tell her grandmother stories about life at work, making it sound so amusing. Once, for several months, she had had a boyfriend called Jason, and in those weeks she bloomed, even losing half a stone. She brought him to meet Mildred, who did not warm to him because he addressed her as "dear" and made no attempt to help clear away the meal she provided. She felt patronized, and she hadn't cared for the pointed manner in which he squeezed past Susie when moving around, exaggerating her bulk. If she wasn't so short, she wouldn't seem so stout.

Mildred was pleased when the romance was over, though Tricia was upset.

"He seemed so nice," she said. "She's had no other boyfriends since Colin in Year Seven at school."

"You can't have wanted her to marry him," Mildred said. "He wasn't a kind man, Tricia."

"What other chance will she get?" Tricia asked. "She loves children."

"She might go far in local government," Mildred declared. "I'm sure she's good at her job."

"Oh yes," Tricia said. "She's bright and conscientious. I'm sure she is." But she looked like a joke, her mother thought. The hair that in Tricia was richly auburn was, in Susie, vivid red, so that she had been called "Ginger" and "Carrots" as a child—and might still be, at work, for all Tricia knew. At college she had dyed it black in an effort to avert the teasing she attracted, but that ended when she joined the dramatic society and was given a comic role for which her red hair was an asset. She survived there by being a bit of a card, playing up the humour, most of it at her own expense, and because she was such a kind girl. She became an excellent cook, which earned her popularity. Mildred thought that perhaps she ought to have gone into catering, but she hadn't seemed drawn to the prospect.

Maybe she was simply too small to lift heavy pots and pans around.

She should wear blue, Mildred thought: a misty blue sweater with a mauve tinge in that soft shaded wool you saw. That would be as becoming to her as the silk blouse was to her mother. It would have to be large, even very large. Mildred herself was still a neat size twelve and bought bargains in the sales, much envied by her daughter who was almost Junoesque.

Mildred went round the shops until she grew quite tired. She found the bird book. She'd get the whiskey from the local pub, to save carrying it far. She bought soap and bath oil and a small purse, and other such things for the day centre people, and a scarf for the librarian. Then she went home. She'd got wrapping paper, too; she could get ahead with her preparations.

On the bus, tired but content, she wondered how the young man whose ticket she had paid for had spent the day. Where had he been going? Had things worked out well for him?

At home, she put on the kettle and eased her feet into comfortable slippers, a thing she never did during the day. That would betray her standards. Only when, once, she had a sprained ankle had she stooped so low. You mustn't let things slide, Mildred always said; if you did, it was difficult to retrieve them.

She picked up the paper and glanced at the crossword, which she did each day, annoyed when she couldn't finish it. Later, she turned on the television for the news, and was watching it when the doorbell rang.

It was Susie. She'd come in her mother's car, and had brought a lasagne from the supermarket, apologizing because she had not had time to make it herself, a bottle of red wine, and a chocolate gâteau. She had come to supper.

Mildred roused herself, kissed Susie warmly and bustled her into the warm sitting room.

Susie was full of the news that, in an office raffle, she had won two tickets to the mayor's Christmas Ball which was held in aid of a charity.

"It's amazing," she said. "It's not like the office party. Much grander." She hated the annual office party, at which the men all seemed to think she was fair game, desired by none and therefore deprived and panting for sex.

She had learned how to walk away, spending time in the ladies' cloakroom. She had endured crude fumblings and lewd suggestive comments, and had been pressed against the wall by sweating heavy drunken men, most of them married. They should have been ashamed of themselves, she thought, but did not say, because she had to work with them later. It never occurred to her that, in the light of their morning's hangover, some of them were.

But now, though excited, she was also despairing.

"Who can I ask to come with me?" she exclaimed. "And what shall I wear?"

Mildred thought immediately of Nick. He was a bit old for her, perhaps, but he was so charming. If he came to see her soon, she might lead the conversation round to ask if he was married—he probably was—and, if he was not, to sound him out as a possibility.

"I'll give you your dress," she said. "It can be your Christmas present."

"Oh no, Gran, I couldn't let you," said Susie. "I'll hire one. After all, I'll never need it again."

What a pity, thought Mildred, but it might be true. Anyway, fashions changed.

"Well, I'll pay for the hire, then," she said, adding, "I had a little windfall the other day, and there's more to come."

"Did you? Have you been backing the horses, Gran?" Susie asked, laughing. When she was happy she was so pretty, Mildred thought.

"Not that," Mildred said. "Let's just say luck went my way. Perhaps you're right to hire. Choose something good, though. Something to set off your hair." Blue, she thought, but I won't suggest it. She knows I think blue suits her.

"I will," said Susie. "Now, let's fix our lasagne, and then you can tell me what you've been up to lately."

• • •

At the office, Susie's win was envied by her colleagues, who thought any one of them was more deserving and better equipped to appreciate the prize. She was mysterious about her partner, saying they would see who it was on the night, but in reality, Susie was desperate. There was no one she could possibly ask. She could give the tickets to someone else. Perhaps that would be the best solution. She could even raffle them again, in aid of some good cause. But that would mean admitting defeat. She felt like Cinderella in reverse, invited to the ball but without a prince.

She could go to an escort agency. They worked for women, not just men; she'd seen their advertisements when she was reading the lonely hearts columns in the local paper, feeling tempted to answer one. Perhaps she should advertise herself. No one except her partner would know.

How was she to solve the problem?

Two days later, Nick returned to Mildred's house.

On his last visit—he'd been three times now, on each occasion buying a pot or bowl or a piece of glass—he'd admired a bureau she had, walnut, once her father's. He'd offered her £250 for it, but she had said she didn't want to sell it.

"It's too big for most modern houses," Nick pointed out. "I'd be doing you a favour, really. You don't need it, do you? And your daughter won't have room for it."

That was true, and £250 would come in very useful for Susie—help her toward a holiday, or the car she was saving up for.

"Are you married?" Mildred asked him.

"No." Nick was startled at the inconsequence of her question.

"Are you busy on December the ninth?" she asked. "It's a Friday."

"Why do you ask?" What could she be leading up to?

"It's my granddaughter," said Mildred. "She's going to the mayor's ball, and her partner's—er—in hospital with a broken leg. She won the tickets, you see." Once launched on her specious explanation, Mildred rattled on, embarrassed. "Would you escort her? I know you can be trusted."

Nick had noticed the bureau on his first visit. His whole aim had been to nurse his victim to the yielding point, to soften her with attention. It was worth a cool fifteen K at least, he knew, and he could place it: a genuine gem, unappreciated because it had been in its owner's possession so long. It was in perfect condition, as far as he could tell. By now he knew about Mildred's daughter Tricia, and her son Jack who had been killed on a scientific expedition in South America. He'd heard of Susie, too. Now he was being offered a deal: take Susie to the ball and get the bureau. Well, what had he to lose? Only an evening. He might even be able to remove the bureau first and then stand the girl up.

But that idea didn't work. The old girl forestalled him.

"You could take the bureau away after you bring Susie back from the ball," she said. "She can stay here that night." Then she'd see Susie in her lovely dress.

Nick agreed to it all. He agreed, too, to meet Susie before then; her grandmother would ask her round to supper. He deplored the waste of time, but if he got the bureau, that would compensate.

He'd done well in this area. He'd picked up a lot of nice bits of porcelain, and some silver, and he'd tipped a mate off who wanted paintings. He came back as planned, some days later, and met Susie.

Could he possibly go through with it? Nick, who spoke the truth when he said he wasn't married, had a girlfriend who helped him in his knocking business; sometimes she went with him. She did the books, such as they were, and minded the shop where he put out stuff for sale.

Nick's girlfriend was twenty-nine, five feet eight inches tall, and very slim. She had black hair permed into wiry ringlets, and wore very short skirts. Her fingernails were long and red; her lips were full. She was experienced, and looked it. Susie was her complete opposite, even down to bitten fingernails.

He used his charm, however.

"I'm so fond of your grandmother," he said.

Susie wondered how they'd met, but neither of them told her. Mildred was not going to confess to any of her sales.

Nick arranged to fetch her on the evening of the ball. He'd come to her grandmother's at eight o'clock. He couldn't stay now, he said.

"Must dash," he declared, remembering to smile at both of them, meanwhile busy scheming. He'd had an idea.

He couldn't get the bureau out of the house unaided; it was much too big and heavy. He'd take Susie to the ball, pretend he was going to the cloakroom and abandon her. She'd simply be bewildered, and he'd be back again before she became suspicious. Meanwhile, he'd have nicked the bureau, tying the old girl up if necessary, but she might already be asleep—old folk notoriously went to bed early. It'd be easy. Jimmy Fox would help him, for a consideration; he'd helped Jimmy out before now, on similar jobs. He'd use his car and Jimmy could bring the van. He'd tell the old woman he'd collect the bureau on Sunday. It'd be like robbing a baby.

Most of the time, Nick did straightforward knocking, calling at houses and picking up good pieces for trifling sums from unsuspecting pensioners. Many old people had something worth a good few pounds more than he offered them and now and then he came upon a real find, like Mildred's desk, and her mugs: she had a full run of coronation and other celebratory mugs ranging from George VI's coronation to the marriage of the Prince of Wales. They were to be another prize, he'd decided. He knew where they were; he'd take them when he took the bureau. And he'd take the Toby jugs. She had others, besides Winston Churchill.

Susie was delighted by Nick, but also frightened. He was a good deal older than she was, and seemed quite a man of the world. She'd given him her telephone number at work; he already had her grandmother's. He'd ring her before the ball, he said, to make a final plan.

Dinner was not included in the ticket deal. People made

their own plans to eat, some having dinner parties, others
dining out, but Susie, who had never been to such a smart
event, did not know that. She'd told Nick that dress was
formal; that meant a dinner-suit, she said. She'd heard some
people in the office mention hiring them.

Nick said he'd got one. It was true.

Friday the ninth arrived, and in the morning Susie received a telephone call. It was Nick. He said he was going
to be delayed and could not arrive in time to fetch her from
her grandmother's. He would meet her at the Town Hall.
She could wait for him in the foyer, or, if she went in to
the reception, she could leave his ticket with the doorman.

Susie's heart sank. She'd imagined making quite an entrance on his arm.

"That's all right," she said, however. "Don't worry."

She rang her grandmother to tell her of the change of
plan. She'd go home to change, she said.

"So I won't see your lovely dress," said Mildred.

"You will when Nick brings me back," said Susie. But
then she had a thought. "Perhaps I'd better get him to take
me home," she said. "I don't want to wake you up, and
it's nearer."

In the end, her grandmother agreed. It made sense, and
Susie's parents would be at the house; they'd know when
she had been delivered safely, after, Mildred hoped, a
lovely evening.

"I'll come and tell you all about it tomorrow," Susie
promised. "I'll take the dress back after I've shown it to
you."

She'd not been sure about it, as it wasn't blue, but the
girl in the shop had talked her into it, saying it and her hair
made a striking combination.

The other women in the department had heard the conversation Susie had with Nick, and one of them felt sorry
for her. Several of them were also going to the ball, not by
luck but because it was a good annual event, and beforehand a group of them—three couples—were joining more
from the office for a Christmas dinner at The Anchor Hotel.
Those going to the ball would go on to the Town Hall, while

the rest made a night of it. Susie, naturally enough, had not been included in these plans, but now her department head suggested she should join them all for dinner.

"Pity about your date," she said. "Still, we'll meet him later." They were intrigued by the mystery man who was going to be her partner. She'd told them nothing about him except to say that he was very good-looking, and about six feet tall.

Susie, rescued, accepted. She'd pay her way, she said, and that was agreed. It would be all right because she had Nick to look forward to.

There were a few grumbles about this plan when Susie went off to the washroom, but on the whole people felt magnanimous about her; after all, it was Christmas and her man had been held up. It could happen to anyone.

"I suppose he does exist," said Margery, and was shushed as Susie returned.

They were to meet at The Anchor, a stone's throw from the Town Hall.

Susie took hours to get ready, bathing, doing what she could about her bitten nails, rubbing cream on her hands. Her newly washed hair stood out around her head in a ginger cloud, and she stepped into her dress, somehow managing to zip it up the back. Her parents had gone out to a different Christmas celebration, so there was no one to help her or to admire her in her finery.

Her dress had such a bouffant skirt that she could not wear a coat over it; she dug out the old cape her mother had had years ago when they were fashionable. Then she was ready. She rang for a taxi and waited till it came; it took only five minutes to drive to The Anchor.

Susie left her cape in the cloakroom. Then she made her way into the bar, where she had been told to meet the others in her party. Afraid of being early, she was, in fact, one of the last arrivals. Without meaning to, she seemed to make an entrance as she hesitated, shyly, in the doorway, looking round for them. She seldom entered bars alone; even as a student, she had not done so, and this one, bedecked with Christmas decorations, was crowded.

Her group was in a corner, and they looked up as she approached. Then, without exception, they all broke into near hysterical laughter, for Susie's dress was the exact shade of her hair. Its satin bodice molded her plump breasts and revealed pale skin above; its skirt, made of many-layered net, billowed out around her like an overgrown tutu, as one witness later said, describing it, as a ballroom dancing costume.

"Susie dear, you look just like an orange," someone said, and so she did, except for her face, which had been flushed with eagerness but now turned pale.

It took her a few moments to realize that they were all laughing at her, that she looked a sight. She'd been doubtful in the cloakroom, but had reassured herself as she remembered the encouragement of the dress agency assistant.

Susie never learned that one girl in the office, jealous of the promotion Susie had recently gained, and knowing she planned to hire a dress, had gone along to the shop and chosen this one, promising the assistant ten pounds if she succeeded in getting Susie to select it.

Now she caught a glimpse of herself in the sheet looking-glass behind the bar. All she saw was garish colour. There had been a green dress that fitted her, very plain, cut straight and loose enough to hide her bulges. She had liked it, really wanted it, but been dissuaded. Wrong! Tears filled her eyes and she turned and fled, not even pausing to collect her cape.

She rushed into the road, saw a bus, and leapt on it, still in her gaudy dress, the tears pouring down her face. The driver gazed at her, expectant, quite unmoved by her grief and by her raiment.

"Where to?" he asked, but she was diving past him to the nearest seat.

"Finchbury," she gulped.

A young man got on behind her.

"I'll pay for her," he said. "Two, please."

He paid, accepting change and tickets, then removed his coat, a padded anorak, quite large, for he was a tall young man. "Put this on," he told her, and he bundled her into it, holding her small gold handbag while he made her insert her arms. "Now, where are you going?" he asked.

"To my gran's," she said, beginning to calm down.

He tried again.

"Where were you going?"

"To the mayor's ball. My dress is ridiculous," she said.

"Your hair's gorgeous," he told her. "Try not to cry."

"I ought to be going home," she said. "To change."

"Where's home?"

"Here. In Sinclair Road," she said.

"Well, we're on the way to Finchbury," he said. "Is that where your gran lives?"

"Yes."

"We'll go there, then," he said. "I'll take you."

She went on crying for a while, but at last grew quiet, blowing her nose on a small tissue which she found in her bag, along with the two tickets for the ball.

"I'm meant to meet Nick at the Town Hall," she said.

"We'll telephone," he answered, unperturbed.

When the bus stopped near Mildred's street, she said, "This is where I get off."

"Keep the coat on," he advised. "I'm coming too."

They left the bus together, and he loped down the road beside her, a tall young man in black trousers and wearing a blue sweater. In her gold slippers with their high heels, Susie was teetering along, and he seized her arm and tucked it through his.

"Where's your gran's house?" he asked.

"It's at the end of the road," she answered. "Where the big tree is."

They walked on together silently, and then, nearing the house, she slowed up, pulling her companion to a halt.

"What's wrong?" he asked.

"There's someone there. At my gran's," she said. "Oh, look! It's burglars!" and she put her hand to her mouth in a gasp of horror.

Her savior looked at her sharply.

"Are you sure?" he said, but it was obvious. A van had been reversed into the short driveway outside the house. Its doors were open, and the front door of the house was also open.

"My grandmother!" she cried.

"Stay there," he said. "No—go back a few houses and bang on the door and ask them to call the police. And stay there," he warned her.

"What are you going to do?"

"See if the keys are in the van for a start," he said. "If not, try to let down the tyres or at least take the number. No heroics," he added, and then, "Get going."

She took off her slippers and ran back up the road in her stockinged feet, turning in three doors down at her grandmother's friend Mrs. Wilson's house, where she was known.

Ten minutes later the police caught Nick and Jimmy Fox carrying the bureau—its drawers, the contents crudely tipped onto the sitting room floor, now loaded with the mug collection, carefully wrapped. Mildred had been tied up and gagged, with a pillow slip placed over her head to act as a blindfold. She was not hurt, but she was very shaken. The two robbers had worn black woollen Balaclava hoods, and she had not recognized Nick. He hadn't touched her; Jimmy Fox had done the tying up.

The story of his deal with Mildred was never revealed; greed had been his undoing, loving folly hers. He did not want to humiliate himself by confessing to the plan, and she would not betray what she had tried to do to help her granddaughter.

When she had been untied, Mildred knew her rescuer at once. And he knew her.

"You paid my bus fare," said the young man. "And today I paid Susie's. You said to do it for someone else another day."

"But why did you?" Susie asked him later, when her grandmother had gone round to spend the night with Mrs. Wilson.

"I saw what happened in the bar," he said. "I was there, waiting to meet my sister. She's the mayoress. Our mother is the mayor. Look—these are my dinner suit trousers; I was going to put my tie and jacket on later. I think you ought to tell me your side of the story while we return to the ball. You must face your friends. My sister will have a dress that you can borrow. Even if we only get there in time for the last waltz, I think you need to do it, Susie.''

"You keep saying my name. You knew it before the police asked me what it was," said Susie.

"I couldn't forget your gorgeous hair," he said. "Do you remember Colin, in Year Seven? I used to carry your recorder for you.''

Before they left Colin made some telephone calls and said his sister had an appropriate dress. They'd go to her house at once, in a taxi. When they arrived, she was waiting for them, having rushed there from the Town Hall. There was no need for Susie to be told that the flowing royal blue gown was a maternity dress, calf length on the sister, full length when worn by Susie. She and Colin danced several numbers together before the ball ended, watched in astonishment by her colleagues. She had said her mystery partner was good-looking, and he was: no wonder she'd kept quiet about his being the mayor's son. Strange, though, about the change of dress: perhaps she had planned it as a joke.

After the ball, Susie went back with him to supper in his mother's kitchen, for both of them were hungry, having missed their dinner. Then he took her home.

Colin was a botanist, back for Christmas from Canada where he was working on a five-year project. He thought there might be an opening there for Susie, since she was so expert at analysing statistics on her computer.

By the time she flew out, in the spring, she had lost two stone.

Nick was sent to prison for two years: his knocking offenses were more difficult to pin down, since money had been handed over, but at least he was removed from circulation for a while. It was no good his pleading that Mildred had agreed to sell her bureau, as she had agreed to sell her other things; why had he needed to wear a mask and tie her up, if that were true?

"He'll find more mugs to fall for his sweet talk, when

he comes out,'' was the rueful comment of the prosecuting counsel.

Alas, it was doubtless true. Mildred, however, never fell victim again to a con man.

Margaret Yorke says she first began reading detective stories when she was ill at the age of twelve. The first of her classic whodunits, featuring amateur detective Patrick Grant, appeared in 1970. Since then she has published numerous crime novels and short stories, and has been Chairman of the Crime Writers Association.

And Broke His Crown

DAVID WILLIAMS

I Crawley, Vicar of King's Minsted, pulling nervously at the hairs sprouting from his right ear. Head bent low, and long frame hunched inside his cassock, he paced the polished wood floor between desk and window like a pained personification of a question mark. "Especially on cu-cu-Christmas Eve," he added, aiming sidelong glances over the desk and his half-glasses at the two men seated in his study.

"No alternative, I'm afraid, vicar. Temptation's far greater with the church full. Collections are better at festival times. Huge at Christmas, as you know. The Christmas Eve carol service tomorrow evening is the perfect time to trap our criminal," countered the dapper Major Clarence Probe-Hyslop, crisp and dogmatic, in military style. The proprietor of the town's largest estate agency, he had not been a serving officer for over sixteen years—to be exact, not since he was invalided out of the army with varicose veins in June 1915. "War wounds," he had explained at the time. He held on to the title "major" because it was good for business—and he was long-serving churchwarden of St.

Oswald's Church for much the same reason. "As Sergeant Jones here says, the fellow's got to be caught red-handed, what?" He sucked hard on the short stemmed, big bowled pipe, and looked across at the Welsh plainclothes policeman for confirmation.

"That's right enough, major. We've got to have evidence, and I've told you how we can get it." The bouncy Handel Jones blinked twice, uncrossed his legs, and leaned well forward in his chair, putting a heavy strain on his trousers. " 'A bruised reed should he not break, and the smoking flax shall he not quench,' " he quoted, almost confidentially, as if he was sharing a racing tip, his dark eyes narrowing before he straightened his back again: "*Isaiah* 42, verse 3," he added, staring meaningfully at the vicar, whose only response was a suspicious glare.

"Quite," commented Major Probe-Hyslop, because he didn't know what else to say. A Bible-thumping policeman was new in his experience.

"But we could so easily have had a quiet word with Rubb," Canon Crawley put in, still pacing. It hadn't been his idea to go to the police. It was Probe-Hyslop who had done that, without consulting anyone. Within his rights as sole churchwarden no doubt, but still an overkill, was the vicar's considered opinion. And now it was too late to turn back. "We could just . . . just have pointed out the ter-ter-temporary error of his ways," he went on, the speech affectation of his undergraduate days returning involuntarily in his agitation. "We shouldn't really have needed to-to-to involve the authorities—"

"Pointed out the error of Alfred Rubb's ways? And then had him sue us for slander, vicar?" the major interrupted. "With no evidence against him yet, we might as well accuse the curate."

"You don't suspect the curate as well, do you, sir?" put in the policeman, less eagerly than would have been excusable in the son of a Primitive Methodist lay preacher predicating moral lapse by a Church of England clergyman.

"Of course we dough-dough-don't suspect the curate,"

countered the vicar, momentarily halting his stride, and clasping and unclasping anguished hands behind his back.

"But the major did mention to me yesterday that the curate sometimes cashed up what's in the collection plates, sir. That's the Reverend G. G. Moxton, isn't it?" Jones smoothed his heavy walrus mustache while consulting a dog-eared notebook, just removed from his fawn raincoat pocket, and which he was perching on the battered trilby hat resting in his lap. He had declined to remove the damp coat on arrival which, in consequence, had now begun to steam gently from the heat of the substantial coal fire behind his chair.

"Mr. Moxton only deals with the collection at one Sunday service." It was Probe-Hyslop who had responded. "That's at the eight o'clock communion, where the attendance is never very big. There hasn't been any falling off in the collections then. That's only happened at the eleven o'clock matins and six o'clock evensong, where I check the totals myself." He failed to remark the policeman's black eyebrows rise a touch as he continued. "That's after Rubb, the verger, has done a first count. Then I enter the totals in the parish account book, and lock the money in the safe."

"I see, sir. So, to go over what you told me at Worchester police station. On Sundays, Mr. Rubb, in a black gown, leads the clergy in procession behind the choir, at the start and end of the two main services. During worship, he sits behind the presiding clergyman, and performs various other tasks. One of those occurs during the singing of the last hymn, when he takes the filled collection plates from the altar table and puts them in the clergy vestry." He looked up from his notes. "The vestry is on the left hand side of the altar, under the church tower, sir?"

"Yes. I'll show you when we go over to the church," Probe-Hyslop provided, while relighting his pipe. He also glanced at the time. It was nearly five, and he'd promised to be home by half past.

"Thank you, sir. And when a service is over, Mr. Rubb goes from the choir vestry, which is at the far end of the church, to the clergy vestry, by himself, to start counting the money, where you usually join him a bit later.''

"Yes, when I've finished speaking to departing members of the congregation about church business. The vicar and the curate stay at the church door for longer than I do, shaking hands with everyone," he completed in a tone that suggested their function was a good deal less vital than his.

"And nobody else can get at the collection plates between the time Mr. Rubb takes them into the vestry and when he comes back after the service, sir?"

"That's right. There are two doors to the clergy vestry. He locks the internal one onto the chancel when he returns from putting the collection away. It's a Yale lock, so he only has to slip the catch. The second door is on the other side of the vestry. It lets out onto the churchyard, and serves the belfry staircase as well as the vestry itself. The staircase comes down beside the door. People using it don't need to come into the vestry, but they're visible from it.''

"This second door's always locked, you said, sir. And the door to the boiler house in the basement is immediately under it . . . outside . . . down some steps. But that's never locked." The sergeant looked up from his notebook, his brow furrowed. "You mentioned that the bell-ringers leave by the external vestry door, sir."

"When they've finished ringing, before matins and evensong, yes. But that's when the services are starting, not ending. The vicar doesn't care to have all eight of them trouping out through the church at that point. Neither do I. Unseemly as well as unsupportive.''

"There's no bell-ringing before the eight o'clock service, sir?"

"No. Too many townspeople object to being woken up so early.''

"And the bell-ringers don't attend any of the services?"

Canon Crawley stopped pacing, and, with feet together, rocked forward onto his toes, then back onto his heels. "Sadly, no," he said, with a sigh that mourned the shortcomings of others. "They tell me their worship is in their ringing. They could be right, I suppose." He stared up at the ceiling as if expecting a heavenly revelation in the matter.

"They spend more time in the bally Mason's Arms than they do in the church," said the major sourly, blowing a good deal of smoke in the sergeant's direction. "That's where they go, in a body, as soon as they stop ringing."

"In a body, sir? You mean all eight of them?"

"That's right. They're all long gone before the time we're concerned with, and the door locked behind them."

"That's a Yale lock too, sir? Like the other?" The major nodded, and Jones ticked something in his book before continuing. "And the eight o'clock service is the only one where you're not there to put the collection in the safe?"

"Yes." Probe-Hyslop fingered the center parting of his glossy hair which he wore brushed very flat. "I can't be at all the services, and we're an officer short at the moment. The other churchwarden had to resign. Pressure of outside work." He fixed the chimer clock on the mantelpiece with a defiant expression, as though daring it to announce that the other man had resigned because he couldn't get on with Clarence Probe-Hyslop.

"So Mr. Moxton has a key to the safe same as you and the vicar, sir?"

"Correct, sergeant."

"But you haven't mentioned our plan to him, sir?" Jones glanced from Probe-Hyslop to Canon Crawley.

"Good God . . . I mean, certainly not," the major answered, too keenly for the vicar, who simply nodded his regretful confirmation.

The major's unguarded exclamation confirmed the policeman's impression that he didn't trust the curate. "Like I said, the fewer who know the better," Jones cautioned. "So if we could keep it just between the three of us? That's for the time being. As we're told in the scriptures, 'A fool uttereth all his mind: but a wise man keepeth it in till afterwards.' That's *Proverbs* 29, verse 11. Very applicable in the present case." He smiled encouragingly at the others, before continuing. "So the verger's always at both main services, vicar?"

"Yes. And a thoroughly conscientious verger he's been over four, no, nearly five years," the canon responded vigorously. "He also polishes the brasses, and helps with the cleaning of the church. He used to stoke the boiler as well, but that had to stop in October of this year, after he was off for two weeks. Bad heart, d'you see?"

"Who took on the stoking, sir?"

"A keen lad called Tobin. Eric Tobin," said the major. "Makes a better job of it, too. Far better. He's a gardener's boy at a big house on the edge of the town. Comes in every weekday, before and after his ordinary work. On Sundays he arrives well before the two main services. He lights and stokes the chancel stove then, too. For extra heat. We're paying him ten shillings a week through the winter. Worth every penny."

"Was that deducted from Mr. Rubb's money, sir?"

"Of course. We're not a charity, what?" This time the major noticed Jones's tight-lipped smile. "I mean, we have a budget for church maintenance, and we have to keep within it," he added, shifting in his chair.

"But Mr. Rubb's income is ten shillings smaller than it used to be?"

"Yes. And four or five pounds a week better than it used to be, if he's been helping himself from the collection plates."

"Quite so, sir."

The vicar sighed loudly, and turned about from examining a framed sepia reproduction of *The Light of the World* hanging near the window. "We've yet to prove he's been doing that," he said. "In the matter of the stoking, Tobin does a better job because he's used to manual work. Alfred Rubb is scarcely a laborer by background. He used to be a bank clerk, before he lost his job."

"He was dismissed, sir?"

"Su-su-certainly not. He was simply laid off at the start of the slump. That's why he's so good with money. I mean, with business generally," he added quickly, after Probe-Hyslop gave a very audible snort. "He's a widower. Lives with his married daughter, quite close to the church. I don't know what St. Oswald's would do without him, I really don't." He pulled out his aged swivel desk chair and subsided into it, much to Probe-Hyslop's relief who had been irritated by his prowling.

"Could I ask how much Mr. Rubb is actually paid, sir?" Jones asked, with studied inconsequence.

The vicar, who wasn't sure, looked at Probe-Hyslop who replied: "Two pounds five shillings a week."

The sergeant made a wan expression, licked the lead of his pencil, and made a note in his book. "A reasonable enough stipend, even for such a paragon, I suppose," he said.

"Others in this country manage on less," the affluent Probe-Hyslop answered stiffly, suspecting irony.

"Indeed they do, sir. Except that . . . opportunity is servant to temptation, and a handmaiden to the avaricious," the Welshman propounded, his voice rising in a crescendo, and so portentously that Probe-Hyslop assumed he was quoting from the Bible again. The vicar figured he wasn't, but then, as if to confuse them both, the sergeant added, " 'And the life of the poor is the curse of the heart,' *Ecclesiasticus* 38, verse 18—"

"Verse 19," Canon Crawley amended, testily for him, but he was finding the other man's sententious scripturizing tiresome.

"Well done, sir," said Jones unabashed, as if he had been testing the vicar. "Just a few last points, about Mr. Rubb's movements. What time does he get to the church on Sundays?"

"An hour before the two main services," said the vicar immediately. "He's never at the eight o'clock, but he's very careful to see things are in order for the eleven and six o'clock."

"And when does he open the vestry door for the bell-ringers, vicar?"

"I believe he lets them in at 10:15 in the morning, and

5:15 in the evening. Although ringing doesn't start until the half hour. Of course, the ringers can come in through the main door of the church at other times if they want, but since I've insisted they must leave by the vestry door, they've taken to arriving that way as well."

"And Eric Tobin?"

The vicar shrugged. "He brings a hod of anthracite up from the cellar, and through the vestry, at just after ten, and again just after five. That's after he's coked up the main boiler."

"Ah, so Mr. Rubb is in the vestry that early to open up the door for him, vicar?"

"I suppose so, yes."

"Does Tobin attend the services?"

"No. I believe he's a Baptist."

"Indeed?" The policemen looked as if he was about to provide some illustrative piece of scripture featuring, perhaps, a deserving Samaritan, but after the earlier correction thought better of it. Instead he asked: "Tomorrow, Christmas Eve, is a Tuesday, but the carol service will be at six, like evensong on a Sunday?"

"Yes. And the services on Christmas Day will be the same as on a Sunday."

"Well, I hope we'll have this business over by then, sir."

"And you'll have two pounds worth of marked half-crowns for me to put in the collection, sergeant?" asked Probe-Hyslop.

"Yes, sir. Sixteen in all. You're still sure it's half-crowns you've been losing?"

"It's what we have to assume, yes. Anyone stealing from the plates would naturally go for them. Each one worth sixpence more than a florin, after all," he completed, stating the obvious. "There used to be thirty or more half-crowns in the collections at matins and evensong. Now it's down to less than a dozen."

Canon Crawley sighed. "And you intend to . . ."

"They think poor Rubb's been palming money from the collection. So the police are putting marked half-crowns in

the plates at the carol service tomorrow, then they're going
to corner him afterwards. Make him empty his pockets.
Daddy's said Mummy and I mustn't tell anyone. But I
know it's all right to tell you, G. G.,'' Priscilla Crawley,
the canon's youngest, unmarried daughter was saying,
around the time the meeting in the vicarage was ending.
Her head and neck were thrust forward, and making up and
down movements, as if she were doing the breast stroke,
except she was walking, not swimming, beside her confi-
dant, the Reverend Geoffrey Gilbert Moxton, known to his
intimates as G. G.

Priscilla was gauche, and lanky, with bobbed, mousy hair
stuffed into a beret, big, innocent blue eyes, and a sharp
patrician nose above a generous mouth. Her strong arms,
presently enveloped in a heavy, wet green mackintosh, were
failing, as always, to keep their boisterous swinging in time
with the long strides of her well-shaped legs. She and her
companion were moving energetically through the rain on
the river path, heading back toward the town.

What Priscilla lacked in poise she made up for in enthusiasm. She loved G. G. with an intensity that transcended
everything else in her twenty-year-old world, but had never
dared to tell him so. Happily, the tall, muscular young
cleric, whose horsy face complemented his initials, felt
about Priscilla much as she felt about him. But since his
earnings were not much larger than those of the St. Oswald's verger, he hadn't presumed to declare his love either, for fear she would assume it amounted to a proposal
of marriage. There was no current prospect of G. G. getting
married, certainly not while he was maintaining his frail
and indigent mother in a private nursing home.

The couple had been checking the condition of a badger
set discovered by Priscilla in the summer. It was badgers
that had first drawn them together.

''Why are they picking on Rubb?'' G. G. questioned,
disturbed that this was the first he had heard of the matter.

''Because the money's been disappearing after he's taken
it to the clergy vestry.''

"But plenty of people have access to the vestry besides him."

"Not when the collection plates are in there, because both doors are locked."

G. G. scowled. "One of the ringers may have been hiding in the ringing chamber."

"But they always leave together before the service starts."

G. G. rubbed his manly chin, which was rather wet from the rain. "Someone else could be hiding up there."

"But there's nowhere to hide. No cupboard or anything."

"There's the bell chamber one level up."

Priscilla shook her head vigorously. "Anyone hiding up there would have to be in place before the bell-ringers arrived, and Daddy says no one could stand being there while the ringing goes on. Not without going deaf, or mad."

"I suppose that's right. So they're saying the vestry's really a locked room. Except Rubb . . ." He paused. "But it can't be Rubb. I know it can't," he ended with such insistence it almost suggested he knew who it could be. He pulled the frayed, turned-up collar of his topcoat tighter over his equally worn muffler.

Forty minutes later the rain had stopped, but there was a rising east wind, and the moon was providing fitful illumination between scurrying clouds. Sergeant Jones was standing on the wide pathway that led from the big lych gate on Church Street to the main door of the church. He was listening to the church bells, when he saw a hatless, strapping lad enter the churchyard through a smaller gate further down the street. The lad went directly to the church tower, which was offset on the north side of the building, at the end of the nave. He then descended the steps beside the vestry door at the tower base, and the wind carried the rasping noise of a bolt opening before he disappeared from sight. Jones rightly assumed the newcomer to be Eric Tobin, who reappeared shortly afterwards, whistling "Good

King Wenceslas,'' as he hurried back to the street, without ever entering the church.

When the bell-ringing ceased, the policeman moved through the gravestones and stationed himself on the narrow path the lad had used. As he expected, the bell-ringers soon emerged in a group from the vestry door—or seven of them did. The eighth followed nearly a minute later, pulling the door shut behind him. Jones heard the click of the lock closing.

"I've been listening to your bells. Beautiful peal,'' he said, as the eighth bell-ringer drew abreast of him.

"We've only been having a short practice this evening,'' the man answered. "Wait till tomorrow night, before the carol service.'' He was a short, burly fellow, with sunken, calculating eyes, of the kind that, in a professional way— and to be on the safe side—Jones usually took to indicate guilt, until innocence was proved.

"Your team-mates are ahead of you.''

"Because I had to change my shoes. I like to ring in plimsolls. Anyway the others won't have got further than the public bar of the Mason's Arms over the road.'' The speaker fixed an appraising stare on Jones. "You a campanologist as well?''

"Not really. I just like the sound of the bells.''

"Welsh, aren't you? Don't get many Welshmen around here. You don't live locally?''

"No, no. Just visiting over the holiday.'' If he had been local, the sergeant wondered if the man would have tried to recruit him as a ringer—or whether the last question had exposed a suspicion of his being a policeman, by a character with something to hide.

Jones's reply had been fairly close to the truth. He was based in Worcester, ten miles away: the small King's Minsted police force didn't include CID officers on its strength. He was planning to catch the 6:50 bus back, in twenty minutes from now. The tour the major had given him of the empty church had been extremely brief. Since then he had been to the local police station to make some arrangements for the next day.

"Merry Christmas," he called after the retreating eighth bell-ringer. The salutation wasn't returned.

When the churchyard was empty, the sergeant, armed with a pocket flashlight, made a quick examination of the ground between the vestry door and the little street gate. He also went down the steps and looked inside the boiler room. He picked up a number of small objects during his foraging, and deposited them in one of the unused envelopes he carried about him. Several of his bullet-sized finds seemed to give him especial satisfaction.

When the internal church lights were extinguished, Jones had ceased his searchings and stationed himself in the street by the big lych gate. "I wonder if you could help me?" he asked, doffing his hat to the slightly built, elderly man who had shortly emerged from the porch of the darkened church.

"I will if I can," said the man. He had moved down the wide pathway at a slow but dogged pace, a walking stick in his gloved right hand. Of medium height, he was wearing a bowler hat, and a dark colored wool overcoat, both of which had seen better days. His steel-rimmed spectacles had been mended with solder at the bridge. Altogether, he didn't look like someone who had tripled his income over the previous few months, but appearances could deceive. "Is it something to do with St. Oswald's? I'm the verger there," he said.

"Well, there's lucky for me. I wanted to know the time of the carol service tomorrow."

"Six o'clock. Oh, that's very kind of you. Thank you." The eyes behind the glasses evinced genuine gratitude as the speaker accepted a Woodbine cigarette from the packet the sergeant proffered. "I'm supposed to be cutting back on gaspers, but since it's Christmas." He lit the cigarette from the match his benefactor was shielding in cupped hands, and which also illumined the verger's gaunt, and deathly pale face.

"Has a service just finished?" asked the sergeant.

"No, but I had to be here for the bell-ringers. For their practice. And to see the church is locked, and ready for tomorrow. We'll be decorating it first thing. The vicar doesn't like that being done before Christmas Eve. Quite right, of course. So will you be joining us for the carols, sir?''

"I hope so. I've still got business to clear up in the town. Right now I'm aiming to catch the next bus back to Worchester.''

"Then I'll walk along with you. I live just this side of the bus station. That's if you'll put up with my dawdling steps.''

The policeman smiled. "I've got quarter of an hour in hand, and you can make sure I take the right turnings. Now it's dark, I feel like 'I have been a stranger in a strange land.' ''

"Ah, Moses said that, when he named his son Gershom. *Exodus*, chapter 2. I'm not sure of the verse.''

"Neither am I,'' said Jones—but, instinctively, he was sure of Alfred Rubb.

It was just after seven o'clock on the following evening when the St. Oswald's carol service was drawing to a tuneful and tumultuous close. The voices of the choir, and a record sized congregation, in the flower and holly decked church, were lifting lustily to match the organ's triumphant rendering of *"Hark! the Herald Angels Sing."*

The collection had been completed during the singing of the first two verses of the carol, and received in the sanctuary by Canon Crawley. Immediately afterwards, the verger had taken the plates to the vestry. He had then returned to his stall in the chancel, closing but not locking, the door behind him.

It was as the last verse of the carol began that Rubb, departing from habit, purposefully put down his hymn-book and returned to the vestry, entering it with unusual alacrity.

Only the two clergymen in the sanctuary, and the members of the choir in the part of the chancel nearest to the vestry, heard the crash—followed by the verger's anguished cry—over the noise of the organ and the singing.

But almost everyone in the church watched in astonishment as the Reverend G. G. Moxton sprang into action from his own position in the sanctuary, vaulting the communion rail, and pounding after Rubb through the door.

Inside the vestry G. G. first came upon an upset collection plate, its contents spread in all directions, and beyond that, the verger's prone body on the floor, the side of his forehead smeared with blood, his right arm stretched out in the direction of the door to the churchyard, and nearly touching it. There were two half-crowns lying beside his open palm.

G. G. knelt beside the body, and was hugely relieved to see Rubb's eyelids flicker, then half open. The verger followed this with an expression of recognition, and the breathless exhortation: "After him! After him!"

The curate jumped for the outside door, and pulled it open. But his further progress was blocked by the solid figure of Sergeant Jones on the step outside.

"I'm from the police," said the sergeant, holding his ground.

"So didn't you catch whoever came out?" demanded G. G.

"Nobody's come out, sir. What's happened to Mr. Rubb?" He pushed past G. G. to the dazed verger who had pulled himself into a sitting position. "Right, sir," he said to the curate, "look after the injured will you, while I arrest our thief?" He turned to the belfry steps and began to mount them to the sound, from within the church of a great "Amen."

"You said you found the vital clue yesterday, sergeant," said the vicar later, sipping tea in the vicarage study with Jones, Probe-Hyslop, G. G., and Priscilla, who had brought in the tea things on a tray.

"That's right, sir. A pair of clues to be exact. Two little bungs of compressed natural moss." He placed the two small objects on the vicar's desk. "One was at the bottom of the boiler room steps. The other was just inside the door. Chucked away by Eric Tobin when he'd done with them last Sunday, I expect. There were others too. Older ones.

The pair he used tonight we found in his trousers pocket when we searched him at the station. Marvellous stuff, pressed moss. Makes the best ear-plugs, by far. They'll even muffle the roar of a big gun, fired at close range. I recognized the plugs straight away. We used them in Flanders, till the greenery gave way to mud. We relied on cotton wool after that.''

"Ah, yes," Probe-Hyslop voiced his agreement, although his nine months' war service in the Pay Corps had all been spent at Aldershot Barracks.

"Don't suppose many people would use moss for making ear-plugs nowadays," mused the vicar.

"A gardener's boy would," said the sergeant. "And it was my wondering for what reason that set me on the right track.''

"So that's how Tobin endured being in the bell chamber, a floor above the ringers?'' said G. G.

"No doubt," answered the policeman. "It's where he went twice every Sunday, after taking the anthracite through to the chancel stove. He went up before the ringers arrived, when people thought he'd left already. He stayed there for the ringing, nipped down the stairs during the last hymn, waited till Mr. Rubb had brought in the collection, helped himself to a handful of half-crowns, and nipped back up again. He didn't let himself out again till everyone had gone. Nice steady income he had going there, too, till he got too greedy, and Mr. Probe-Hyslop noticed the shortage of half-crowns.''

"He must have had a terrible shock when Rubb appeared in the vestry a second time tonight," put in Priscilla, while pressing G. G. to another Marie biscuit.

"Didn't we all. Or most of us," remarked the sergeant pointedly.

"But why didn't Tobin make a run for it to the churchyard, instead of going back to the belfry staircase?''

"Partly force of habit, miss, and partly because it was quicker than getting the door open. He hoped Mr. Rubb hadn't had time to see who he was, or where he was heading, before he'd thrown the plate at his head.'' He turned to the vicar. "I suppose it was you, sir, who told Mr. Rubb he was suspected?"

"No, it was me. Just before the service," the curate intervened.

"And it was me who snitched to G. G., after Daddy told me," Priscilla admitted, chin up, tone impenitent. She firmly intended to marry G. G. (which she did after his mother recovered, and married the owner of the nursing home), and she knew already that she could never keep any secrets from him.

"Well, since Mr. Rubb is expected to recover, there's no real harm done," said Jones magnanimously. "Lucky that. The blow could have killed him, and then we'd have had murder on our hands for Christmas." He made a pained face at the unseasonable thought. "He won't be at the services tomorrow, of course. Which reminds me, it's time I was going." He picked up his hat. "Well, a happy Christmas to all. And remember, only he who sins by defiling the feast deserveth to sojourn in the lonely pit," he completed, thinking of Eric Tobin.

"Very appropriate," said Probe-Hyslop. "Another quotation from the Bible?"

"No, no," said the Welshman, cheerfully. "I just made it up."

David Williams has written nineteen intriguing and amusing whodunits since 1976: two were shortlisted for the CWA Gold Dagger Award. Most have featured urbane merchant banker/amateur sleuth Mark Treasure, but his two latest, *Last Seen Breathing* and *Death of a Prodigal*, introduced widower DCI Merlin Parry of the South Wales Constabulary and his portly assistant DS Gomer Lloyd.

Bearing Gifts

◆

NICOLE SWENGLEY

"I can't write *another* Christmas story!" wailed Alice with the anguish of a seasoned journalist faced with the annual nightmare of short December deadlines.

Elaine Bloom's Chanel-red mouth pursed like a spurt of blood. Alice Villiers was the only person in the department to have caused her any real angst about a promotional somersault over the heads—and raised eyebrows—of several more experienced colleagues when she'd been made lifestyle editor of *The Globe*'s weekly magazine.

Ever since Alice had torn holes in a health piece she'd commissioned from a dodgy source, taking her complaint straight to the Editor, Elaine had adopted a strategy of keeping her rival busy with dud jobs no one else was prepared to tackle.

"This is consumer hell," complained Alice. "I've already covered 'How the Stars Dress Their Trees,' 'Fifty Ways to Stuff a Turkey' and 'Wrap Your Gifts the Experts' Way.'"

Her pale face and panda eyes were barely visible behind

the quivering Manhattan-style high-rise blocks of press releases lining her desk.

'You've had me testing Christmas tree lights, discussing Christmas tree price wars and weighing the comparative merits of different brands of artificial tinsel,'' she continued. ''I've scoured the shops for wacky decorations, captioned twenty varieties of door-wreaths and analyzed the tensile strength of decorative paper napkins. Can we *please* forget Christmas now and move on to something more interesting?''

Elaine frowned. She had no intention of being told which stories to run in her magazine section. Not by Alice, anyhow. She leaned forward and spoke in a low menacing voice, hoping that Nosy Nikki, the department's long-eared secretary, couldn't hear from the depths of the fashion cupboard where she was bagging up a rack of spangly evening dresses on loan for a photographic shoot.

''Now we're caught up in a cover price war with *The Daily Planet*, all department budgets are being slashed. The Editor told me yesterday that he may need to shed staff in the New Year. I wouldn't try skating on thin ice if I were you.''

Alice sighed and wondered for the fifteenth time that week whether she should try to transfer to *The Globe*'s women's page. It couldn't be worse than being at Elaine's beck and call despite tighter lead-times on the newspaper.

''What's the story?'' she asked wearily, eyeing Elaine's new Nicole Fahri outfit with an emotion suspiciously close to envy.

''A charity auction at Cholmondley's. It's in aid of the Children at Christmas appeal. *The Globe* will donate a sum equivalent to the top bid at a gala dinner in The Dorchester which readers have the pleasure of attending for £50 a head. It's a neat way of promoting the paper and increasing revenue, don't you think?''

Elaine smoothed back her neat black bob. The Christmas Appeal Dinner had been one of her brighter ideas, she thought. Who was to know—or care—that she'd gleaned it from a back issue of *Tatler*?

"What's being auctioned?" Alice asked dully, too tired for genuine curiosity.

Elaine screwed up her perfect nose. "Mangy old teddy bears," she replied, turning on a neat black heel and heading for her office.

Alice recollected Elaine's comment as she wandered around Cholmondley's basement with Richard Hunt, an associate director of the auction house.

It was typical of Elaine that she had no affection for old bears, Alice thought. She was all designer labels, flash perfume and chic high heels. If her bedroom was as fashion-conscious as the outfits she wore, what place would there be for an old threadbare teddy?

Alice was very fond of bears. At home, she chatted to her five furry friends frequently and, although they remained stubbornly silent, they seemed to perk up when she paid them some attention. If she ignored them, their fur looked even more bedraggled and their worn black eyes conveyed reproach.

Cholmondley's bears were lined up on slatted wooden shelves waiting patiently to be catalogued. As she idled past the racks Alice felt that the range of expressions on their faces defied description. Some appeared petulant while others seemed bored by the long wait for new owners. Some looked cross while their cousins appeared curious, sad-eyed or snooty. Far more was conveyed by cocked heads and raised paws than words might express.

"It's the cuddle factor that appeals," explained Richard Hunt. "No matter how threadbare, people are enchanted by them. Buyers always ask for their names and as much history as we can give them."

"Are they antiques?" asked Alice.

"Not strictly speaking. The earliest in our sale dates from 1904. But these days teddies really are a serious collector's item. When Christie's sold a blue plush bear by Steiff, the German manufacturers, a couple of years ago, he fetched £49,500."

"Gosh! Was he very rare?"

"He was a one-off sample made for Harrods and came to London in a small batch of colored bears. But the store buyer didn't like his fancy blue fur so he was never manufactured commercially."

They stopped in front of a embarrassed-looking bear whose paws had been patched with yellow face-cloth.

"He won't fetch much," remarked Richard unsympathetically. "It's always best to leave torn paws unmended or make repairs as close to the original as possible."

"But how can anyone part with them?" cried Alice, feeling hopelessly sentimental as she picked up a cinnamon-colored bear with black boot-button eyes and gave it a squeeze.

"Some people are really sad to sell their bears but they need the money," explained Richard. "One old lady came in with her childhood bear because she hadn't got a family of her own and she wanted to make sure he went to a good home when she died. Another client stipulated that a pair of bears should be sold together in a single lot because they had never been separated. And someone else brought in a chair on which the bear had always sat and insisted that the seat was sold along with Ted."

Alice laughed and cuddled a pale gold bear with fat spoon-shaped feet. "How much will this one go for?" she asked.

"The estimate is between £3,000 and £4,000," replied Richard. "Steiff bears always command a good price. But not all the bears in our sale are as expensive as that one. We've got some with estimates from £50. Only the rarer ones in good condition will fetch a lot of money."

"But what are the advantages of buying an old bear when you can nip off to a department store and get a brand new one?" asked Alice, jotting down Richard's comments for her article.

"Hand-made bears have so much more character than today's mass-produced bears," he replied. "They're made of better quality materials—mohair plush with wood-shaving stuffing. Modern bears generally have synthetic fibers and their kapok stuffing makes them much squishier."

Alice stroked a dirty white bear with short stubby arms. "This one has quite a different sort of expression," she said.

"He's an early Merrythought. English bears have flatter faces and shorter limbs than the old Steiff bears," explained Richard. "Steiffs were originally designed from sketches of real bears, so they have pointed snouts, big paws and long limbs. Look, here's a more recent version of a Steiff. You can see that the design hasn't changed much from the very early ones."

"So who's the star of the show?" asked Alice, scribbling in her notebook.

"Hugo," replied Richard. "Come over here and I'll introduce you."

Hugo was sitting on Richard's desk with his head on one side. Alice recognized Steiff's signature snout, large shaped paws and humped back. One elongated jointed arm was raised as if in welcome, and below Hugo's black stitched nose lurked a black stitched smirk.

"Brilliant condition," enthused Richard. "The seller told us he was found wrapped in newspaper in an attic."

"What do you think he'll fetch?" Alice and Hugo studied each other cautiously.

"Our estimate is between £5,000 and £6,000. But he may go for much more. With any luck we'll find bidders throwing caution to the winds because a percentage of the sale receipts are being donated to the Children at Christmas appeal."

Alice thought of her own bears at home and wondered whether Harry, her beloved grubby polar bear, or threadbare tangerine Fred would object to a new, rather dilapidated, companion.

Alice sensed something was wrong as soon as she stepped into the office. Heads were lowered in front of computer terminals and apart from the clatter of keyboards and the incessant ringing of telephones it was unusually quiet for a busy Tuesday afternoon.

She slid into her seat, stubbing her toes on a couple of boxes shoved inside the desk's kneehole. The towering pile of press releases had acquired a further tier in her absence, and a stack of unopened mail littered the desk as if it had been raining paper all morning.

"What's been going on?" she whispered to Nikki sitting opposite her.

Nikki's sharp nose popped up above her computer like a mechanical automatum.

"There's been a row about the holiday rota," she confided in a low voice. "Elaine's changed it so she can have a whole week off after Christmas. You and Jackie have got to come in on Boxing Day."

"Shit," said Alice and switched on her computer. A flashing green signal indicated that a message was waiting in her queue. She called it up on the screen. It was the re-organized holiday rota.

Alice reached for the telephone. She would have to alter the booking she'd made for a three-day Christmas break at a hotel in the West Country. Since she had no family of her own she normally stayed in London during the so-called festive season and invited other waifs and strays to Christmas Day dinner at her Notting Hill flat. This year, she'd decided to let someone else do all the work even if it meant Christmassing with strangers.

It was typical of Elaine to snaffle some extra days off, Alice thought sourly. If challenged, she'd plead that she needed to spend time with her five-year-old daughter. As Alice and Jackie were both single there was really no argument over who should come into the office on Boxing Day to put the magazine to bed.

Elaine's shrill voice broke into her reverie. "Alice, have you fixed up a photo shoot with one of the Children at Christmas kids?"

"You never—" Alice stopped. She had learned long ago that it was useless to argue with Elaine. The goal-posts moved like a hologram every time.

"I want the pictures on my desk by lunchtime tomorrow.'' Elaine's dark head withdrew into her goldfish bowl office. The door slammed shut. She obviously wanted to make a private telephone call.

Alice bit her lip. It was going to be a difficult 24 hours. How was she going to get ''Fill Your Own Christmas Crackers'' finished as well as organizing a photographic session sufficiently early to have prints ready by lunchtime?

Ludicrous Elaine. Hateful Christmas. Scrooge was right after all, Alice thought savagely.

She picked up the telephone. ''Richard, I need to ask a really *big* favor. You know that *The Globe* is going to match the highest bid in the bears sale with a donation to charity? Well, I need to get a picture shot early tomorrow of a kid from the children's home hugging Hugo. Do you think you could send him over to my office by courier? I promise I'll look after him and bring him back to Cholmondley's tomorrow afternoon.''

There was a long pause.

''I'm sorry, Alice, I really can't do that. It would be more than my job's worth if Hugo vanished before the sale.''

''I'll be with him all the time. Hand in paw. Honest.'' Alice racked her brains. ''Tell you what, Richard, I'll persuade Elaine to run a piece on your maritime sale in our Boat Show Special in January.'' This was a reckless promise. Alice knew very well that she had no more influence with Elaine than silent, stuffed Hugo.

''Well . . .'' Richard hesitated. He'd been trying to get *The Globe* to cover the maritime sale for the last three years. ''If you absolutely promise not to let him out of your sight you can have him for two hours in the morning. But I want him back here by twelve o'clock. We've got the preview tomorrow evening.''

Alice relaxed. All she had to do now was find a nice-looking kid, ask the picture desk to book a photographer and set up a sentimental shot of child and bear somewhere quiet like the boardroom.

''Lot six. A fine Steiff pale golden plush-covered teddy bear with large deep-set black boot-button eyes, pronounced snout, black stitched nose, mouth and claws, swivel head, elongated jointed shaped limbs, large shaped paws, large spoon-shaped feet, felt pad and hump, 28 inches tall, circa 1910.''

The auctioneer paused for breath and swept a knowing glance over his captive audience.

''What am I bid? £100? £150 here . . . £200 . . . £500. I'm offered £500 on my right . . . £1,000 . . . £1,500 . . . Going on, sir? £2,000 . . . £2,000 for this original Steiff bear. Any more?''

A Cholmondley's man, who was sitting behind a desk at the side of the room with a telephone glued to his ear, raised a lean finger.

The auctioneer peered at him over his gold-rimmed half-glasses. ''A telephone bid of £4,000,'' he announced.

A gasp united the ursine-loving crowd.

''Going on, sir? £4,500 . . .'' The auctioneer's beady eye swept the room then flicked back to the Cholmondley's man. ''£5,000 . . .''

Alice squirmed in her seat. Hugo had acquired a slight squint since yesterday, despite the best efforts of the woman at the Doll's Hospital, but it seemed that no one had noticed.

''£5,500 . . . £6,000 . . . £6,500 . . .''

The auctioneer's glance swerved between the back row and the telephone as rhythmically as if he had been following a ball on court.

''£7,000 . . . £7,500 . . . £8,000 . . . £8,500 . . . £9,000 . . .''

There was a pause as the motley crowd in Cholmondley's wood-panelled sale room held its collective breath.

''Going on, sir? I have £10,000 on the telephone.''

Pause.

''All done? I'm selling for £10,000.'' The gavel cracked down. ''That's yours on the telephone.''

Alice chewed her lip as she scribbled in her notebook. £10,000 for dear old Hugo. Nearly double the estimate. Someone somewhere must be desperate for a Christmas bear. She wondered if Richard Hunt would give her the name of the telephone bidder. There was still time to interview him or her before the story went to press.

As she slipped away from the auction house Alice mentally promised that she'd send an old woman with nimble sewing fingers the largest bunch of flowers Interflora could deliver.

The following morning Alice was engrossed in checking a page proof when the telephone rang for the twentieth time.

"We've had Hugo's buyer on the phone." Richard Hunt's voice crackled with suppressed fury. "He says that the eyes aren't the bear's original ones. Our expert has had a word with the buyer over the phone and he agrees."

"Well?" Alice held her breath.

"You said you wouldn't let him out of your sight."

"I didn't," lied Alice. "Maybe your expert made a mistake when he catalogued the bear."

Richard Hunt laughed hollowly. "I wish that was true."

"Look, he had hundreds of bears to catalogue. Maybe he didn't examine Hugo very carefully," Alice argued, sounding considerably more confident than she really felt.

"The bear was in perfect condition," Richard retorted. "Until he came back from your office."

"Prove it," challenged Alice. Attack might still prove the best line of defense, she thought nervously.

There was a pause.

"You know I can't," replied Richard tersely. "I've had to tell the buyer that the catalog description is a statement of opinion only."

"Well, there you are!" exclaimed Alice triumphantly. "In any case, Richard, I can't see what you're worried about. I take it that Cholmondley's received its full £10,000 plus 10 percent premium plus VAT?"

"Yes," Richard's tone softened slightly. "But you owe me for this Alice and you can be sure I'll call in my dues."

The line went dead.

Alice gave a sigh of relief and thumbed through the phone book to find the listing for Interflora.

•   •   •

Alice was still at her desk at 8:30 p.m. She had purposely waited for the last person to leave the office. Now she began scrabbling in Nikki's desk drawer for the spare office keys.

Elaine's desk was as neat as Alice's was untidy. Apart from a small stack of plastic wallets it was a paper-free zone. A fat leather desk diary was given pole position beside the computer terminal.

Alice flicked it open and noted the number of lunches Elaine had enjoyed at expensive restaurants around Kensington over the previous few weeks. But it was Wednesday in which she was most interested. The day Hugo came to have his picture taken. The horrific morning when she'd returned to the boardroom to find the kid from the children's home crying over an eye-less bear.

The photographer had said he'd only been out of the room for two minutes answering an urgent call of nature. Alice herself had been at her desk battling with "Fill Your Own Christmas Crackers."

Yet some mean soul had flashed into the boardroom, grabbed the bear and savagely plucked out its eyes, leaving poor old Hugo sightless and worth potentially much less than before.

The stuttering child volunteered that the woman was tall, had gold hair like an angel and smelled fruity. There wasn't anyone in the office who answered that description. Yet Alice was convinced that somehow the theft was linked with Elaine. *The Globe Magazine*'s lifestyle editor was the only person, apart from herself, who knew that Hugo was due to visit the office that day.

Was she allowing her dislike of Elaine to get out of proportion? Alice asked herself. What on earth would soignée Elaine, with her designer child and banker husband, want with Hugo's black boot-button eyes? If this was a warped attempt to get Alice into trouble it was certainly a pretty bizarre scam.

According to her desk diary, Elaine had interviewed someone called Lady Arabella Jagger at 11 a.m. on Wednesday. This had obviously taken place in the office because Alice remembered seeing Elaine raiding the coffee machine around mid-morning. But she had no recollection of Nikki collecting a stranger from the lift and ushering her into the office as she usually did with visitors.

Alice closed the door to Elaine's office and locked it. Then she shuffled through the phone book. Much to her disappointment Lady Arabella Jagger wasn't listed, either in the business directory or the residential book. She tried looking under Jagger, Arabella and Jagger, A., without success.

Disappointment clawed at her throat. As she swivelled away from her desk, Alice's black wool leggings snagged on its ragged edge, yanking her eyes from page to knee. In that fluid movement she found her answer: Jagger's Jewellery was printed in large bold type at the bottom of the list.

Within minutes Alice had left the office and was chugging toward Knightsbridge in her yellow *deux-chevaux*.

Jagger's Christmas window was a stunning black-and-silver Art Deco fantasy. Gleaming geometric brooches and triangular earrings perched on circular silver pillars of mixed height. Fake snow, dotted with a dew of diamonds and pearls, frothed around the elliptical bases. Jet necklaces twined around the columns like glittery spider's webs. Silver studs and links pocked a black velvet back-cloth like a starry night sky at sea.

A tiny silver salver in the center of the display masqueraded as a face. Its pouting black mouth held a glossy sheath-knife. A perspex bubble floated overhead. Inside, black and silver lettering read: Give Your Loved One A Jagger This Christmas.

Alice winced at the festive slogan and was about to turn back to her car when she caught sight of two black boot button eyes staring out from the silver salver face. In the reflected glow of London's haloed streetlamps they appeared to be winking. Despite the drizzle, it was a while before Alice moved away from the damp pavement outside the shop.

• • •

"Mr. Durham won't be free till lunchtime," quacked the secretary. "Then he's in meetings all afternoon."

"Well, when can I speak to him?" Alice was irritated by the stone wall at the other end of the line. "I've got a deadline and I need to talk to him before then."

"I'm sorry, I can't tell you when he'll be able to speak to you," said the stone wall unhelpfully. "What's it about?"

"The Cholmondley's sale."

"I don't know anything about that," came the flat reply. "You could try ringing in the morning."

Alice threw the handset back on the receiver in disgust. Then a light-bulb flashed in her head and she pressed the re-dial button.

Adopting a tone several degrees higher than normal she asked the switchboard operator to put her through to Mr. Durham's office.

"Interflora here," she announced brightly. "I've got a gorgeous bouquet of Christmas roses for Mrs. Durham but I'm afraid my silly assistant has mislaid the address. I wonder if you'd be kind enough to tell me where they should be delivered."

"Ooh, he's got a heart of gold, hasn't he?" cooed the stone wall. "But she won't be at home so you'd better send them around to her at work. It's a jeweller's in Knightsbridge. I'll give you the address."

A smile curved the corners of Alice's lips as she replaced the receiver and looked at the note she'd jotted on her pad.

"Nikki, my love?"

Nikki's pointed nose rose, doglike, from her desk. Alice *never* called her that. Was she going mental with all the work Elaine was piling on her?

"Do you remember if Elaine asked you to meet a visitor at the lifts on Wednesday morning by any chance?"

Nikki quickly reviewed her position. She wanted to avoid getting caught up in any fresh fracas between Elaine and Alice. She liked working on the magazine—it was so much more relaxed than the news desk—and she wanted to keep her job. Moreover, she had pretensions about turning, chameleon-like, into a journalist. So far she'd only been allowed to caption a few photographs and compile listings for the fashion editor. But even this was a start and she didn't want to jeopardize her chances for the future.

"What if I did?" she replied warily.

Sensing her anxiety, Alice sought to reassure her. "Oh, there's nothing wrong," she said sweetly. "I know Elaine was interviewing Lady Arabella Jagger and I just wondered if you'd had the pleasure of meeting her."

Nikki relaxed. "Sure. Did you see that amazing necklace she was wearing? When I admired it she said she'd let me have a press discount card if I wanted to buy anything at her shop." Seeing Alice studying her closely, she added hastily, "Only ten percent off, mind you."

"Did you take her into Elaine's office straight away?"

Nikki frowned. Wednesday seemed a long time ago. Forty-eight hours of black coffee, cigarettes, curly office sandwiches and boozy evenings at her local fogged the memory of Wednesday around the edges like an old sepia photograph.

"No, Elaine said she wanted to go somewhere quiet to interview her because Jackie was sorting out transparencies on the light-box in her office. So I took her along to the boardroom."

"And left her there?" Alice suggested calmly.

"There was a photo-shoot going on. So I got her a cup of coffee from the machine and came back here to ask Elaine if she wanted me to check whether the spare office along the corridor was free."

"So Lady Arabella met our handsome photographer?" joked Alice.

Nikki grimaced. "Handsome? You must need your eyes tested. I suppose Dave must have been around somewhere because all his gear was set up. I left Lady A with a little girl and her cuddly toy."

"Thank you, Nikki, you've been extremely helpful," said Alice.

I have? Nikki thought. And does Santa Claus exist? But

she diplomatically said nothing and gave a beatific pre-Christmas holiday smile instead.

"You suggested I called Mr. Durham this morning," Alice objected sourly when the stone wall informed her that he was in a meeting.

"He's a very busy man, dear. Try later."

"When's the best time to catch him?"

"Oh, there's no knowing that. You'll just have to call back."

Alice threw the handset down with a wail of frustration and returned to her page proofs.

Minutes later, she re-dialed. This time the telephone rang for quite a while before it was answered. The stone wall must have left her perch temporarily.

"Yup?" The voice was fierce, self-important and unlikely to belong to a man who liked bears.

"Alice Villiers of *The Globe* here. The Editor suggested I had a quick word with you about your success at the Cholmondley's sale." Alice poured as much cool efficiency into her voice as possible.

"Do we have to discuss this now? I'm extremely busy," came the brusque reply.

"So's the Editor," replied Alice tautly. "This won't take two minutes of your time and since he will be inviting you personally to the Children at Christmas Appeal dinner I think it would be courteous if you allowed me to put a few questions to you regarding the sale."

"Two minutes then."

Alice took a deep breath. "Ten thousand pounds is a lot to pay for an old teddy bear. Why were you so keen to buy it?"

There was a half-second pause during which it occurred to Alice that she was about to hear a lie.

"I actually bought it for my mother." The gravelly voice sounded slightly embarrassed. "She saw it in Cholmondley's catalog and recognized it as a childhood toy that she lost years ago"

"So it's a Christmas present for her?" suggested Alice.

"If you like." The voice was suddenly disinterested. Jock Durham had no desire to become *The Globe*'s latest human interest story.

"Is your mother very old?"

"Eighty-six."

"So the bear could be seen as an excellent investment should you eventually inherit it?" Alice held her breath as she waited to hear how this comment would be received.

Gruff laughter.

Jock Durham wasn't in the futures and derivatives market for nothing. He liked to think he knew a potentially sound investment when he saw one.

"If you like," he conceded.

"The Editor wondered if it might be possible to take a photograph of you with the bear," Alice lied smoothly.

"I haven't got it," Jock Durham replied, relieved that he could avoid getting mixed up with some idiotic photographic session. "I asked Cholmondley's to send it directly to my mother."

"So you haven't ever seen it in the flesh—I mean, fur?" Alice asked with surprise.

"No. Now if you don't mind . . ."

"Thank you, Mr. Durham," said Alice politely. "You've been very kind." She paused. "There's just one more thing. Would it be possible to have a word with your mother just to hear how pleased she is to have the bear back in the family again?"

"Out of the question," snapped Jock Durham rudely and the line went dead.

Puzzled, Alice strolled over to the coffee machine and bought herself a wilting plastic mug of hot chocolate. Then she returned to her desk still deep in thought.

If Jock Durham hadn't seen Hugo, either before or after the sale, how had he been able to inform Richard Hunt that the bear's eyes weren't Steiff originals?"

She re-dialed.

"Interflora here."

"Again?" said the stone wall. "But I gave you the delivery address yesterday."

"I'm so sorry to trouble you once more but it's the address of the *older* Mrs. Durham I need."

"Oh!" said the stone wall, surprised. "She's in a home. Hang on."

Alice could hear some scrabbling at the other end of the line.

"Well, you're in luck," said the woman triumphantly. "I knew I'd put it some place but I wasn't sure where. Hibiscus Lodge, Church Road, Brighton."

"Thanks," said Alice quietly.

Nikki had certainly done her stuff. She'd booked the appointment with Lady Arabella Jagger and here she was, on cue, ringing the shop again.

Alice edged over to the window display. All she had to do was to stand with her back to the window and slide her hand down inside the black velvet curtain.

"It's *The Globe* again," hissed Lady Arabella's assistant. "She wants to talk to you personally and won't take no for an answer."

Alice was faintly amused by Nikki's persistence. Maybe she would make a good investigative journalist one day.

She felt the assistant's eyes on her and her hand—poised halfway to the silver salver—trembled. Suddenly the black velvet curtain detached itself from the wall. To avoid discovery, Alice swung her fist across the display sending the jewelry flying. There was a crash of falling pillars and a splatter of stones against the plate glass window.

Diamonds dripped onto the shop floor and rolled along the pale polished floorboards. Pinned to the telephone, Lady Arabella Jagger was powerless to rescue her precious stock. Her eyes darted insanely around the shop as she sprang from her seat and performed a mad Irish jig giving off potent whiffs of expensive citrus perfume.

Seeing her assistant scrabbling head-down in a corner on hands and knees, Alice seized the salver and ripped the black eyes off their matching double-sided sticky pads. In seconds they were safely in her pocket.

"I'm *so* sorry," Alice gushed. "I really *do* apologize.

What can I say? I'm overcome with embarrassment. *Such a stupid clumsy thing to do.''*

The assistant scowled at her while Lady Arabella Jagger—still glued to the telephone—gestured wildly at her assistant and mouthed obscenities quite at odds with her sleek golden appearance.

''You'd better wait until I've accounted for everything,'' said the assistant coldly.

Alice plonked herself down in the black leather chair beside the woman's desk.

''I think these were attached to the plate,'' she said casually, placing the sheath-knife carefully on the desk along with two black boot-button eyes which the Doll's Hospital had been kind enough to sell her for the princely sum of £1.50 each.

''Only a few minutes, mind you,'' said the starchy white nurse.

''She's been sleeping very badly and tires quickly.''

At first Alice could see little while her eyes adjusted to the shadows in the room of the private nursing home. The blinds were skewed to let in a shaft of afternoon sunlight, but other than that the small space was cool and dark.

''Mrs. Durham?'' she ventured, crossing over to the armchair where a frail figure was wrapped in a thick patchwork blanket.

Alice knelt down by the chair and touched her arm.

''Mrs. Durham, I've come to visit Hugo,'' she said softly.

The eyes blinked open and Ethel Durham stared blankly at Alice while her mind re-grouped itself.

''Do I know you?'' she quavered.

Alice stood up and swept Hugo off the bed and onto Mrs. Durham's knee. Propelling his paw up and down, she made the bear wave slowly at his new mistress.

The old woman gave a tinkling laugh like fine bone china breaking on a terracotta floor.

''Can you tell me when you first met Hugo?'' Alice asked.

Ethel Durham beamed. Far-off memories were much easier to recall than what she'd had for dinner the night before.

"Oh, my dear, I was six. We were living in a grass hut and my Daddy gave him to me for my birthday. I was worried he'd be too hot with all that fur."

Alice wondered whether the old woman's mind was wandering.

"Where were you living then?" she asked gently.

"The Cook Islands. We were living on Rarotonga. My father went there as a missionary in 1908."

"Is that where he met your mother?"

"No, they met at a dance in Keighley."

"Did both your parents come from Yorkshire?"

"My father was Irish."

"And how long did you live in the Cook Islands?"

"Till I was twelve. Then I was sent to live with my aunt in Keighley because they didn't think it proper to bring up a young lady where there were—so many rough men."

"Did Hugo come with you to England?"

"Yes." Ethel Durham's eyes looked dreamy. "Shall I tell you a story?"

"Oh yes, please do," said Alice enthusiastically. She glanced at her watch, wondering how long she'd got before the starchy white nurse would spirit her away.

"The men were savages, you know. They lived in the mountains and wore hardly anything at all. Grass skirts for ceremonial occasions. They cooked their food in underground ovens and ate with their fingers.

"My father met up with a trader called Tom Donovan who'd spent some time there and was able to speak a bit of the language. He and my father talked to the village chiefs and persuaded them to stop warring among the different clans and to move from the mountains to the coastal plain.

"When my father burned down a statue of one of their heathen gods the village chiefs were so impressed with the power of Jesus that they converted to Christianity and ordered all their people to be baptized.

"But Tom was always warning mother that it was too

good to be true. He said that cannibals didn't change their spots. And he was right. He ended up in the pot after a huge dispute with one of the chiefs about fishing rights.

"After that, my mother took a few precautions in case we had to leave the island quickly. She gave me strict instructions about what I had to do if anything happened to her or my father. She showed me how to pack my bag and took me to meet a half-caste who had a boat. She gave him money and he was to take me to Samoa where I could board a freighter, which called once a month, and make my way to a cousin in New Zealand.

"She insisted that the one thing I should take with me, apart from my bag, was Hugo. Tom had given her a present, she said, which she had sewn onto Hugo. If ever I was without money I was to take Hugo's eyes to a jeweller. My mother was a very clever woman, don't you know?"

Ethel Durham's fingers stroked Hugo while her mind hovered half in the present, half in the past.

"You wouldn't guess that Hugo's eyes are valuable Cook Island black pearls, would you? They're only found in a certain part of Polynesia which makes them very rare. I suppose they must be antiques by now."

Alice was stunned. For a moment she couldn't think of anything to say, then quickly pulled herself together.

"What a wonderful story, Mrs. Durham. No wonder he's such a precious bear."

Alice gave Hugo's head a perfunctory pat while she thought rapidly. There was no point in telling Mrs. Durham—who obviously couldn't see too well—that Hugo's eyes had cost £1.50 each from the Doll's Hospital in London. Nor was there any reason to explain how her son had unwittingly betrayed her secret to a treacherous daughter-in-law.

"How did you come to lose Hugo?" she asked. "Cholmondley's said the seller found him in an attic wrapped in newspaper."

"Ah, that was when my aunt died. There was a dispute in her family over her will and the estate was frozen for ages while it was all sorted out. By then I'd qualified as a nurse and emigrated to Canada. I kept asking my cousins to let me have the bear but it was never sent on. I suppose poor Hugo was forgotten and got left behind when my aunt's house was sold.''

"But at least you're reunited now," said Alice kindly.

Much to Alice's amazement Elaine agreed to run a feature on Cholmondley's maritime sale in the Boat Show Special. Collaring her on Christmas Eve exploited the guilt factor to the full. Alice decided to give Richard Hunt a quick call to give him the good news.

"Heard anymore from Hugo's buyer after your article appeared?" Richard asked, slurring his words slightly.

"Hugo is in very good hands," Alice replied firmly.

"Glad to hear it," replied Richard unevenly. It sounded as if his Christmas Eve lunch had been a long and alcoholic one.

Alice seized her opportunity with characteristic slyness.

"Richard, I don't suppose you could tell me when Cholmondley's next jewelry sale takes place, could you?" she asked sweetly. "I've inherited something I can hardly bear to part with but, like everyone else these days, I need the money."

Nicole Swengley is a regular contributor to *The Times* and *Daily Telegraph* and the author of two non-fiction books. She writes: "The most satisfactory experience of Christmas long past was waking in the early hours and feeling the bulky weight of a well-stuffed Christmas stocking across my childish legs. Oddly enough, I felt no desire to peep. The sleepy knowledge that Santa had visited yet again was pleasure enough until morning came.

"One year—I must have been about nine—my Christmas present was a bright red shiny sit-up-and-beg typewriter with circular black and silver keys which clacked in a deeply authentic manner. Rival comics soon began appearing in our household. Whether this early editorial experience presaged my future career as a freelance journalist is open to interpretation."

Season of Goodwill

MIKE SEABROOK

I generally try and give Harry Peacock a lot of personal space, because people who get too close to him have a nasty tendency to find themselves helping Old Bill with his enquiries. He's a wiry little short-arse of a geezer, half black and half Indian, from Mauritius. He once had a twenty-dollar name, but he stopped being Harrington Push-pathakaraghavan or whatever piece of elasticated Tamil it was and became Harry Peacock, because he thought it would make people trust him better. Seeing that he could call himself Mr. Justice Peacock and a blind man still wouldn't trust Harry with a bent penny, scarlet and ermine and wig and all, it wasn't a great success in his case; still, at least people could pronounce it better—rather like me when I dropped my real name, which was Jayantibhai, of all things, and became just plain Jack Patel.

The next thing I know about Harry is that he's in the *Guinness Book of Records*, and the Scotland Yard Book of Records also, for being on the highest number of bank, credit card and finance house wanted lists at one time, and the third is that he covered himself in immortality one time when we were celebrating after getting a result in some job with a slap-up Chinkie at a restaurant run by a mate of mine out Hounslow way. I read a story one time about someone called Cortes, who went and conquered South America back in the time of Henry the Eighth or Lord Nelson or somebody. Apparently he ran into this geezer called Montezuma, who was king of the Aztecs, or it may have been the Incas, and Montezuma put a solid gold fingerbowl in front of him, and this Cortes thought it was a glass of water and drank it. It sounds like a perfectly reasonable mistake to make to me, but anyway, Harry did the same thing at the Jade Garden, Hounslow, and had the piss taken right royally for a long time afterwards.

Not that that's got anything to do with anything, but it's the thing everybody knows about Harry, and seems to have stuck, because he's known as Fingerbowl to some of the geezers on the manor now, or Fingers for short. But I'm sure you'll forgive me if I continue calling him Harry: I've known him longer than most, and always called him plain Harry, and it's too late to change; besides, "Fingers" sounds so naff, as if I was telling some crime story to the kids.

The other thing that's worth knowing about Harry is that the one thing he's never short of is ideas, and that's really where we come in now, because I got the idea for my Christmas special from him, and a right bleeding catastroscope it turned out to be.

Harry's a Catholic like I'm a Hindu—that is, he goes to Mass when his old woman really looks as if she's going to make life not worth living for him if he resists. But, also like me, he's equally respectful of all faiths and denominations in his observation of holidays. Personally, I celebrate Christmas and Easter as cheerfully as I celebrate Diwali. And Muhammad's birthday, Buddha's birthday and my birthday. I'd celebrate the principal feasts of Shinto, Taoism and ancient Egyptian sun worship, if I knew the dates; all the same, Christmas is somehow special to both of us; and we both like to celebrate these happy occasions properly, with the maximum amount of brotherly love spread around; so it only remains for someone to supply the brotherly love, in the form of plenty of grub, booze and presents. Especially booze.

To this end, Harry told me on the fatal day, he always gets himself a job with one of the big department stores when Christmas approaches. When I'd finished registering astonishment at the idea of him taking any kind of a job at all, naturally I asked why, and he told me.

It seems that he doesn't take just any old job, but always driving one of the store's delivery vans. The stores are always desperate to take on extra delivery drivers at the heaviest time of the year for orders, so they never bother to give his credentials even a cursory once-over. If anyone starts as much as looking like doing any of the normal checks, Harry says, he's had it on his feet before the geezer can get his clipboard into the "Off" position. But nobody ever does, and last year it was Selfridges who drew the short straw.

The main idea behind this unaccustomed period in employment is obvious enough: Harry delivers all sorts of special orders to all sorts of addresses, lots of them of the poshest. All he has to do is to make a mental note of what he's delivered and where, and he's in business. Tuesday: delivered one mink, one silver fox and six cases of Glen McSporran to number 123 The Bishops Avenue. Wednesday: one five-foot square flat-screen TV, one high-class video and one economy size service of Waterford Crystal to an address in your Ham and High. Thursday: one set of solid platinum taps for all six baths somewhere in Golders Green. Well, you've got my drift, of course. All Harry has to do then is get his little team organized, wait for the residents at number 123 The Bishops Avenue or wherever to set off to the next Christmas party, and it's up the drainpipe—or more likely, straight in through the French windows—and it's one mink and one silver fox for the fence, and six cases of Glen McSporran to split between Harry and the lads as a nice Christmas bonus.

Sometimes he gets a team together, for the heavy stuff, with a wheelman and all. Other times, for the really valu-

able small items he goes in up the drainpipe himself—
Harry's a very fair B&E man himself, though he's getting
a bit of old for that kind of lark now. However, for the
solid gold, diamond-encrusted item, he'll still go in alone.
But there's always one bit of special help Harry needs, and
that's a driver. I should explain that, unless you take a
wheelman, there are sound professional reasons for not
driving to a job of this kind. Basically, it's just too risky:
there's always a chance of random breath-test stops—especially around Christmas, when Plod positively overflows
with the spirit of brotherly love and goodwill to all men;
and there are all the normal problems of parking, getting
pranged by some other idiot and getting turned over as part
of the normal routine, and so on. Whereas no one, not even
the keenest figure-hunting young probationary rookie, often
pulls a cab, let alone a bloke on a bus. So what Harry does
on a job of this kind is to go to the scene by bus, and call
a cab for the getaway. What more obvious? So at a prear-
ranged time, when he knows he'll be leaving the premises,
a car is on hand, supplied by a friendly minicab firm, at a
given corner of the street, waiting to pick up Harry and the
gear. He always uses the same minicab firm, and always
asks for a driver he knows well. It's usually, in fact, me.
There's always a little Christmas bonus in it for me, and
often we can do Harry a favor in return by taking the bent
gear off his hands straight off—if it's the sort of stuff
they'll be interested in, like perfume, or booze, or a vanload
of videos, we've quite often simply taken it back to the
office and flogged the lot to the drivers in the course of a
night.

Well, this year I'm talking about, Harry had been doing
all his usual preparation, clocking what he'd been delivering and where to and all that, when a surprise bonus presented itself. He was sloping out through the goods outward
bay, slipping like a shadow between the close lines of vans,
when he noticed that the glass security box was empty for
a minute. Well, that's simply more than someone like Harry
can be expected to resist. It's the work of less than thirty
seconds for him to find a van that some prat of a driver's

left well stocked up and with the keys in the ignition, start her up and off into the dense Christmas traffic. An hour and a half later the gear's safely stowed in the lock-up garage Harry rents in Hounslow, and the van's safely back in the goods outward back at the shop. The security blokes are back in their little glass box when Harry drives it back in of course, but who's going to notice which of the forty or fifty drivers—or maybe, being Christmas, the hundred and odd—drives a van back *into* the yard? Quite right.

So, later that night, our office smells like a whore's boudoir as all the drivers try out the merchandise—but a very expensive whore: some of the girls I've got an arrangement with for specially vetted fares I pick up from time to time late at night from certain hotels and casinos smell like that. Because the load happens to have been perfume, so Harry knows he can flog it to our lot, and save himself the trouble of fencing it. All our drivers have solved their last-minute Christmas present problems for their girlfriends, Harry's had a result and saved himself a hefty cut to his fence, the goods is safely dispersed so Plod's got more chance of being struck by lightning than tracking any of it down: technically, the job's down to West End Central CID, being committed at Selfridges; the gear was stowed briefly at Hounslow, Harry lives in Wembley and our office is in Brentford; and a whole fleet of drivers' girlfriends and the odd wife or two all stink of Poison for six months after.

Anyway, I suppose it's time I came to the point. You'll have been wondering how all this came to bring about my downfall. Well, this Christmas I'm talking about I'd been doing all right, but then took one of the dives that happen occasionally. It's all part of life's pattern, and you get used to it, but it's never nice, and especially not at Christmas. As it happened I'd just had a bit of an up and a downer with one of the casinos I have an arrangement with. Normally I take, maybe, a couple of dozen specially selected punters who hire my minicab to this casino every week. I take them inside, signal to DJ-wearing types lurking in reception, they come forward and usher the Jap or Arab punter—it's almost always a Jap or an Arab, though the Chinks are getting into it pretty big nowadays, as well, come to think of it—anyway, these DJ-wearing types take the punter off my hands, and a bit later I return to collect the wreckage, and a cut from the grateful casino out of his losings.

Sadly, I'd taken them a couple of duff numbers, one way and another lately, and they'd had some bad trouble, even bringing the patter of enormous feet into the premises on one occasion, which is something they do *not* appreciate. Also, on account of services rendered they would let me play a bit myself now and then, only I'd had a very big winning streak—big for me, that is—and that they don't appreciate either. So there was a certain coolness in the air between them and me, and it was affecting my earning power something bloody disastrous.

So, all in all, what with the Missus starting to ask questions about why the minicab business was suddenly taking a downturn just when I ought to have been as busy as a one-legged cat in a sandbox with all the Christmas party business, and me as miserable as sin anyway on account of being denied my little flutter, which is one of my greatest pleasures in life, I was unusually receptive when Harry started bending my ear about the joys of driving for the big stores over the Christmas period. We had a few bevies and Harry talked about it some more, and told me about some of the ramps and scams he'd got going for him courtesy of Selfridges, and before I knew what I was saying I'd decided to give it a go myself.

Well, the first part went off reasonably well, though it could have been better. Harry made discreet enquiries on behalf of this mate of his, and they duly called me in to interview me. The interview was, as you might imagine, nothing more than a joke, but as it turned out they hadn't got any driving jobs right that minute. However, they had got one batch of jobs coming up right away, and would I care to take one of them on, while I waited for one of the temporary drivers to drink his wages and get breathalyzed, or bend one of the firm's vans and get fired, or, most likely,

just to get fed up with the unaccustomed rigours of working
and not turn up the day after pay-day—one of which was
certain to happen within the week? Harry gave me a firm,
enthusiastic nod, I accepted, and half an hour later I was
installed. As one of a dozen brand new Santa Clauses, scarlet suit, long white whiskers and all.

Well, Harry was OTM. Personally, I had my doubts. But
he led me aside and started congratulating me as if I'd
personally prevailed on the management to give me the
combination of the safe. I was mystified, but he rapidly
explained. "You're fireproof," he crowed. "You couldn't
have asked for a better cover if you'd specified it yourself."
And he went on to explain what I had to do. Starting at
eight o'clock the next morning, I got down to it.

It was simple enough. There was Harry, with a family
size supply of criminal intent and a van to take the results
away in. And there, in the very midst of Aladdin's cave,
was me, with a large sack. The camouflage was the best
imaginable: who takes any notice of Father Christmas
shambling toward his grotto with his sack of presents over
his shoulder for the little horrors? Who's going to suspect
anything amiss if a van marked "Selfridges" in letters two
feet high comes out of Selfridges' yard? We creamed it for
nearly a week. Harry did all the casing. All I had to do was
vary the way I walked throughout the giant store to my
grotto every shift, after breaks and so on; and who's going
to notice that one out of a dozen Santa Clauses goes one
way from the staff canteen to his pitch after his tea break,
and another way after his lunch? Even if anybody's ever
thought Father Christmas was on the wrong sledge path,
with about a million staff there for the pre-Xmas rush,
who's going to notice, or know which Father Christmas it
was? Or have the time to take any notice? In any case,
who's going to care?

So every evening when we met up in the boozer back
home in Wembley, Harry told me what he'd seen in the
store that looked nickable and easy to fence, where it
was, how many staff there were to worry about in that
department, and next day I'd be found bumbling my way

through that department on the way to my daily encounter with the flower of the nation's youth, lugging my lolloping great sack of plastic dustbin-bait behind me ... and slipping the odd unconsidered trifle into the same sack's capacious maw as I passed through; and for a week we made this very nice little killing. Somewhere along the route Harry would be waiting quietly with his own container, apparently on its way to be loaded onto his van, and brandishing a clipboard with delivery note and invoice, all as kosher as could be. And no one so much as glanced up as we did the business.

I lifted all the usual stuff, small enough to be easy to sweep into my sack, easy to get rid of and not too noticeable when it first disappeared—perfumes, whole canteens full of silver cutlery, ornaments, clocks, even a bit of tom they were unwise enough to display on a pedestal without a lockable cabinet. That was a bottle tester, but we got away with it, and even then it was over half an hour before the alarm went up.

All this gear went out on Harry's regular runs, and we fenced most of it at my minicab office when I went in to drive the night shift. And then, just as my nerves were beginning to settle down and I was beginning to think we were on the easiest pickings since the Enclosures Acts, we got found out.

Actually, we got found out twice, and the first time we managed to see the danger off without any trouble. The second time, it was just pure farce. Harry, to be sure, has had the occasional bit of grief with Old Bill, you know, like everybody has, and most times it was his own fault or, more often, just bad luck, wrong person in wrong place at wrong time, copper comes around corner, have it on feet by instinct, can't run as fast as copper, "Guilty, your Honour," "Pay a fine of ...," or, more recently, "Disgraceful record. You will go to prison for ..." As for me, I've always managed to keep my nose clean, or, at least, out of the same frame as the pursuing copper in the official photograph for first place—all bar once, anyway, and that was different, as you may remember if you read the account of it I gave in one of these little case-histories of mine.

As I say, the first time we got caught it was no big thing. Like most of the great detective work in history, it was pure chance. Another of the temporary drivers, taken on like Harry for the Christmas rush, went by mistake to the wrong van. And, of course, he had to pick Harry's van to go to. While he was rummaging through the load wondering why it didn't look familiar, he found a lot of very suspicious-looking bent gear.

Well, that might have been that. If he'd been a lot of the blokes, he'd have simply grassed us; we'd have received separate, innocuous looking summonses to pop into the office, and there would be the reception committee, and maybe Plod also, all looking terribly stern and (with the important exception of Plod, who'll be looking so gleeful it'd make you want to throw up) disappointed and more-in-sorrow-than-in-anger, like missionaries who've discovered one of the converts sneaking out the back door of the old witch doctor's tent, and giving us the old "How could you betray our trust in you like this?" act, and all that sanctimonious cant, which ignores the fact that the whole place is all got up to be a giant-sized open invitation to tea-leaves of every description, and if they insist on leaving jam out in open bowls to attract a lot of fat, greedy blue-bottles (if you'll forgive the expression), they're going to get the odd wasp as well . . . still, I shouldn't start doing the old philosophy bit, or we'll be here all night; and anyway, like I say, it wasn't one of the honest Joes who found us out. Oh, no.

What this bastard did was very neat. Having found out what Harry and I were up to by sheer chance, he then watched us carefully for—well, it must have been a couple of days. Then he followed us off the premises at the end of one day, and came up to us while we were having a jar and discussing plans for the morrow back home on the manor. So there's Harry and me, sitting in the Ferret happily deciding what we'll be having off the next day, when this big, beefy Englishman comes up. He sort of looms over us at our table for a moment, looking down at us. Then,

"Hmmm," he goes, very sneering and nasty, "one short-arse spade, one wily oriental gentleman from the sub-continent. *Not* a great credit to centuries of benevolent British rule, I fear."

Harry looks at me, and I look at Harry, and then we both, as if moved by the same spring, glance across in the direction of Georgie Clarke, who's a sort of freelance hard man, and a good pal of mine. He helped me in one of my minor adventures once, and turned out to be very valuable, given the right management—Georgie doesn't keep a great deal of furniture on mahogany row, so to speak, but he's a terribly efficient Number Two. Besides, he wouldn't like the idea of miscellaneous hard cases from other manors coming running blazers on us. However, before we had a chance to do anything, the newcomer had sat down with us at our table. We didn't want a scene, so we let him, and sat there glaring at him in an angry, heavily charged silence, waiting for him to say something.

In the end, of course, he put the bite on us, claiming to have the goods, the whole goods and nothing but the goods on us. It was all interspersed with a lot of unpleasantness of a highly racialist kind, and we thought about calling the police, but in the end we just made a late-night appointment to meet him to hand over some of what he was demanding with menaces, and then got George to keep it on our behalf. After that the geezer was too busy recovering in traction to worry about Harry and me. I don't like to think about what happened on that dark night in the even darker place we'd arranged to meet the geezer, but these things have got to be stamped out.

Well, with this bloke suddenly indisposed, I finally got my promotion from Father Christmas to driver. That was the most annoying and frustrating part of it all: there I was, sitting pretty, all ready to come into what was rightfully my own high estate, only to be brought low by the last possible source imaginable—a foolish, ignorant woman, with far more money than she knows what to do with and no sense at all.

It was our immediate misfortune that I knew this woman,

or rather, that she knew me. When I married my Banu, it was an arranged match, she coming from a very well-to-do Bombay family; and this Meherbai Shroff was a very close friend of her family. Her old man's a hot-shot lawyer, and also a Parsee, which means he rakes in hugh amounts of loot from all the rich Parsees out there, including a lot of Tata and Irani money, from that side, plus plenty from the Birlas and others on the Hindu side. Well, now, Mehrnosh-Uncle is a very sprightly, jovial old boy, of the rotund tendency—indeed, he's almost circular—with a permanent sunny smile behind big around glasses like the bottoms of Vimto bottles. It's always struck me he must have tremendous eyesight to be able to see through glasses that thick. Anyway, he's often over here, smuggling some of his money out to stash it in various Swiss bank accounts; and when he's here, he keeps Meherbai in order. But sometimes she takes it into her head to come over on her own, just to see Banu and other members of her enormous circle of family and friends; and then there's always trouble.

Meherbai is a typical woman of her type, class and station in Bombay life. Nothing to do with caste—you don't want to listen to all that nonsense—but everything to do with her money—or, anyway, Mehrnosh's money. This means, cutting a long story short, that she lives like a Maharani of the old order, she keeps half a suburb of Bombay in employment as servants in their huge house, and she wouldn't know her way to her own kitchen, let alone how to boil an egg if she got there. Not that she'd ever try to find her way there: she'd regard it as far beneath her dignity to be seen dead, buried and decomposed in such a part of the building. This is all right: about the only thing that might bring her contented and well-paid staff out on strike is if she started interfering in their part of the house. The whole place runs like a Swiss watch, and the only thing you have to remember when you're there is not to forget yourself and say "Thank you" to any of the servants when they wait on you at table and so on, because she thinks this is lowering yourself and will give them ideas above their station.

Occasionally she takes herself off into the city to buy something she doesn't think she ought to entrust to one of the servants, and this, too, is all right. A price-tag in Bombay is never more than a basis for negotiation, and that goes even in the biggest, smartest shops, like in Jhaveri Bazaar. So everybody indulges in the national pastime of bargaining. This applies even to the very wealthiest, like Meherbai. So, for example, she'll have herself driven down to K. Wadia's—that's their Asprey's—and select, say, a diamond necklace, with a price tag of five lakhs—half a million rupees to you and me. She'll offer the sales assistant one lakh. He'll say four. She'll say one and a half, he'll suggest three and a half, until they agree on a sale price of three lakhs, and everybody's happy. There's nothing unusual or untoward about all this: everybody does it, it's expected, and nobody would be more surprised if the rich lady didn't dicker over the price than the shop assistant. Indeed, if she didn't she'd get a *lot* of stick from all her rich mates, who'd all start in on her angrily, demanding to know how they're to be expected to get fair prices if she's going to start letting the side down by paying the price asked—and so on. You can imagine the rest.

Well, as I say, this is all very well in its proper place, which is Bombay. The trouble with people like Meherbai is that they're totally insulated from reality. This has two consequences: first, they haven't a clue how the real world, including the rest of us, who live there, works. Second, and interlocking with this, is the fact that they combine this fathomless ignorance with a sublime confidence that they know all there is to know about everything, the real world included. If you live in the midst of a swarm of servants, not one of whom is ever going to breathe the suspicion of a word of contradiction to your lightest or silliest word, from saying an egg costs ten times what they actually *know* it costs, since it's them who pay for the eggs in the house, to saying the world is flat, it doesn't do a lot for your humility.

So someone like Meherbai goes sailing majestically through life, taking it utterly for granted first of all that the remainder of the human race exists solely, or at least mainly, to serve her, and secondly that there is nothing that she doesn't know—nothing, at any rate, that she needs to know that she doesn't know.

The result of this was that on my last morning as Santa I was strolling through the store on my way to my grotto and the day's ration of little bastards, with my mind's eye firmly on a beautiful golden ocelot jacket and a very nice canteen of silver-plated cutlery that weighed enough to sink the *Titanic* that I'd already got stuffed in the top of my sack, when what should I see but a fracas in full swing around the perfume counter. And who should it be but— yes, you guessed it—Meherbai Shroff.

I groaned silently at the prospect—I hadn't known she was over here—slung my sack of assorted junk and carefully selected non-junk properly over my shoulder and started sidling off toward the nearest exit. Maybe I went into automatic pilot, but it so happened that the exit I slipped through was the one I usually went through to get my swag to the loading bay to get it stowed in Harry's van. But, as you'll have worked out for yourself, I was too late. A piercing shriek of recognition rang through the gigantic store like a car alarm going off in a trombone factory, and in a moment she was after me. Unfortunately she forgot to put down the *very* expensive bottle of Joy she was clutching, which caused several assistants to come hot-footing after her, and I came panting and spluttering into the loading-bay only a short head in front of the field, totally confused by panic, surprise and shortness of breath. And as I came charging out onto the dock, two things happened: Meherbai caught up with me, angrily demanding why I had gone sloping off like that and clawing equally infuriatingly at my shoulder in a mixture of hysteria, excitement, infuriated hauteur at the insolence of the counter assistant who had looked superciliously down his long, thin nose at her when she attempted to offer him one quarter of the asking price for the Joy, and relief at seeing a friendly face. The second thing that happened was that as Meherbai came crashing up from one side, Harry came scooting around the side of his van and up onto the dock from the other, carrying a soft cloth bag containing *his* morning's work.

So, as I came out onto the tailgate-height stone dock where the vans are loaded, Meherbai came charging out after me like a frightened sheep, pursued by her entourage of sales assistants, all trying to pacify her and assure her that there was no need for alarm at the same time as they were trying to carry on a furious argument among themselves, each trying to blame the others for letting the silly old bag try to dicker over price in the inner sanctum, and their boss puffing fatly along twenty yards behind the young girls and boys trying to bollock all of them at once and uttering blood-curdling threats of the sack, or, what seemed to be worse, demotion to household linens or some such thing, sounding all the time as if he was about to expire of a heart attack, acute asthma or both.

As Meherbai came barging into me amidships at a rate of knots, the others, unable to put their brakes on in time, all came piling into the fray like motorists in one of those fifty-vehicle pile-ups on the M1 in fog. I'd have been bowled over under this lot, and probably have gone sailing over the edge of the dock like an Olympic diver going off the five-meter board, if it hadn't been for little Harry coming scuttling furtively around the looming side of his van, clutching the soft cloth bag. He got in my path neatly in time to stop me from taking a header into the oily, gungy dispatch bay, and went flying himself. His cloth bag went sailing through the air, and landed like a perfect nine-iron shot, right at the feet of the fat bastard chasing the assorted kids who were after Meherbai.

I went crashing on top of Harry, crushing every bit of breath out of him and scuppering any chance he might have had of doing a runner—even assuming he'd have had enough presence of mind left to think of it in the first place, which is a bit unlikely, Harry not being a contender for the world quick thinking title. I am a contender, but any chance I might have had was promptly snookered by Meherbai landing in my solar plexus.

Meherbai eats like a rich woman with no looks to consider, and I expired with a noise like a football getting punctured in a burping competition; and just as Harry's cloth bag was landing at the fat bastard's feet, my Santa Claus sack went flying, and landed under the noses of the rugby scrum of kids trying to set Meherbai on her feet, brush her down, stop her hysterical tears and, most of all, to recover the pint and a half bottle of Joy, which must have been worth one of the smaller South American countries' gross domestic product, and which she was still clutching in a convulsive, vice-like grasp. All through the whole of this lot Merherbai was still producing a series of sound effects that sounded like a troop of howler monkeys swinging through the Amazon jungle, and would have drowned out the Last Trump.

I sat up, rubbing various bits of myself, and glanced fearfully around to survey the damage. "Can't someone shut that silly cow up?" came in groaning tones from somewhere underneath me, and I shifted a bit to let Harry out from under me. He sat up dizzily, shaking his head and making a sort of panting "wough-wough-wough" noise like a cross between a pair of old-fashioned bellows and an old dog snuffing it.

We looked at each other, looked around and back at each other. The extent of the disaster reflected in his face and, I dare say, in mine too. Fat Bastard had totally forgotten Meherbai and the vengeance he had been threatening his sales kids with, and was peering instead, in mingled astonishment and delight, at a sparkling assortment of small but very expensive items trawled from a highly unguided tour of the store undertaken by Harry that morning, now strewn at his feet where they had spilled out of Harry's soft cloth bag when it landed there. Meanwhile the kids were marveling at the unexpected appearance of my beautiful golden ocelot coat, and scrabbling around on the filthy floor of the dock gathering up the heavy, curlicued knives and forks and spoons from the canteen I'd lifted, which had shot from my sack and burst open in their midst.

That was it, really. Harry and I were well nicked, of course, and taken under heavy escort by the kids to the lock-up, under the eagle and self-satisfied eye of Fat Bastard, who was already quite visibly working out his story of how he had planned it all, and equally visibly wondering how much a year the promotion he expected to get out of it would come to. The only minor consolation Harry and I got was that Meherbai was also nicked, for a short time, when Fat Bastard got carried away and thought she was in on it with us.

In the end, however, we had a happy Christmas after all. After much long and hard thought the store decided not to prosecute, on account of the bad publicity and not wanting to announce to the world through a megaphone that its security arrangements were as watertight as the *Spirit of Free Enterprise*. The moral of the story is, first, that if you ever decide to go bent, don't pick Harry as your partner, because the juju on him is as potent as ever; second, it's not other villains who'll screw it up for you, but innocent silly old ladies; and third, doing good to others really *is* the best way of spending Christmas. I know what I shall be doing with my spare time next year when the season of goodwill to all men comes round: lobbing out soup for the Silver Lady to the winos in the Embankment Gardens. You can't get into trouble that way. I hope.

Mike Seabrook has unhappy memories of Christmas, particularly the three occasions when he was a policeman at Bow Street Station and spent the festive season on the beat. The author of four novels and compiler of several sporting anthologies, he has also written *Coppers*, about life in the British police, as well as a life of the composer Peter Maxwell Davies. He now lives in the Jura mountains on the Franco-Swiss border.

More Than Flesh & Blood

SUSAN MOODY

◆

Looking back, he was always to remember the place as like a honeycomb, full of golden light. The walls of the houses, made of some yellowish local stone, were glazed with it. Roofs, covered in ochre-edged rings of lichen, dripped it back into the single narrow street, where the front doors opened straight into what would once have been called the parlor.

After the long journey through the barren hills, the village welcomed him. Driving across the humped stone bridge, he knew at once that he'd found what he was looking for. He stopped the car and got out. There were no shops, no pub, no one to ask the way. At the far end of the street there were cows, creamy-gold in the fierce light of the starting-to-set sun, sauntering toward an open farm gate. Beyond it, stone buildings, mud and hay, metal churns, indicated a dairy. He followed them.

A woman was already clamping the first cow to the nozzles of an electric milking-machine. She looked up at him without straightening, her face strong from confronting the weather unprotected for fifty or sixty years.

"I'm trying to find this house," he said, city-diffident in the presence of elemental sources. He showed her the photograph, thumb and fourth finger grasping the edges of the thick cardboard.

"Aye," she said.

"Beckwith House, I believe it's called."

"Aye."

"Is it here? In the village?"

"Noo." Her voice was soft, rounded as the cows she tended. "Noo, it's not."

That shook him a little. He had been so sure it would be here, friendly with other houses, neighbored.

"Where then?"

"It's up t'dale a way." She nodded toward the road behind him and the deep hills into which it led. Already, shadows were tumbling down the slopes, only the higher crests fully daylit, though he could still see the outlines of the dry-stone walls which criss-crossed the lower slopes, and the occasional brooding bulk of a barn.

"How far?"

"Two, three miles. Mebbe four. It's right on t'road."

"Thank you."

As she moved back toward the gate, she called after him: "Does she know you're coming?"

He stopped. "Does who know I'm coming?"

"The missus."

He smiled and shook his head. "No," he said. "She doesn't."

Back in the open again, after the temporary closing in of the village, he could feel wind sweeping down from the high fells, gusting the car toward the edge of the black road. Now that he was close to where he had been heading for most of his life, he felt none of the excitement he had anticipated, merely a sense of a waiting void about to be filled.

"... *somewhere* ..." she used to say, cruelly. But where? Until today, he had not known. Now, the place, the time, the night edging down on him from above, fitted around him as though tailor-made.

The road began to wind. In the bend of a turn, he saw stone gateposts, iron gates twice as tall as he was, laurels massed behind walls. He parked on the verge, tucking the car in close. Behind the gates was a short drive curving toward a house, square and two-storied. Though he had never been here before, he knew precisely how the path led around behind the house, past deep-silled windows to a porched side door. He knew it would come out onto a flag-stoned terrace looking over an enclosed garden. He knew the view from the windows at the rear of the house, and where the plums and apples would stand on either side of the wrought-iron gate set in the garden wall, through which, like a photograph, could be seen a segment of landscape. There would be a pond, too, beside the terrace, and a rock-ery full of alpines, little crawling plants that overflowed and spilled down the edges of white stones. On one of the gate-posts there was a round slate plaque. Beckwith House. He traced the two meniscal curves of the B with his finger. He turned the handle of the right-hand gate. It whimpered me-tallically. The iron bars resisted as he pushed, then opened, following a deep groove in the gravelled earth behind it.

   . . . *somewhere* . . .

Here. He'd found it at last, been drawn to it, almost, though perhaps that was a trifle fanciful. He had had so little to go on, just the whispered, half-heard word— "Garthway . . ." Garthway? The more he tried to re-run the sequence in his head, the dying eyes filming even as they looked at him, the huge body heaving, the lips puckering as they tried to form the word while one hand twitched slowly on the turndown of the linen sheet with the border of drawn-thread work, the less he could remember what exactly had been said.

His feet made no sound on the earth. The gravel had long since sunk into the soil and now lay embedded in it like the eyes of drowning men below the surface of the water. Neglect entombed the house. He walked between the leaves of dark unpruned laurels. There was a faint light in one of the windows, its dirt-streaked panes almost hidden by creeper long left untended.

There was a glow, too, from the ornate fanlight above the front door. He banged the knocker and felt the house pause, listening, questioning. Footsteps came along the passage toward him, brisk, almost eager.

The woman who opened the door stared at him for a time. Later he could not have said for how long. Two or three seconds? Or had they been minutes? Her mouth moved toward a welcoming smile, then let it be. She brushed her hand against the side of her head, even though her hair was neatly tidy.

"Martin," she said. Not a question.

"Yes."

"I knew you'd come."

"Yes."

"It's taken you long enough."

"I wasn't sure where to look." Even with the help of the police computers, it had taken weeks of work to pinpoint this place, this woman.

She nodded, as if she knew what the difficulties in tracing her had been.

"You'd best come in, then." She stood aside, flat against the wall of the narrow hall to let him pass in front of her. "Straight through. I'm in the kitchen."

The kitchen was warm, pined, full of good smells. They were part of the things which had been denied him. He saw that the room had been redecorated: the wallpaper had been changed and there was shelving that had not been there before.

In the fuller light, he was able to see her properly. She was younger than he had expected. And much less sad. It seemed to him that she ought to have been sad.

"What are you now?" she said. "Thirty-two?"

"Next birthday," he said.

"Early June, isn't it?"

He nodded, not minding that she had forgotten the precise date; though they had not met for over thirty years, she knew the month, just as he knew that behind the door to the left of the range was the larder, that although there were only five brass dish-covers hanging above it, there had once been seven. She leaned back against the warm curves of the Aga and shook her head. "I'd have known you anywhere," she said.

"Yes." Of course she would.

She frowned. "You're with the police, aren't you?" she said.

"Am I?"

She frowned. "That's what she said, last time I heard. That you were with the police."

Was he? Sometimes, he could scarcely remember who he was or where he came from. Sometimes he could scarcely remember that he didn't really know the answer to the question. Which was why he was here now.

He reached into the pocket of his coat and pulled out a package. He spread the contents on the shiny oilcloth which covered the kitchen table. And as he did so, the voices which never seemed to be far away, came back.

"*. . . somewhere . . .*"

"*Where?*"

"*Somewhere.*"

"*Where, Gran?*"

"*Up north.*"

"*Where up north?*"

"*That would be telling, wouldn't it now?*"

"*Tell me Gran. Tell me.*" Because even then, a child, six, seven, ten years old, he had known it was important. If she would just pinpoint the place for him, just give it space, meaning, then he himself would finally be rooted.

"*What happened, Gran?*"

She would start again. "*It was Christmas Eve.*" Then stop, laughing at him, the heavy rolls of her flesh shaking up and down her body. She was all too aware of the depth of the desire to know that filled him. Only to know.

"*Christmas Day, Gran.*" It was part of the cruel ritual that the beginning must never vary.

"*Oh yes. You're a knowing little monkey, aren't you?*" A nod of the head, a stare over the tops of her glasses, a small not-quite-pleasant smile. "*It was Christmas Day, and there was champagne in a silver bucket . . .*"

Ah, that champagne. For years he hadn't really known what it was. "Wine, dear, with a sparkle," she'd told him. "It made you feel good. Or bad, depending on your viewpoint." And she had giggled, an old woman scratching at memories.

When he was older, of course, he'd seen real, not imagined champagne, seen the big bottles, the shiny tops, the labels, special, rich, different from other labels on other bottles. Later still, drunk it, felt the bubbles at the top of his mouth. The sparkle of it was entwined in his earliest memories: that Christmas, that champagne.

"Yes, Gran. The champagne."

"There was champagne in a silver bucket, and then your mother . . ."

And she would stop. Always. Her fingers would float above the photographs, her hands small and delicate against the grossness of her bulk, and he would see the past in her eyes, the something terrible that she would never tell him. He knew it was terrible by her silence. And always, briefly, her face would register again the shock of whatever it was had happened that Christmas Day, before she turned off into a story of Santa Claus or mince pies or some other yuletide banality which he knew had nothing to do with the one which lurked behind her eyes.

"Then what, Gran? What?" But there would be no force in his voice now. She wasn't going to tell him. Not then. Not ever.

Now, the woman came forward, stood beside him, stirred the photographs on the table with her finger.

"Still got all the snaps, then?" she said.

"Yes."

"I suppose she's dead."

"Yes."

"About time. How did she die?"

Slowly, he wanted to say, but did not.

"Because I hope it hurt her to let go of life," the woman said. "I hope she fought against it, knowing she would lose."

That was exactly how it had been. He said nothing.

"I hope it was . . . violent." Her voice shook. "Like his." She sifted through the photographs and picked one out. "Like his."

He was young. Dark. Hair falling over his forehead. A military cap held under one arm.

The woman moved her head from side to side. "He was so beautiful," she said, lifeless. "So . . . *beautiful.*"

"My father."

"Yes. What did she tell you about him?"

"She told me nothing. Except that he was dead."

"I don't imagine she told you why."

"No. Not even that this was his picture. At least—not until very recently." He'd managed to choke that from her, squeezing and relaxing the soft flesh of her throat, alternately giving her hope, then removing it. And my mother, he'd said. Tell me where she is, where she is. And almost left it too late. "Garthway," she had managed. That was all.

Outside the window, at the edge of the garden, he could see how the last of the sun caught the green hill through the iron gate which led out onto the moors. It shone like a transparency between the shadowed walls on either side.

"And now you've come back to see for yourself where it all happened, have you?" The woman filled a kettle at the tap and set it on top of the red Aga.

"She never told me what exactly . . ." He picked two photographs out of the pile on the table. ". . . but I knew something must have."

Somewhere in his mind he heard the echo of the hateful voice: "*It was Christmas Day, somewhere up north . . .*"

Two photographs. Christmas dinner, every detail clear: the turkey, the sausages, the roast potatoes and steaming sprouts, a cut glass dish of cranberry sauce, a china gravy boat. Beside the table, a silver bucket. The people leaned toward each other, smiling, holding up glasses, about to celebrate. At the head of the table was a woman of maybe forty, big-boned, fair-haired, her dress cut low over prominent breasts. She was handsome, ripe. His workmates at the police station would have whistled if he'd shown them

the photo, would have nudged each other, said she was
pleading for it, they wouldn't have minded a bit of that
themselves. She was leaning toward the young girl sitting
at her right, saying something.

"That's you, isn't it?" he said, his finger brushing across
the girl's face.

"It is. It was."

And the same scene, seconds later. Glasses still in the
air, but the smiles gone as they stared toward something
out of frame, their faces full of horror and shock. The girl
was gone. The woman at the head of the table looked
straight ahead at the camera, smiling a small not-quite-
pleasant smile.

"What happened?" he said. "I have to know." Because
the body down in Wandsworth would never tell now. The
swollen protruding tongue was silent at last. Had been for
weeks. The small white hands would never again turn and
turn through the photographs, reliving a past that a cata-
clysm had destroyed.

The woman lifted her shoulder and released a sighing
breath. "You have a right, if anybody does," she said. "I
didn't know Bobby was taking photographs then."

"Bobby?"

"My youngest brother. He was camera mad. He took all
of these, photographed everything. 'It'll be a record for
posterity' he'd say.

"It's been that, all right."

Staring down at the photographs, the woman said softly:
"She hated me, of course."

"Who did?"

"My mother." She indicated the woman at the head of
the table. "It must have been some kind of madness, some
pathological obsession. Or maybe she was just jealous because Dad loved me more than he loved her. They'd have
a word for it today, I suppose. Perhaps they did then, but
I never knew what it was, just that she was dangerous. My
brothers tried to protect me, even little Bobby. So did Dad,
while he was alive. I think she would have killed me, if
she could." A silence. "She did the next best thing."

"Tell me."

Again the shuddering sigh. "Edward. Your father. He lived further up the dale. His family was rich, owned a lot of land. Edward was ten years older than I was, but it never mattered. Right from the beginning there was never anyone else for either of us." She turned her gaze on him. "We *loved* one another." On the Aga the kettle began to fizz, water drops skittering like ants across the surface of the hot plate. The woman got up, found a teapot, cups, saucers. "Do you understand that?"

"Yes," he said, though he knew nothing of love.

"I was sent away to school, to keep me from my mother, but the first day of the holidays, Edward would be there, outside the garden gate, and then it was like summer, like fireworks, like roses shooting out of the ground and birds singing." She smiled, looking back. Her voice was without emotion.

"What happened?"

"On my sixteenth birthday, in the middle of September, Edward wrote to me at school—he was in the Army by then—and said he was being posted overseas after Christmas and wanted me to come with him. He said I was old enough, he'd ask my mother if we could get married, since Dad had died the year before."

"What did she say?"

"That it was out of the question, that I was far too young. I wrote and said I didn't need her consent, I was legally able to get married and I was going to, soon as I came home at Christmas, so I could go abroad with Edward. She was furious."

He nodded. He knew Gran's furies. The violence, the hatred, flowing out of her like champagne from a shaken bottle.

"Edward said he thought my brothers could persuade her. And in the end, she gave in. She invited Edward to have Christmas dinner with us." She checked, touched her forehead, closed her eyes. "I really thought that she . . ."

Softly, he said: "It was Christmas Day, somewhere up north."

Equally softly, she said: "It was snowing that day and Edward was so late that we were about to start without him. Then he suddenly appeared at the door of the dining room. He stood there, looking at me. Just—looking. Not smiling. And then my mother leaned over to me and said . . . she said . . ."

"What?" All these years, and he could feel the inner emptiness begin to fill at last with what should always have been there.

"She must have planned it, decided exactly when she would tell me, right down to the second. Normally I would never have sat next to her at the table but that day she made me. So nobody but me heard her say that she and Edward . . . that they were lovers. That she'd seduced him, that it had been easy, that it was not me he loved but her."

"Did you believe her?"

"No. Not all of it. Not . . . everything."

"What then?"

"Edward knew what she was doing. He called my name. He said he loved me, that in spite of everything, I was to remember he loved me. Then he—suddenly, he was gone, out through the front door. We heard a shot."

"My God."

"I ran and ran across the grass, in my new shoes. I could see him lying on the ground with his gun beside him, and I knelt in the snow and held him while he died. His blood was so red against the white. She put her arm around me for the first time in her life. She said they would have married. That Edward had no choice, not in the circumstances."

"Did you believe her?" he said again.

"Not at first." She sighed. "Later, I went into a . . . hospital for a while."

"Of course. If you were carrying . . . I suppose in those days . . . more of a stigma . . . unmarried . . ." His voice died away.

"When I came out, Bobby had died in a car crash and my elder brothers had both gone out to Australia. She'd gone, too. She took you away with her, down south. You were all that was left of my Edward."

"You poor thing."

"Because of course, she and Edward *had* . . . not that I ever blamed him. It was all her fault."

"Poor darling Mother." He covered her hand. They would be friends, she and he. They would make up for all the years that the evil old woman, Gran, had taken from them both. He thought swiftly about Gran's dying, wished it had taken her longer, that she had suffered more, that he had been, perhaps, more brutal at the beginning. "Why didn't you come looking for me?"

She moved from under his hand. "Why would I? It would only have brought it back. The trauma. Besides, eventually I got over the shock of it all."

He wished she did not sound so indifferent. "I didn't," he said.

"Jim and I started courting, we got married, had the children . . ." She shrugged. "You know how it is."

"But, Mother . . ." The word hung in his mouth, succulent, unaccustomed.

She started at him for a moment. "I'm not your mother," she said, giving the word a hard emphasis.

"What?" He did not take in what she was saying.

She smiled a small, familiar, not-quite-pleasant smile. "Not me, Martin. Your father and I didn't . . . hadn't . . . I was a virgin when I wed Jim."

"Then . . . who?"

She didn't answer.

"*Gran*?" he said.

"If that's what you called her."

"She told me my parents were dead," he said. Tears filled his eyes. Hatred, raw and red-edged, filled him. Was Gran, that blowsy, disgusting old woman, was she the mother, the flesh and blood, it had taken him so long to find?

The woman looked at him. "In a way, she was right, wasn't she?"

"No! Don't say that!" His hands were around her neck.

He could feel the bone at the base of her skull and the convulsive movements of her throat. He shook his head. "She can't be . . . not Gran," he said.

He squeezed harder, trying to force the right words from her mouth, while her white fingers tore at his hands and her face darkened. "Tell me it wasn't Gran," he screamed, but she did not answer.

When he let her drop back in her chair her eyes, so like his own, had grown dull. In one of her small hands she still held the photograph of that long-past never-finished lunch-eon, and the champagne in a silver bucket, on Christmas Day.

Susan Moody's fourth Christmas was marked by a visit to *Mother Goose*, from which she had to be removed, scream-ing. At the age of six, her Christmas treat was *Bambi*, an experience which imbued her with the melancholy for which she is now famous. Her Christmases have gone steadily downhill since then. In spite—or perhaps because— of the dolorist streak such disappointments have encour-aged, she has written a number of crime and suspense nov-els, the most recent of which is *King of Hearts*, featuring Cassandra Swann, a bridge-playing amateur sleuth.

The Proof of the Pudding

PETER LOVESEY

Frank Morris strode into the kitchen and slammed a cold, white turkey on the kitchen table. "Seventeen pounds plucked. Satisfied?"

His wife Wendy was at the sink, washing the last few breakfast bowls. Her shoulders had tensed. "What's that, Frank?"

"You're not even bloody looking, woman."

She took that as a command and wheeled around, rubbing her wet hands on the apron. "A turkey! That's a fine bird. It really is."

"Fine?" Frank erupted. "It's nineteen forty-six, for Christ's sake! It's a bloody miracle. Most of them around here will be sitting down to joints of pork and mutton—if they're lucky. I bring a bloody great turkey in on Christmas morning, and all you say is 'fine'?"

"I just wasn't prepared for it."

"You really get my goat, you do."

Wendy said tentatively, "Where did it come from, Frank?"

Her huge husband stepped toward her and for a moment

she thought he would strike her. He lowered his face until it was inches from hers. Not even nine in the morning and she could smell sweet whiskey on his breath. "I won it, didn't I?" he said, daring her to disbelieve. "A meat raffle in the Valiant Trooper last night."

Wendy nodded, pretending to be taken in. It didn't do to challenge Frank's statements. Black eyes and beatings had taught her well. She knew Frank's rule of fist had probably won him the turkey, too. Frank didn't lose at anything. If he could punch his way to another man's prize, then he considered it fair game.

"Just stuff the thing and stick it in the oven," he ordered. "Where's the boy?"

"I think he's upstairs," Wendy replied warily. Norman had fled at the sound of Frank's key in the front door.

"Upstairs?" Frank ranted. "On bloody Christmas Day?"

"I'll call him." Wendy was grateful for the excuse to move away from Frank to the darkened hallway. "Norman," she gently called. "Your father's home. Come and wish him a Happy Christmas."

A pale, solemn young boy came cautiously downstairs, pausing at the bottom to hug his mother. Unlike most children of his age—he was nine—Norman was sorry that the war had ended in 1945. He had pinned his faith in the enemy putting up a stiff fight and extending it indefinitely. He still remembered the VE Day street party, sitting at a long wooden bench surrounded by laughing neighbors. He and his mother had found little to celebrate in the news that "the boys will soon be home."

Wendy smoothed down his hair, whispered something and led him gently into the kitchen.

"Happy Christmas, Dad," he said, then added unprompted, "Did you come home last night?"

Wendy said quickly, "Never you mind about that, Norman." She didn't want her son provoking Frank on this of all days.

Frank didn't appear to have heard. He was reaching up to the top shelf of a cupboard, a place where he usually kept his old army belt. Wendy pushed her arm protectively in front of the boy.

But instead of the belt, Frank took down a brown paper parcel. "Here you are, son," he said, beckoning to Norman. "You'll be the envy of the street in this. I saved it for you, specially."

Norman stepped forward. He unwrapped his present, egged on by his grinning father.

He now owned an old steel helmet. "Thanks, Dad," he said politely, turning it in his hands.

"I got it off a dead Jerry," Frank said with gusto. "The bastard who shot your Uncle Ted. Sniper, he was. Holed up in a bombed-out building in Potsdam, outside Berlin. He got Ted with a freak shot. Twelve of us stormed the building and took him out."

"Outside?"

"Topped him, Norman. See the hole around the back? That's from a Lee Enfield .303. Mine." Frank levelled an imaginary rifle to Wendy's head and squeezed the trigger, miming both the recoil and report. "There wasn't a lot left of Fritz after we'd finished. But I brought back the helmet for you, son. Wear it with pride. It's what your Uncle Ted would have wanted." He took the helmet and rammed it on the boy's head.

Norman grimaced. He felt he was about to be sick.

"Frank dear, perhaps we should put it away until he's a bit older," Wendy tried her tact. "We wouldn't want such a special thing to get damaged, would we? You know what young boys are like."

Frank was unimpressed. "What are you talking about— 'special thing'? It's a bloody helmet, not a thirty-piece tea service. Look at the lad. He's totally stunned. He loves it. Why don't you get on and stuff that ruddy great turkey, like I told you?"

"Yes, Frank."

Norman raised his hand, his small head an absurd sight in the large helmet. "May I go now?"

Frank beamed. "Of course, son. Want to show it off to all your friends, do you?"

Norman nodded, causing the helmet to slip over his eyes. He lifted it off his head. Smiling weakly at this father, he left the kitchen and dashed upstairs. The first thing he would do was wash his hair.

Wendy began to wash and prepare the bird, listening to Frank.

"I know just how the kid feels. I still remember my old Dad giving me a bayonet he brought back from Flanders. Said he ran six men through with it. I used to look for specks of blood, and he'd tell me how he stuck them like pigs. It was the best Christmas present I ever had."

"I've got you a little something for Christmas. It's behind the clock," said Wendy, indicating a small package wrapped in newspaper and string.

"A present?" Frank snatched it up and tore the wrapping away. "Socks?" he said in disgust. "Is that it? Our first Christmas together in three bloody years, and all you can give your husband is a miserable pair of socks."

"I don't have much money, Frank," Wendy reminded him, and instantly wished she had not.

Frank seized her by the shoulders, practically tipping the turkey off the kitchen table. "Are you saying that's my fault?"

"No, love."

"I'm not earning enough—is that what you're trying to tell me?"

Wendy tried to pacify him, at the same time bracing herself for the violent shaking that would surely follow. Frank tightened his grip, forced her away from the table and pushed her hard against the cupboard door, punctuating each word with a thump.

"That helmet cost me nothing," he ranted. "Don't you understand, woman? It's the thought that counts. You don't need money to show affection. You just need some savvy, some intelligence. Bloody socks—an insult!"

He shoved her savagely toward the table again. "Now get back to your work. This is Christmas Day. I'm a reasonable man. I'm prepared to overlook your stupidity. Stop snivelling, will you, and get that beautiful bird in the oven.

Mum will be here at ten. I want the place smelling of turkey. I'm not having you ruining my Christmas.''

He strode out, heavy boots clumping on the wooden floor of the hallway. ''I'm going around to Polly's,'' he shouted. ''She knows how to treat a hero. Look at this dump. No decorations, no holly over the pictures. You haven't even bought any beer, that I've seen. Sort something out before I get back.''

Wendy was still reeling from the shaking, but she knew she must speak before he left. If she didn't remind him now, there would be hell to pay later. ''Polly said she would bring the Christmas pudding, Frank. Would you make sure she doesn't forget? Please, Frank.''

He stood grim-faced in the doorway, silhouetted against the drab terraced houses opposite. ''Don't tell me what to do, Wendy,'' he said threateningly. ''You're the one due for a damned good reminding of what to do around here.''

The door shook in its frame. Wendy stood at the foot of the stairs, her heart pounding. She knew what Frank meant by a damned good reminding. The belt wasn't used only on the boy.

''Is he gone, Mum?'' Norman called from the top stair.

Wendy nodded, readjusting the pins in her thin, blond hair, and drying her eyes. ''Yes, love. You can come downstairs now.''

At the foot of the stairs, he told her, ''I don't want the helmet. It frightens me.''

''I know, dear.''

''I think there's blood on it. I don't want it. If it belonged to one of our soldiers, or one of the Yankees, I'd want it, but this is a dead man's helmet.''

Wendy hugged her son. The base of her spine throbbed. A sob was building at the back of her throat.

''Where's he gone?'' Norman asked from the folds of her apron.

''To collect your Aunt Polly. She's bringing a Christmas pudding, you know. We'd better make custard. I'm going to need your help.''

"Was he there last night?" Norman asked innocently. "With Aunt Polly? Is it because she doesn't have Uncle Ted anymore?"

"I don't know, Norman." In truth, she didn't want to know. Frank's widowed sister-in-law was welcome to him. Polly didn't know the relief Wendy felt to be rid of him sometimes. Any humiliation was quite secondary to the fact that Frank stopped out all night, bringing respite from the tension and the brutality. The local gossips had been quick to suspect the truth, but she could do nothing to stop them.

Norman, sensing the direction her thoughts had taken, said, "Billy Slater says Dad and Aunt Polly are doing it."

"That's enough, Norman."

"He says she's got no elastic in her drawers. What does he mean, Mum?"

"Billy Slater is a disgusting little boy. Now let's hear no more of this. We'll make the custard."

Norman spent the next hour helping his mother in the kitchen. The turkey barely fitted in the oven, and Norman became concerned that it wouldn't be ready in time. Wendy knew better. There was ample time for the cooking. They couldn't start until Frank and Polly rolled home from the Valiant Trooper. With last orders at a quarter to three, it gave the bird five hours to roast.

A gentle knock at the front door sent Norman hurrying to open it.

"Mum, it's Grandma Morris!" he called out excitedly as he led the plump old woman into the kitchen. Maud Morris had been a marvelous support through the war years. She knew exactly when help was wanted.

"I've brought you some veggies," Maud said to Wendy, dumping a bag of muddy cabbage and carrots on the table and removing her coat and hat. "Where's that good-for-nothing son of mine? Need I ask?"

"He went to fetch Polly," Wendy calmly replied.

"Did he, indeed?"

Norman said, "About an hour ago. I expect they'll go to the pub."

The old lady went into the hall to hang up her things. When she returned, she said to Wendy, "You know what people are saying, don't you?"

Wendy ignored the question. "He brought in a seventeen-pound turkey this morning."

"Have you got a knife?" her mother-in-law asked.

"A knife?"

"For the cabbage." Maud turned to look at her grandson. "Have you had some good presents?"

Norman stared down at his shoe-laces.

Wendy said, "Grandma asked you a question, dear."

"Did you get everything you asked for?"

"I don't know."

"Did you write to Saint Nick?" Maud asked with a sideward glance at Wendy.

Norman rolled his eyes upwards. "I don't believe in that stuff anymore."

"That's a shame."

"Dad gave me a dead German's helmet. He says it belonged to the one who shot Uncle Ted. I hate it."

Wendy gathered the carrots from the table and put them in the sink. "I'm sure he was only doing what he thought was best, Norman."

"It's got a bullet hole."

"Didn't he give you anything else?" his grandmother asked.

Norman shook his head. "Mum gave me some chocolate and the *Dandy Annual*."

"But your dad didn't give you a thing apart from the helmet?"

Wendy said, "Please don't say anything. You know what it's like."

Maud Morris nodded. It was pointless to admonish her son. He'd only take it out on Wendy. She knew from personal experience the dilemma of the battered wife. To protest was to invite more violence. The knowledge that her second son had turned out such a bully shamed and angered her. Ted, her dear first-born Ted, would never have harmed a woman. Yet Ted had been taken from her. She took an apron from the back of the door and started shredding the cabbage. Norman was sent to lay the table in the front room.

Four hours later, when the King was speaking to the nation, they heard a key being tried at the front door. Wendy switched off the wireless. The door took at least three attempts to open before Frank and Polly stumbled in to the hallway. Frank stood swaying, a bottle in his hand and a paper hat cocked ridiculously on the side of his head. His sister-in-law clung to his coat, convulsed in laughter, a pair of ankle-strap shoes dangling from her right hand.

"Happy Christmas!" Frank roared. "Peace on earth and goodwill to all men except the Jerries and the lot next door."

Polly doubled up in uncontrollable giggling.

"Let me take your coat, Polly," Wendy offered. "Did you remember the pudding? I want to get it on right away."

Polly turned to Frank. "The pudding. What did you do with the pudding, Frank?"

"What pudding?" said Frank.

Maud had come into the hall behind Wendy. "I know she's made one. Don't mess about, Frank. Where is it?"

Frank pointed vaguely over his shoulder.

Wendy said despairingly, "Back at Polly's house? Oh no!"

"Stupid cow. What are you talking about?" said Frank. "It's on our own bloody doorstep. I had to put it down to open the door, didn't I?"

Wendy squeezed past them and retrieved the white basin covered with a grease-proof paper top. She carried it quickly through to the kitchen and lowered it into the waiting saucepan of simmering water. "It looks a nice big one."

This generous remark caused another gale of laughter from Polly. Finally, slurring her words, she announced, "You'll have to make allowances. Your old man's a very naughty boy. He's took me out and got me tiddly."

Maud said, "It beats me where he gets the money from."

"Beats Wendy, too, I expect," said Polly. She leaned

closer to her sister-in-law, a lock of brown hair swaying across her face. "From what I've heard, you know a bit about beating, don't you, Wen?" The remark was not made in sympathy. It was triumphant.

Wendy felt the shame redden her face. Polly smirked and swung around, causing her black skirt to swirl as she left the room. The thick pencil lines she had drawn up the back of her legs to imitate stocking seams were badly smudged higher up. Wendy preferred not to think why.

She took the well-cooked bird from the oven, transferred it to a platter and carried it into the front room. Maud and Norman brought in the vegetables.

"Would you like to carve, Frank?"

"Hold your horses, woman. We haven't said the grace."

Wendy started to say, "But we never . . ."

Frank had already intoned the words, "Dear Lord God Almighty."

Everyone dipped their heads.

"Thanks for what we are about to receive," Frank went on, "and for seeing to it that a skinny little half-pint won the meat raffle and decided to donate it to the Morris family."

Maud clicked her tongue in disapproval.

Polly began to giggle.

"I can't begin to understand the workings of your mysterious ways," Frank insisted on going on, "because if there really is someone up there he should have made damned sure my brother Ted was sitting at this table today."

Maud said, "That's enough, Frank! Sit down."

Frank said, "Amen. Where's the carving knife?"

Wendy handed it to him, and he attended to the task, cutting thick slices and heaping them on the plates held by his mother. "That's for Polly. She likes it steaming hot."

Polly giggled again.

The plates were distributed around the table.

Not to be outdone in convivial wit, Polly said, "You've gone overboard on the breast, Frankie dear. I thought you were a leg man."

Maud said tersely, "You should know."

"Careful, Mum," Frank cautioned, wagging the knife. "Goodwill to all men."

Polly said, "Only if they behave themselves."

A voice piped up, "Bill Slater says that—"

"Be quiet, Norman!" Wendy ordered.

They ate in heavy silence, save for Frank's animalistic chewing and swallowing. The first to finish, he quickly filled his glass with more beer.

"Dad?"

"Yes, son."

"Would we have won the war without the Americans?"

"The Yanks?" Frank scoffed. "Bunch of part-timers, son. They only came into it after men like me and your Uncle Ted had done all the real fighting. Just like the other war, the one my old Dad won. They waited till 1917. Isn't that a fact, Mum? Americans? Where were they at Dunkirk? Where were they in Africa? I'll tell you where they were—sitting on their fat backsides a couple of thousand miles away"

"From what I remember, Frank," Maud interjected, "you were sitting on yours in the snug-bar of the Valiant Trooper."

"That was different!" Frank protested angrily. "Ted and I didn't get called up until 1943. And when we were, we did our share. We chased Jerry all the way across Europe, right back to the bunker. Ted and me, brothers in arms, fighting for King and country. Ready to make the ultimate sacrifice. If Dad could have heard what you said just then, Mum, he'd turn in his grave."

Maud said icily, "That would be difficult, seeing that he's in a pot on my mantelpiece."

Polly burst into helpless laughter and almost choked on a roast potato. It was injudicious of her.

"Belt up, will you?" Frank demanded. "We're talking about the sacred memory of your dead husband. My brother."

"Sorry, Frank." Polly covered her mouth with her hands. "I don't know what came over me. Honest."

"You have no idea, you women," Frank went on. "God knows what you got up to, while we were winning the war."

"Anyway," said Norman, "Americans have chewing gum. And jeeps."

Fortunately, at this moment Frank was being distracted. Wendy whispered in Norman's ear and they both began clearing the table, but Maud put her hand over Wendy's. She said, "Why don't you sit down? You've done more than enough. I'll fetch the pudding and custard. I'd like to get up for a while. It's beginning to get a little warm in here."

Polly offered to help. "It is my pudding, after all." But she didn't mean to get up because, unseen by the others, she had her hand on Frank's thigh.

Maud said, "I'll manage."

Norman asked, "Is it a proper pudding?"

"I don't know what you mean by proper," said Polly. "It used up most of my rations when I made it. They have to mature, do puddings. This one is two years old. It should be delicious. There was only one drawback. In 1944, I didn't have a man at home to help me stir the ingredients." She gave Frank a coy smile.

Ignoring it, Wendy said, "When Norman asked if it was a proper pudding, I think he wanted to know if he might find a lucky sixpence inside."

With a simper, Polly said, "He might, if he's a good boy, like his dad. Of *course* it's a proper pudding."

Frank quipped, "What about the other sort? Do you ever make an improper pudding?"

Before anyone could stop him, Norman said, "You should know, Dad." His reflexes were too quick for his drunken father's, and the swinging blow missed him completely.

"You'll pay for that remark, my son," Frank shouted. "You'll wash your mouth out with soap and water and then I'll beat your backside raw."

Wendy said quickly, "The boy doesn't know what he's

saying, Frank. It's Christmas. Let's forgive and forget, shall we?''

He turned his anger on her. ''And I know very well who puts these ideas in the boy's head. And spreads the filthy rumors all over town. You can have your Christmas Day, Wendy. Make the most of it, because tomorrow I'm going to teach you why they call it Boxing Day.''

Maud entered the suddenly silent front room carrying the dark, upturned pudding decorated with a sprig of holly. ''Be an angel and fetch the custard, Norman.''

The boy was thankful to run out to the kitchen.

Frank glanced at the pudding and then at Polly and then grinned. ''What a magnificent sight!'' He was staring at her cleavage.

Polly beamed at him, fully herself again, her morale restored by the humiliation her sister-in-law had just suffered. ''The proof of the pudding . . .'' she murmured.

''We'll see if 1944 was a vintage year,'' said Frank.

Maud sliced and served the pudding, giving Norman an extra large helping. The pudding was a delicious one, as Polly had promised, and there were complimentary sounds all around the table.

Norman sifted the rich, fruity mass with his spoon, hoping for one of those coveted silver sixpenny pieces. But Frank was the first to find one.

''You can have a wish. Whatever you like, lucky man,'' said Polly in a husky, suggestive tone.

Frank's thoughts were in another direction. ''I wish,'' he said sadly, holding the small coin between finger and thumb, ''I wish God's peace to my brother Ted, rest his soul. And I wish a Happy Christmas to all the blokes who fought with us and survived. And God rot all our enemies. And the bloody Yanks, come to that.''

''That's about four wishes,'' Polly said, ''and it won't come true if you tell everyone.''

Wendy felt the sharp edge of a sixpence in her mouth, and removed it unnoticed by the others. She wished him out of her life, with all her heart.

Norman finally found his piece of the pudding's buried treasure. He spat the coin onto his plate and then examined it closely. "Look at this!" he said in surprise. "It isn't a sixpence. It doesn't have the King's head."

"Give it here." Frank picked up the silver coin. "Jesus Christ! He's right. It's a dime. An American dime. How the hell did that get in the pudding?"

All eyes turned to Polly for an explanation. She stared wide-eyed at Frank. She was speechless.

Frank was not. He had reached his own conclusion. "I'll tell you exactly how it got in there," he said, thrusting it under Polly's nose. "You've been stirring it up with a Yank. There was a GI base down the road, wasn't there? When did you say you made the pudding? 1944?"

He rose from the table, spittle flying as he ranted. Norman slid from his chair and hid under the table, clinging in fear to his mother's legs. He saw his father's heavy boots turned toward Polly, whose legs braced. The hem of her dress was quivering.

Frank's voice boomed around the small room. "Ted and I were fighting like bloody heroes while you were having it off with Americans. Whore!"

Norman saw a flash of his father's hand as it reached into the fireplace and picked up a poker. He heard the women scream, then a sickening thump.

The poker fell to the floor. Polly's legs jerked once and then appeared to relax. One of her arms flopped down and remained quite still. A drop of blood fell from the table edge. Presently there was another. Then it became a trickle. A crimson pool formed on the wooden floor.

Norman ran out of the room. Out of the house. Out into the cold afternoon, leaving the screams behind. He ran across the street and beat on a neighbor's door with his fists. His frantic cries of "Help, murder!" filled the street. Within a short time an interested crowd in party hats had surrounded him. He pointed in horror to his own front door as his blood-stained father charged out and lurched toward him.

It took three men to hold Frank Morris down, and five policemen to take him away.

The last of the policemen didn't leave the house until long after Norman should have gone to bed. His mother and his grandmother sat silent for some time in the kitchen, unable to stay in the front room, even though Polly's body had been taken away.

"He's not going to come back, is he, Mum?"

Wendy shook her head. She was only beginning to think about what happened next. There would be a trial, of course, and she would try to shield Norman from the publicity. He was so impressionable.

"Will they hang him?"

"I think it's time for your bed, young man," Maud said. "You've got to be strong. Your mum will need your support more than ever now."

The boy asked, "How did the dime get in the pudding, Grandma Morris?"

Wendy snapped out of her thoughts of what was to come and stared at her mother-in-law.

Maud went to the door, and for a moment it appeared as if she was reaching to put on her coat prior to leaving, but she had already promised to stay the night. Actually she was taking something from one of the pockets.

It was a Christmas card, a little bent at the edges now. Maud handed it to Wendy. "It was marked 'private and confidential' but it had my name, you see. I opened it thinking it was for me. It came last week. The address was wrong. They made a mistake over the house number. The postman delivered it to the wrong Mrs. Morris."

Wendy took the card and opened it.

"The saddest thing is," Maud continued to speak as Wendy read the message inside, "he is the only son I have left, but I really can't say I'm sorry it turned out this way. I know what he did to you, Wendy. His father did the same to me for nearly forty years. I had to break the cycle. I read the card, love. I had no idea. I couldn't let this chance pass by. For your sake, and the boy's."

A tear rolled down Wendy's cheek. Norman watched as the two women hugged. The card drifted from Wendy's lap and he pounced on it immediately. His eager eyes scanned every word.

My Darling Wendy,
    Since returning home, my thoughts are filled with you, and the brief time we shared together. It's kind of strange to admit, but I sometimes catch myself wishing the Germans made you a widow. I can't stand to think of you with any other guy.
    My heart aches for news of you. Not a day goes by when I don't dream of being back in your arms. My home, and my heart, will always be open for you.
    Take care and keep safe,

Nick

Nick Saint, (Ex-33rd US Reserve)
221C Plover Avenue
Mountain Home
Idaho

P.S. The dime is a tiny Christmas present for Norman to remember me by.

Norman looked up at his grandmother and understood what she had done, and why. He didn't speak. He could keep a secret as well as a grown-up. He was the man of the house now, at least until they got to America.

Peter Lovesey writes: "I'm old enough to remember some wartime Christmases, each one, thank God, totally unlike the one in this story. A treasured memory is of a party for bombed-out London kids given at a US Army base in 1944, with cartoon films, gifts, clowns and a Santa with a cigar and a Texan drawl. I used some of it in a book called *Rough Cider*. My affection for Americans is stronger than ever now that I have a granddaughter born in Brooklyn."

Charades, Anybody?

♦

H. R. F. KEATING

Christmas is coming, Assistant Superintendent of Police Jack Partington said to himself. Suppose Christmas in India won't be much like Christmas at Home, though. Didn't Old Stamper say something about it being not only my duty to organize charades at the Club party but that I've got to carve one of the peacocks at tiffin too? Oh God, will I get that right? How do you carve a peacock? Why didn't I watch last year when Pater was carving the goose? Golly, I'd only just left school then, but it seems years ago. Years and years ago. And anyhow, do you carve a peacock the same way?

Old Stamper was Jack's name for his superior officer, District Superintendent of Police Mortimer Staples. Who had been known in moments of extreme displeasure actually to stamp his foot in red-faced rage. Or at least Jack had seen him do that more than once. There had been, for instance, the wrinkled collar time. He had come into the daftar to begin work, five minutes early on parade, feeling confident he had got everything right, and Old Stamper had at once pointed his swagger-stick at his throat—only it turned out it was actually at the shirt collar—and had shouted at him, in a voice that must have penetrated easily to Havildar Bulaki Ram standing at attention just outside.

"Your collar. It's disgusting. Abominable. Why can't you see your dhobi irons your shirts properly? Good God, man, have some thought for prestige. Do you think the natives are going to have any respect for a man with a collar in that state? You're letting down the Empire, Partington. Letting down the British Empire."

And then had come that stamped foot. Or had that been at one of the other times he'd got something wrong? Heaven knows there had been enough of them. If it hadn't been for the occasional compensating piece of good luck he would have been tempted more than once to shoot himself. But, thank goodness, something generally seemed to have turned up. Like the way, a little later, the dhobi who had seemed incapable of beating clothes clean without losing every single button on them had suddenly vanished from the chummery he shared with two fellows from the Forestry Department, to be replaced by an aged Muslim, an absolute wizard with the iron.

Still, Christmas next week. And surely then—season of goodwill and all that—Old Stamper would ease up a bit.

On Christmas Day Old Stamper did seem to be noticeably less pernickety. At the carol service at St. Peter's he had darted one sharp glance at the collar of his shirt as he took around the collection plate—another of a junior officer's duties, it seemed—but he hadn't even produced a single one of his angry snorts. And at the Club tiffin, even under glances from his beady eye as he wielded the knife at the other table, his own peacock had carved beautifully, though perhaps this was actually because it had been properly hung. Old Stamper himself had gone out into the jungle and shot both birds a few days earlier. "I don't propose to rely on you, Partington. I make no doubt your head's full of some nonsense or other about not killing the Hindu sacred bird."

Thank goodness old Bulaki Ram had said something a

little earlier about the peacock being sacred "excepting for British officers like Staples Sahib." So he had been able to take in his stride the jibe about his reliability and had even come up with a piece of India knowledge that should have pleased Old Stamper, always going on and on about "You've got to get to know this country, Partington. In all its ways."

"Yes, sir, the peacock being the vehicle of Lakshmi, isn't it? Goddess of wealth and learning."

Not that he had got much credit for that. Perhaps it had been one of the ways of the country Old Stamper wasn't sure about.

And now, another piece of luck, one chair at tiffin had been left empty. By Mrs. Wendy Wilson, the Widow Wendy as she was called behind her back. The Widow Wendy, in her lean and stringy forties, notorious for her vicious temper when anything or anybody crossed her, and notorious too—not that, of course, anything was openly said—for her sexual appetite. Young men in particular were, so Jack had gathered somehow, her special fancy. He had taken care ever after to steer well clear.

But he had had a nasty feeling that today, when it came to the time to organize the charades, he would find it hard to escape her. The Widow Wendy, Old Stamper had said, was always the star turn at acting out the syllables.

"She won't take a hand at bridge nowadays, used to snap at all her partners and say we were too stupid. So she just sits there in her bungalow playing some damn complicated kind of Patience—if she isn't entertaining herself in another manner. It's only when it comes to amateur dramatics that the bloody woman ever makes an appearance now. Likes to show off. Gaudy kind of fly to cast in front of some silly fat young mahseer swimming up the river."

Jack had at that moment taken a resolution not to be that fat young fish. He had made an excuse and withdrawn his offer to take a part in the forthcoming Club production of Noël Coward's *Red Peppers*.

Happily, however, when plum pudding and mince pies had been manfully disposed of by one and all—the heat notwithstanding, traditions must be kept up—and party games were getting into full swing, there was still no sign of the Widow Wendy. So it was with a considerable feeling of relief that Jack began to organize the choosing of teams for the charades. He had worked out well beforehand a list of good, two-syllable words to suggest if members' inspiration failed—*tin-sel, hum-bug, lime-light, white-wash* (easy to show the first part by contrast to a comical black native), *big-wig, pom-pous* (pom, the little dog, and puss). He was specially pleased with that last one, and even felt a twinge of regret that Old Stamper had disappeared from the scene, to the bar likely as not, and would not be there to see his subordinate for once running a good show. But none of those carefully devised words was destined to puzzle the wits of the assembled sahibs and memsahibs. Because scarcely had Jack got his teams into opposite corners of the big anteroom ready to play when Havildar Bulaki Ram came bursting in.

"Partington Sahib, Partington Sahib," he shouted. "Terrible thing has happen. Wilson Memsahib dead, sahib. Sahib, it is horrible murder."

Jack followed the stout little havildar out at a run. Behind him, he was just aware of the paper-hatted Club members leaving their corners and drawing together into a protective huddle.

Bulaki Ram led him to the bungalow Wendy Wilson had occupied ever since her husband, in the Public Works Department, had succumbed to a sudden, particularly vicious attack of malaria. Its door was gaping wide. They hurried through the drawing room, a scene of total disarray, the table overturned, a scatter of playing cards all over the floor, the chair beside it lying on its side, and there in the bedroom she lay. A sprawled figure in a half-open orange-and-white kimono.

Round her neck, appallingly plain to be seen, was a ring of deep bruises.

"Strangled," Jack heard himself say. "The servants. Bulaki Ram, have you rounded up the servants? Staples Sahib is always saying he expected something like this to happen."

"Sahib," the stocky little havildar replied. "It is Christmas *lamasha* today. Sahibs, memsahibs and chota sahibs at Club. All servants also having jolly time. In Club servants' quarter, sahib."

"All of them? All? Are you sure?"

"Oh, yes, sahib. Not one would be missing. I have seen."

"Well then, some dacoits must have come up from the black town."

"Sahib, no. Nothing stolen, not at all dacoit work."

"Well, yes. Yes, I suppose you're right about that. But then . . . Look, if no one was about, as you say, how did anyone get to know this had happened?"

"Oh, sahib, it was Little Brown Gramophone."

Jack knew about Little Brown Gramophone. Everyone in the Station did. He was a small boy, occasionally employed at the Club, who possessed nothing, except for one extraordinary gift. He could imitate perfectly any sound he heard. Jack once had swung around in sweat-rising dismay when he had heard what he took to be Old Stamper's voice saying "Partington, Partington, what the devil are you doing now?" Hence the name that the little monster had been given by, at first, Major Smith, the Club Secretary, and later by everyone, even servants who had no other English.

"And what was Little Brown Gramophone doing in Wilson Memsahib's bungalow?"

"No, no, sahib, he was not at all inside. I was questioning. Slapping also. He was sitting at backside of bungalow compound when *ek dum* he was hearing Wilson Memsahib shouting 'No, Jack. No, Jack.' Then when it was time, after sahibs' tiffin was finish, he went to join other servants for Christmas khana, sahib. But after some time someone was saying Wilson Memsahib had not come to Club for charades. Then he was telling what he had heard. Was telling, and screaming out same in Wilson Memsahib voice. Then I was going to bungalow and finding Wilson Memsahib here, where you are seeing also."

"But did Little Brown Gramophone see anyone? Anyone hurrying out of the bungalow?"

"Oh, sahib, I was asking. With ear-pulling also. But, no, sahib. He was at the backside, and door is at the frontside. He was seeing no one."

"And when you'd discovered the body you came and told me straight away? Yes?"

"Yes, sahib. As soon as I was not finding DSP Staples."

"Yes. Well, where is the DSP?"

"Sahib, I am not knowing. He was at Christmas tiffin, sahib, but now no one is able to find."

Jack felt a sinking of pure dismay. He would never have thought he would be delighted to see Old Stamper. But at this moment he would have given anything to hear that familiar fault-finding bark.

Because, until the DSP was located, plainly he himself was in charge of the investigation into the Widow Wendy's murder, if only for the first vital half an hour. But, worse, far worse, if all the servants had been safely under the eye of Bulaki Ram and no dacoits were involved, then the murder can only have been committed by—

By a sahib.

It was plain enough, in fact. "No, Jack. No, Jack," Little Brown Gramophone had heard Wendy scream out. It could only be her protest at the attack that had ended her life. He could see it all. The man, whoever it was, Jack, must have come to see Wendy, no doubt by appointment at a time when, with in theory everyone sitting down to Christmas tiffin, the coast would be clear for an assignation. And then there must have come a quarrel. No doubt it would have been about—well, about sex. The table in the drawing room overturned, Wendy running to her bedroom, the man, Jack—who was he?—following, and . . .

At last he turned away from the body in its wide-flung orange-and-white kimono. Good God, the thought struck him, the woman must have been proposing to go to bed with the man who had murdered her on Christmas Day. On Christmas Day itself.

In the bungalow drawing room he found Havildar Bulaki

Ram setting the place to rights, painstakingly picking up the scattered cards, putting the table and Wendy Williams' chair back in place.

"Leave that, man," he snapped. "For God's sake, we've got a murderer to find."

The sight of the little havildar down on his knees on the floor in a hopeless effort to restore order brought back to him with a new jolt of depression the extent of the task before him. To go questioning and prying among all the people of the Station to find one chap who had been absent at tiffin and whose name was Jack.

And who, anyhow, was Jack? Who could he possibly be? As far as he could remember there was in fact no one called Jack in the whole Station.

Except, he thought suddenly, me. But I didn't strangle the Widow Wendy. At least I'm sure of that much.

But Old Stamper. When someone finds him and he takes charge, what's he going to think when he hears Little Brown Gramophone repeat that cry of "No, Jack. No, Jack?" And what will he have to say about what I've done so far?

However, that fear proved to be one he did not have to worry about. Because Old Stamper was found eventually in the Station hospital. He had been admitted late that afternoon, Matron said, with a bad case of heatstroke. At present he was delirious and in a high fever.

So now it really is up to me, Jack thought. Just six months in the Indian Imperial Police, and I'm faced with a murder. And not just some bazaar knifing, either. A real murder. And the big problem is that I know that name of the murderer. Jack. It's Jack. But, as far as I know, there just isn't anyone called Jack in the whole darn place.

But that evening he set to grimly with a list Havildar Bukali Ram had provided for him of every white male in the district. There were not so very many of them, but the list confirmed that there was not a single Jack among them all. There were more than enough other names, however, to make it extraordinarily difficult to check who had been where during the Christmas tiffin. To begin with, there had been no particular places allocated at the two long tables, except for the DSP and himself carving and the padre at the far end of Old Stamper's table, saying grace. So everyone had sat just wherever they liked. Then, once the peacocks had been carved, served and eaten, people had moved about. They had moved again, too, when the plum pudding had been despatched. And when the mince pies had been consumed in full proper quantity there had been yet another general move. So no one was certain when or whether they had seen anybody else.

Alibis, he thought. Yes, this is an absolute Agatha Christie story come to life. And hardly anyone with a proper alibi.

But Poirot had never been faced with finding a man called Jack who simply did not exist. And Poirot's faithful Captain Hastings, dull-witted though he was, was more help in his investigations than Havildar Bulaki Ram could possibly be now.

Because the plain fact of the matter was that any particular questioning of any of the Station sahibs was all too likely to bring to the fore matters that an Indian ought not to know about. Any mention really, Jack thought, of Wendy Williams' amours ought to be totally taboo in front of any native. If anything came out in Bulaki Ram's hearing, decent fellow though he was, it was almost certain that the ramifications of the whole disreputable business—already he himself had been told in strict confidence by two Club members, not without a certain boastfulness, that they had visited Wendy—would be all around the bazaar in less time than it took to tell. What would that do for British prestige?

Until late in the night he worked away at his increasingly muddled list, checking and cross-checking, striking out and putting back in again, and all the while getting more and more fed up with Bulaki Ram's attempts to be helpful. Didn't the fellow realize the list, with all its annotations, was no longer a document he was entitled to see? At last in exasperation he sent him off duty.

"As sahib is wishing. But if you are wanting some more of help I would stay till day itself is coming."

"No, no. Off you go to bed, havildar. There'll be plenty for you to do tomorrow."

"Very good, Partington Sahib. Perhaps then you will tell me I must be asking Little Brown Gramophone once more if he was seeing any person leaving Wilson bungalow after he was hearing scream of 'No, Jack. No, Jack.' "

"Oh, I don't think anything Little Brown Gramophone can tell us will help. It won't be any use getting him to repeat yet again what Wilson Memsahib shouted. I've heard all I want of that."

"Very good, sahib."

He had tried, after getting rid of Bulaki Ram, to bring some order to the muddle of his list. But in only a few minutes had given up, gone back to his chummery and flopped into bed himself. And in the morning there was a messenger from the hospital. "DSP Staples is wanting to see. *Ek dum*, he is saying."

He found Old Stamper in his hospital cot looking very ill, although apparently out of his delirium. In answer to a series of feeble barks, he told him every detail of the circumstances of the murder that he could bring to mind.

"Well, man, if Bulaki Ram, who happens to be about as reliable as any Indian ever is, has made certain all the damn servants were out of the way, and if no dacoits were involved, then you'll just have to find this fellow Jack, won't you?"

"Yes, sir. Only . . ."

"Only what, man? Don't stand there and gibber like a blasted monkey. All you've got to do is to go to anybody in the Station called Jack, and make them give you their alibi for tiffin time yesterday. That should be something even you can manage."

"Well, sir, yes. Except, sir, no one is called Jack. No one in the whole Station, as far as I know."

"Then you'll have to get to know a little more, won't you? And don't just stand there. Go away and get on with it. Can't you see I'm a sick man? You're not to come both-ering me with every little damn detail. I'm not your blasted mother, you know.''

"No, sir, no."

And he got away. As quickly as his legs would take him.

To get Bulaki Ram to make him out a new copy of his list of white sahibs. Armed with this, he then set off to go around to each and every name it held with the object of finding out if any one of them was sometimes called Jack. Or had ever been called Jack. Or had a Christian name that was sometimes distorted into Jack.

This, again, was the sort of inquiry that he felt Bulaki Ram should not be privy to. Supposing someone had been given the pet-name of Jack as—Well, as a sort of love token by the Widow Wendy. You never really knew.

So, when Bulaki Ram suggested he should go and finish clearing up in the locked Wilson bungalow, he told him that this was something that had to be done and the sooner it was put in hand the better.

There were six first-name Johns among the people on his list, and four others whose second or third name it was. But each of them assured him, rather insultingly in view of the name he was called himself, that they abominated Jack as a nickname and always had done. And when he asked the wife of the first of them to confirm this he got his nose put out of joint so firmly that he abandoned the thought of asking any other wife.

If I've exhausted the whole damn list without finding anything out, he told himself, I suppose I'll have to go back to them. But that'll be a last resort.

But then the thought came over him that, if he found he had reached a point on the list when he knew who "Jack" was, he would be in the position of having to arrest some respected member of the Club for the murder of a lady who, whatever her morals might be, was after all a white woman.

How could he ever do it?

Then halfway through the morning he discovered some-thing about the padre. The Rev. Michael Fowler had once been a naval chaplain.

"Oh, yes," he had said, with a cheerful clergyman grin when this had come out, "the boys of the lower deck used to call me Parson Jack. Parson because—Well, I was not really a parson, but I was in Holy Orders. And Jack because I was, well, a sort of Jack Tar, you know."

The padre. Could it be? The padre going in secret to the Widow Wendy's bungalow when everybody else was tucking into a decent Christmas tiffin? And . . . ?

But then he remembered. Parson Jack had said grace before his own carving knife at his table or Old Stamper's at the other one had so much as caressed any plump peacock breast. And he had, too, said a thanksgiving grace, "For what we have just received may the Lord make us truly thankful," when the last morsel of mince pie had vanished. Could he have slipped out between the two of them? No, he himself had heard that droning parson's voice and honking laughter throughout the whole meal. He was certain of that.

Back to going around from person to person with his increasingly stupid-sounding question.

"I wonder—it's been suggested to me that someone called Jack may have seen someone near the Wilson bungalow yesterday morning—I wonder, you're never called that by any chance?"

"What the hell are you rabbiting on about, old chap?"

Or, more pointedly, "Hadn't you better catch whatever damn native it was who did for poor old Wendy instead of badgering people with work to do? The British Raj doesn't run itself, young man."

For a moment he had thought of explaining then how, as it so happened, no damn native could have been responsible for the Widow Wendy's death. That it had to be someone called Jack, a member of the Club. One of us. But the man he had been talking to, Charles Sumner, a fifty-year-old planter, a real old India hand, was not going to be told he was wrong by a whipper-snapper just out from England.

"I'll do my best, sir," he had said.

And had scuttled away.

So he felt somehow entitled, when he found little Hav-

ildar Bulaki Ram waiting for him just outside the Summer
bungalow, to be pretty sharp with him.

"Well, havildar, what is it you want now?"

"Sahib, to see if you are needing some help."

"No, I do not. For God's sake, I've got enough trouble
on my plate to last me a lifetime."

And that, he added to himself, is about how long it's
going to take me to solve this bloody case. Unless Old
Stamper's fever goes down, and he can take over.

"Sahib, nothing at all Bulaki Ram can do?"

"Oh, for God's sake, havildar. Have you—Have you—
Oh, have you cleared up Wilson Memsahib's bungalow?
Didn't I tell you to do that?"

"Yes, sahib. All finished. Everything present and correct.
Just only one card from pack missing, *ek tash ka gulam.*"

"Well, go back and find it, man. If you can. It may be
a clue. Or, I don't know, whoever strangled Wilson Memsahib may have taken it away with him, or something. Get
back there and see if it isn't somewhere about after all."

But, tramping around to the Club again to see if he could
find anymore of the people on his list, any Jack, however
unlikely, he felt a sudden jab of shame. He oughtn't to have
spoken like that to old Bulaki Ram. The fellow was only
trying to do his best. It wasn't his fault that he was totally
unequipped to deal with a business like this, the murder of
a memsahib by a sahib.

Good heavens, I'm getting as bad as Old Stamper.

And my Hindustani isn't up to much either. God knows
what it was Bulaki Ram was saying then. *Tash ka* some-
thing-or-other. Ought to look it up, I suppose. When this
beastly business is over. If it ever is.

He paid a visit to Old Stamper at the hospital that evening.
But the fever seemed to have got worse again and he wasn't
really able to take in much.

Which was perhaps a good thing, as there was nothing
really to report. Except that he had spoken to every man
on the list Bulaki Ram had made out, and that the only

possible Jacks he had come across were the padre and the various Johns.

Or . . . a possibility he had not dared to explore. The District Commissioner's wife. From some official document he had once had to countersign he had remembered that her name in full was Frances Jacqueline Lee-Powers. But—But this wasn't possibly a woman's crime. It couldn't be. It mustn't be.

Thank goodness, before he could put forward this awful possibility, Old Stamper had closed his eyes and fallen into a feverish doze.

He crept out.

But, he said to himself, if tomorrow something hasn't given me the clue to it all—and what could that possibly be?—then it'll be . . . Going to see Mrs. Lee-Powers. Mrs. District Commissioner Frances Jacqueline Lee-Powers. The burra memsahib. Jacqui? Jackie? Jack? And asking her if, for some unthinkable reason, she had strangled the Widow Wendy.

Should he have an early night? There was nothing more really he could think of to do. And he was dog-tired. Both the Forestry fellows in the chummery had gone on tour. He could go to bed straight away and sleep and sleep and sleep.

But outside the chummery he found Havildar Bulaki Ram, patiently waiting.

Offering help yet again? What could he give the fellow to do now? All the routine had long ago been tidied away.

"Good evening, havildar. You waiting for me?"

"Oh, yes, sahib. Reporting, sahib."

"Reporting? What on earth about? I didn't give you anything to report on, did I?"

"*Ek* missing playing-card, sahib."

"What? Oh, yes. Yes, that. Well, did you find it? What did you say it was? *Tash ka* something?"

"No, I was not at all finding, sahib. It is one *tash ka gulam*. What angrezi sahibs are calling *jack*. From pack Wilson Memsahib had for playing the game of Patience."

"A jack? A jack. That's odd, when here I am looking

for a man . . . You say, you found on the floor there a jack
missing from the pack of cards that had been sent flying . . .
You're sure it was missing? Absolutely sure?''

"Oh, yes, sahib. Not at all in cards-pack."

Jack felt thoughts racing through his mind, tumbling and
twisting, almost too fast to be caught.

But not quite.

"Do you know what," he said, speaking more to himself
than to Bulaki Ram standing at a little distance apparently
giving himself up to admiring the huge stars glowing in the
night sky. "Do you know what? I think we may have
been barking up the wrong tree all along over this business.
If . . . well, if the Widow Wendy—" In his growing excitement he quite forgot that this was a name that, for the
prestige of the British Raj, someone like Bulaki Ram should
not be allowed to hear. "If Wilson Memsahib was just sitting there alone in her bungalow, playing Patience. And
then . . . then she suddenly found the pack she was using
was missing a jack, wouldn't a woman like her shout out
something like 'No jack. No jack'?''

Bulaki Ram, if he had heard all that, made no reply,
apparently still lost in his study of the familiar stars above
him.

"You know," Jack went on, happy in his almost absent
audience, "if all that happened when Little Brown Gramophone heard those words was that the Widow Wendy leapt
up and overturned her table in her rage. And that's something pretty likely if what Old Stam—if what I've been
told about her is true. Then she was not murdered at that
moment, but at some time later."

"Oh, sahib," Bulaki Ram said, suddenly returning from
the stars. "You are most clever. Most clever. Altogether
one Sheer Luck Hoomes."

"Listen, havildar," Jack went on eagerly. "What time
was it exactly when you found the body? Have you any
idea? You can tell the time and all that, can't you?''

"Oh, sahib, I am knowing when it was. Sahibs' tiffin in
Club was finish. All had gone from dining room to anteroom for fun and games."

"I see. But you can't put an exact hour and minutes to it?"

"No, no, sahib. Bulaki Ram isn't having any watch. All he can say, it was some time after DSP Sahib was leaving to take one walk in sun."

"Yes. Poor fellow. That must have been when he got his go of heatstroke. They said at the hospital that he came wandering in without his topee on his head."

"Oh, yes, sahib. First time such thing has happen for Staples Sahib. Him very careful officer. Well knowing India."

"Yes. I wonder why he suddenly decided to . . ."

Jack came to a halt.

He had almost asked the stocky little havildar if he had had any idea why the DSP should have left the Club when all the other people on the Station were in the comparative cool underneath the anteroom's big, slowly whirring fans getting ready to play charades.

On his way to the hospital to make the arrest, he wondered if some of the credit should not go to Bulaki Ram. After all, it had been he, really—hadn't it?—who had realized the significance of the missing jack from the Widow Wendy's pack.

It was true, in fact, that his own thoughts had been sort of guided by the little havildar. And not only, when you came to think about it, over the business of what those words, "No jack. No jack," had actually meant. Hadn't he been steered the whole way to the answer, if you looked at it in the right light?

And, more, was this only the first time he had been kept right by the little man? What about the way that terrible dhobi had been mysteriously replaced by such a first-class ironing wallah when Bulaki Ram had heard Old Stamper bawling him out about his collar? And, now he came to look at it, surely it had been when by chance he had heard the little havildar chatting to a friend that he had learnt about Wilson Memsahib's habit of putting her claws into young newcomers? So Bulaki Ram had known about the

Widow Wendy all along. And, surely, it had not even been by chance that he had chatted about her liking for young men at a time when he himself could hear?

He strode on through the velvety darkness of the Indian night.

But, if he did insist on telling everyone who was the real Sheer Luck Hoomes—only no question of sheer luck about it—would Bulaki Ram want that?

No.

No, Jack said to himself as in the far distance a jackal gave one of its long, mournful howls. No, I see it now. Bulaki Ram likes things to be the way he arranges them. The white sahib playing his part, and the native, however much he quietly learns, staying always in the background.

Yes, that's it. The charade must go on. Bulaki Ram actually wants it to. And it suits me as a sahib, of course, that it should. It suits all of us sahibs, actually.

But that's all right. Provided I'm one of the ones—there must be some of us—who always remembers that it is all a charade.

H. R. F. Keating wrote his first crime story as long ago as 1969. Best known for his crime novels, many of which feature Inspector Ghote of the Bombay CID, he has also written several books about crime fiction and is the editor of *Agatha Christie: First Lady of Crime*. A respected reviewer and critic, he is a former chairman of both the Crime Writers' Association and the Society of Authors.

The Mistletoe Murder

◆

P. D. JAMES

One of the minor hazards of being a best-selling crime novelist is the ubiquitous question, "And have you ever been personally involved with a real-life murder investigation?"; a question occasionally asked with a look and tone which suggest that the Murder Squad of the Metropolitan Police might with advantage dig up my back garden. I invariably reply No, partly from reticence, partly because the truth would take too long to tell and my part in it, even after fifty years, is difficult to justify. But now, at seventy, the last survivor of that extraordinary Christmas of 1940, the story can surely safely be told if only for my own satisfaction. I'll call it "The Mistletoe Murder." Mistletoe plays only a small part in the mystery but I've always liked alliteration in my titles. I have changed the names. There is now no one living to be hurt in feelings or reputation, but I don't see why the dead should be denied a similar indulgence.

I was eighteen when it happened, a young war-widow; my husband was killed two weeks after our marriage, one of the first RAF pilots to be shot down in single combat. I had joined the WAAF, partly because I had convinced my-self it would have pleased him, but primarily out of the need to assuage grief by a new life, new responsibilities. It didn't work. Bereavement is like a serious illness. One dies or one survives, and the medicine is time, not a change of scene. I went through my preliminary training in a mood of grim determination to see it through, but when my grand-mother's invitation came, just six weeks before Christmas, I accepted with relief. It solved a problem for me. I was an only child and my father, a doctor, had volunteered as a middle-aged recruit to the RAMC; my mother had taken herself off to America. A number of school friends, some also in the forces, wrote inviting me for Christmas, but I couldn't face even the subdued festivities of war-time and feared that I should be a skeleton at their family feast.

I was curious, too, about my mother's childhood home. She had never got on with her mother and after her mar-riage the rift was complete. I had met my grandmother only once in childhood and remembered her as formidable, sharp-tongued, and not particularly sympathetic to the young. But I was no longer young, except in years, and what her letter tactfully adumbrated—a warm house with plenty of wood fires, home cooking and good wine, peace and quiet—were just what I craved. There would be no other guests, but my cousin, Paul, hoped to be on leave for Christmas. I was curious to meet him. He was my only surviving cousin, the younger son of my mother's brother and about six years older than I. We had never met, partly because of the family feud, partly because his mother was French and much of his childhood spent in that country. His elder brother had died when I was at school. I had a vague childhood memory of some disreputable secret, whispered about but never explained. My grandmother, in her letter, assured me that, apart from the three of us, there would only be the butler, Seddon, and his wife. She had taken the trouble to find out the time of a country bus which would leave Victoria at five p.m. on Christmas Eve and take me as far as the nearest town, where Paul would meet me.

The horror of the murder, the concentration on every hour of that traumatic Boxing Day, has diminished my memory of the journey and arrival. I recall Christmas Eve in a series of images, like a gritty black-and-white film, disjointed, a little surreal. The bus, blacked out, crawling, lights dimmed, through the unlit waste of the countryside under a reeling moon; the tall figure of my cousin coming forward out of the darkness to greet me at the terminus; sitting beside him, rug-wrapped, in his sports-car as we drove through darkened villages through a sudden swirl of snow. But one image is clear and magical, my first sight of Stutleigh Manor. It loomed up out of the darkness, a stark shape against a gray sky pierced with a few high stars. And then the moon moved from behind a cloud and the house was revealed; beauty, symmetry and mystery bathed in white light.

Five minutes later I followed the small circle of light from Paul's torch through the porch with its country paraphernalia of walking-sticks, brogues, rubber boots and umbrellas, under the black-out curtain and into the warmth and brightness of the square hall. I remember the huge log fire in the hearth, the family portraits, the air of shabby comfort, and the mixed bunches of holly and mistletoe above the pictures and doors, which were the only Christmas decoration. My grandmama came slowly down the wide wooden stairs to greet me, smaller than I had remembered, delicately boned and slightly shorter even than my five foot three. But her handshake was surprisingly firm and, looking into the sharp, intelligent eyes, at the set of the obstinate mouth, so like my mother's, I knew that she was still formidable.

I was glad I had come, glad to meet for the first time my only cousin, but my grandmother had in one respect misled me. There was to be a second guest, a distant relation of the family, who had driven from London earlier and arrived before me. I met Rowland Maybrick for the first time when we gathered for drinks before dinner in a sitting room to the left of the main hall. I disliked him on sight and was grateful to my grandmother for not having suggested that

he should drive me from London. The crass insensitivity
of his greeting—"You didn't tell me, Paul, that I was to
meet a pretty young widow"—reinforced my initial prej-
udice against what, with the intolerance of youth, I thought
of as a type. He was in the uniform of a flight-lieutenant
but without wings—Wingless Wonders, we used to call
them—darkly handsome, full-mouthed under the thin mustache, his eyes amused and speculative, a man who fancied
his chances. I had met his type before and hadn't expected
to encounter it at the Manor. I learned that in civilian life
he was an antique dealer. Paul, perhaps sensing my disappointment at finding that I wasn't the only guest, explained
that the family needed to sell some valuable coins. Rowland, who specialized in coinage, was to sort and price them
with a view to finding a purchaser. And he wasn't only
interested in coins. His gaze ranged over furniture, pictures,
porcelain and bronze, his long fingers touched and caressed
as if he were mentally pricing them for sale. I suspected
that, given half a chance, he would have pawed me and
assessed my second-hand value.

My grandmother's butler and cook, indispensable small-
part characters in any country house murder, were respectful and competent but deficient in seasonal goodwill. My
grandmother, if she gave the matter thought, would probably have described them as faithful and devoted retainers,
but I had my doubts. Even in 1940 things were changing.
Mrs. Seddon seemed to be both over-worked and bored, a
depressing combination, while her husband barely contained the lugubrious resentment of a man calculating how
much more he could have earned as a war-worker at the
nearest RAF base.

I liked my room; the four-poster with its faded curtains,
the comfortable low chair beside the fire, the elegant little
writing-desk, the prints and water-colors, fly-blown in their
original frames. Before getting into bed I put out the bedside light and drew aside the blackout curtain. High stars
and moonlight, a dangerous sky. But this was Christmas
Eve. Surely they wouldn't fly tonight. And I thought of
women all over Europe drawing aside their curtains and

looking up in hope and fear at the menacing moon.

I woke early next morning, missing the jangle of Christmas bells, bells which in 1940 would have heralded invasion. Next day the police were to take me through every minute of that Christmas, and every detail remains clearly in my memory fifty-two years later. After breakfast we exchanged presents. My grandmother had obviously raided her jewel-chest for her gift to me of a charming enamel and gold brooch, and I suspect that Paul's offering, a Victorian ring, a garnet surrounded with seed pearls, came from the same source. I had come prepared. I parted with two of my personal treasures in the cause of family reconciliation, a first edition of *A Shropshire Lad* for Paul and an early edition of *Diary of a Nobody* for my grandmother. They were well-received. Rowland's contribution to the Christmas rations was three bottles of gin, packets of tea, coffee and sugar, and a pound of butter, probably filched from RAF stores. Just before mid-day the depleted local church choir arrived, sang half a dozen unaccompanied carols embarrassingly out of tune, were grudgingly rewarded by Mrs. Seddon with mulled wine and mince pies and, with obvious relief, slipped out again through the black-out curtains to their Christmas dinners.

After a traditional meal served at one o'clock, Paul asked me to go for a walk. I wasn't sure why he wanted my company. He was almost silent as we tramped doggedly over the frozen furrows of desolate fields and through birdless copses as joylessly as if on a route march. The snow had stopped falling but a thin crust lay crisp and white under a gun-metal sky. As the light faded, we returned home and saw the back of the blacked-out manor, a gray L-shape against the whiteness. Suddenly, with an unexpected change of mood, Paul began scooping up the snow. No one receiving the icy slap of a snow-ball in the face can resist retaliation, and we spent twenty minutes or so like schoolchildren, laughing and hurling snow at each other and at the house, until the snow on the lawn and gravel path had been churned into slush.

The evening was spent in desultory talk in the sitting

room, dozing and reading. The supper was light, soup and herb omelettes—a welcome contrast to the heaviness of the goose and Christmas pudding—served very early, as was the custom, so that the Seddons could get away to spend the night with friends in the village. After dinner we moved again to the ground-floor sitting room. Rowland put on the gramophone, then suddenly seized my hands and said, "Let's dance." The gramophone was the kind that automatically played a series of records and as one popular disc dropped after another—"Jeepers Creepers," "Beer Barrel Polka," "Tiger Rag," "Deep Purple"—we waltzed, tangoed, fox-trotted, quick-stepped around the sitting room and out into the hall. Rowland was a superb dancer. I hadn't danced since Alastair's death but now, caught up in the exuberance of movement and rhythm, I forgot my antagonism and concentrated on following his increasingly complicated lead. The spell was broken when, breaking into a waltz across the hall and tightening his grasp, he said:

"Our young hero seems a little subdued. Perhaps he's having second thoughts about this job he's volunteered for."

"What job?"

"Can't you guess? French mother, Sorbonne educated, speaks French like a native, knows the country. He's a natural."

I didn't reply. I wondered how he knew, if he had a right to know. He went on:

"There comes a moment when these gallant chaps realize that it isn't play-acting anymore. From now on it's for real. Enemy territory beneath you, not dear old Blighty; real Germans, real bullets, real torture-chambers and real pain."

I thought: And real death, and slipped out of his arms hearing, as I re-entered the sitting room, his low laugh at my back.

Shortly before ten o'clock my grandmother went up to bed, telling Rowland that she would get the coins out of the study safe and leave them with him. He was due to drive back to London the next day; it would be helpful if he could examine them tonight. He sprang up at once and they left the room together. Her final words to Paul were:

"There's an Edgar Wallace play on the Home Service which I may listen to. It ends at eleven. Come to say good-night then, if you will, Paul. Don't leave it any later."

As soon as they'd left Paul said: "Let's have the music of the enemy," and replaced the dance-records with Wagner. As I read he got out a pack of cards from the small desk and played a game of patience, scowling at the cards with furious concentration while the Wagner, much too loud, beat against my ears. When the carriage-clock on the mantelpiece struck eleven, heard in a lull in the music, he swept the cards together and said:

"Time to say goodnight to Grandmama. Is there any-thing you want?"

"No," I said, a little surprised, "Nothing."

What I did want was the music a little less loud and when he left the room I turned it down. He was back very quickly. When the police questioned me next day, I told them that I estimated that he was away for about three minutes. It certainly couldn't have been longer. He said calmly:

"Grandmama wants to see you."

We left the sitting room together and crossed the hall. It was then that my senses, preternaturally acute, noticed two facts. One I told the police; the other I didn't. Six mistletoe berries had dropped from the mixed bunch of mistletoe and holly fixed to the lintel above the library door and lay like scattered pearls on the polished floor. And at the foot of the stairs there was a small puddle of water. Seeing my glance, Paul took out his handkerchief and mopped it up. He said:

"I should be able to take a drink up to Grandmama with-out spilling it."

She was propped up in bed under the canopy of the four-poster, looking diminished, no longer formidable, but a tired, very old woman. I saw with pleasure that she had been reading the book I'd given her. It lay open on the around bedside table beside the table-lamp, her wireless, the elegant little clock, the small half-full carafe of water with a glass resting over its rim, and a porcelain model of a hand rising from a frilled cuff on which she had placed her rings. She held out her hand to me; the fingers were limp, the hand cold and listless, the grasp very different from the firm handshake with which she had first greeted me. She said:

"Just to say goodnight, my dear, and thank you for coming. In wartime, family feuds are an indulgence we can no longer afford."

On impulse I bent down and kissed her forehead. It was moist under my lips. The gesture was a mistake. Whatever it was she wanted from me, it wasn't affection.

We returned to the sitting room. Paul asked me if I drank whiskey. When I said that I disliked it, he fetched from the drinks-cupboard a bottle for himself and a decanter of claret, then took up the pack of cards again, and suggested that he should teach me poker. So that was how I spent Christmas night from about eleven-ten until nearly two in the morning, playing endless games of cards, listening to Wagner and Beethoven, hearing the crackle and hiss of burning logs as I kept up the fire, watching my cousin drink steadily until the whiskey bottle was empty. In the end I accepted a glass of claret. It seemed both churlish and censorious to let him drink alone. The carriage-clock struck one forty-five before he roused himself and said:

"Sorry, cousin. Rather drunk. Be glad of your shoulder. To bed, to sleep, per chance to dream."

We made slow progress up the stairs. I opened his door while he stood propped against the wall. The smell of whiskey was only faint on his breath. Then with my help he staggered over to the bed, crashed down and was still.

At eight o'clock next morning Mrs. Seddon brought in my tray of early morning tea, switched on the electric fire and went quietly out with an expressionless "Good morning, madam." Half awake, I reached over to pour the first cup when there was a hurried knock, the door opened, and

Paul entered. He was already dressed and, to my surprise, showed no signs of a hangover. He said:

"You haven't seen Maybrick this morning, have you?"

"I've only just woken up."

"Mrs. Seddon told me his bed hadn't been slept in. I've just checked. He doesn't appear to be anywhere in the house. And the library door is locked."

Some of his urgency conveyed itself to me. He held out my dressing-gown and I slipped into it and, after a second's thought, pushed my feet into my outdoor shoes, not my bedroom slippers. I said:

"Where's the library key?"

"On the inside of the library door. We've only the one."

The hall was dim, even when Paul switched on the light, and the fallen berries from the mistletoe over the study door still gleamed milk-white on the dark wooden floor. I tried the door and, leaning down, looked through the keyhole. Paul was right, the key was in the lock. He said:

"We'll get in through the French windows. We may have to break the glass."

We went out by a door in the north wing. The air stung my face. The night had been frosty and the thin covering of snow was still crisp except where Paul and I had frolicked the previous day. Outside the library was a small patio about six feet in width leading to a gravel path bordering the lawn.

The double set of footprints were plain to see. Someone had entered the library by the French windows and then left by the same route. The footprints were large, a little amorphous, probably made, I thought, by a smooth soled rubber boot, the first set party overlaid by the second. Paul warned:

"Don't disturb the prints. We'll edge our way close to the wall."

The door in the French windows was closed but not locked. Paul, his back hard against the window, stretched out a hand to open it, slipped inside and drew aside first the black-out curtain and then the heavy brocade. I followed. The room was dark except for the single green-shaded lamp on the desk. I moved slowly toward it in fascinated disbelief, my heart thudding, hearing behind me a rasp as Paul violently swung back the two sets of curtains. The room was suddenly filled with a clear morning light annihilating the green glow, making horribly visible the thing sprawled over the desk.

He had been killed by a blow of immense force which had crushed the top of his head. Both his arms were stretched out sideways, resting on the desk. His left shoulder sagged as if it, too, had been struck, and the hand was a spiked mess of splintered bones in a pulp of congealed blood. On the desk-top the face of his heavy gold wrist-watch had been smashed and tiny fragments of glass glittered like diamonds. Some of the coins had rolled onto the carpet and the rest littered the desk-top, sent jangling and scattering by the force of the blows. Looking up I checked that the key was indeed in the lock. Paul was peering at the smashed wrist-watch. He said:

"Half-past ten. Either he was killed then or we're meant to believe he was."

There was a telephone beside the door and I waited, not moving, while he got through to the exchange and called the police. Then he unlocked the door and we went out together. He turned to re-lock it—it turned noiselessly as if recently oiled—and pocketed the key. It was then that I noticed that we had squashed some of the fallen mistletoe berries into pulp.

Inspector George Blandy arrived within thirty minutes. He was a solidly built countryman, his straw-colored hair so thick that it looked like thatch above the square, weather-mottled face. He spoke and moved with deliberation, whether from habit or because he was still recovering from an over-indulgent Christmas it was impossible to say. He was followed soon afterwards by the Chief Constable himself. Paul had told me about him. Sir Rouse Armstrong was an ex-colonial governor, and one of the last of the old school of Chief Constables, obviously past normal retiring age. Very tall, with the face of a meditative eagle, he greeted my grandmother by her Christian name and followed her upstairs to her private sitting room with the grave conspiratorial air of a man called in to advise on some urgent and faintly embarrassing family business. I had the feeling that Inspector Blandy was slightly intimidated by his presence and I hadn't much doubt who would be effectively in charge of this investigation.

I expect you are thinking that this is typical Agatha Christie, and you are right; that's exactly how it struck me at the time. But one forgets, homicide rate excepted, how similar my mother's England was to Dame Agatha's Mayhem Parva. And it seems entirely appropriate that the body should have been discovered in the library, that most fatal room in popular British fiction.

The body couldn't be moved until the police surgeon arrived. He was at an amateur pantomime in the local town and it took some time to reach him. Dr. Bywaters was a rotund, short, self-important little man, red-haired and red-faced, whose natural irascibility would, I thought, have deteriorated into active ill-humour if the crime had been less portentous than murder and the place less prestigious than the Manor.

Paul and I were tactfully excluded from the study while he made his examination. Grandmama had decided to remain upstairs in her sitting room. The Seddons, fortified by the consciousness of an unassailable alibi, were occupied making and serving sandwiches and endless cups of coffee and tea, and seemed for the first time to be enjoying themselves. Rowland's Christmas offerings were coming in useful and, to do him justice, I think the knowledge would have amused him. Heavy footsteps tramped backwards and forward across the hall, cars arrived and departed, telephone calls were made. The police measured, conferred, photographed. The body was eventually taken away shrouded on a stretcher and lifted into a sinister little black van while Paul and I watched from the sitting-room window. Our fingerprints had been taken, the police explained, to exclude them from any found on the desk. It was an odd sensation to have fingers gently held and pressed onto what I remember as a kind of ink-pad. We were, of course, questioned, separately and together. I can remember sitting opposite Inspector Blandy, his large frame filling one of the armchairs in the sitting room, his heavy legs planted on the carpet, as conscientiously he went through every detail of Christmas Day. It was only then that I realized that I had spent almost every minute of it in the company of my cousin.

At seven thirty the police were still in the house. Paul invited the Chief Constable to dinner, but he declined, less, I thought, because of any reluctance to break bread with possible suspects, than from a need to return to his grandchildren. Before leaving he paid a prolonged visit to my grandmother in her room, then returned to the sitting room to report on the results of the day's activities. I wondered whether he would have been as forthcoming if the victim had been a farm laborer and the place the local pub.

He delivered his account with the staccato self-satisfaction of a man confident that he's done a good day's work.

"I'm not calling in the Yard. I did eight years ago when we had our last murder. Big mistake. All they did was upset the locals. The facts are plain enough. He was killed by a single blow delivered with great force from across the desk and while he was rising from the chair. Weapon, a heavy blunt instrument. The skull was crushed but there was little bleeding—well, you saw for yourselves. I'd say he was a tall murderer, Maybrick was over six foot two. He came through the French windows and went out the same way. We can't get much from the footprints, too amorphous, but they're plain enough, the second set overlaying the first. Could have been a casual thief, perhaps a deserter, we've had one or two incidents lately. The blow could have been delivered with a rifle-butt. It would be about right for reach and weight. The library door to the garden may have been left open. Your grandmother told Seddon she'd see to the locking up but asked Maybrick to check on the library before he went to bed. In the black-out the murderer wouldn't have known the library was occupied. Probably tried the door, went in, caught a gleam of the money and killed almost on impulse.''

Paul asked: ''Then why not steal the coins?''

''Saw that they weren't legal tender. Difficult to get rid of. Or he might have panicked or thought he heard a noise.''

Paul asked: ''And the locked door into the hall?''

''Murderer saw the key and turned it to prevent the body being discovered before he had a chance to get well away.''

He paused, and his face assumed a look of cunning which sat oddly on the aquiline, somewhat supercilious features. He said: ''An alternative theory is that Maybrick locked himself in. Expected a secret visitor and didn't want to be disturbed. One question I have to ask you, my boy. Rather delicate. How well did you know Maybrick?''

Paul said: ''Only slightly. He's a second cousin.''

''You trusted him? Forgive my asking.''

''We had no reason to distrust him. My grandmother wouldn't have asked him to sell the coins for her if she'd had any doubts. He is family. Distant, but still family.''

''Of course. Family.'' He paused, then went on: ''It did occur to me that this could have been a staged attack which went over the top. He could have arranged with an accomplice to steal the coins. We're asking the Yard to look at his London connections.''

I was tempted to say that a faked attack which left the pretend victim with a pulped brain had gone spectacularly over the top, but I remained silent. The Chief Constable could hardly order me out of the sitting room—after all, I had been present at the discovery of the body—but I sensed his disapproval at my obvious interest. A young woman of proper feeling would have followed my grandmother's example and taken to her room. Paul said: ''Isn't there something odd about that smashed watch? The fatal blow to the head looked so deliberate. But then he strikes again and smashes the hand. Could that have been to establish the exact time of death? If so, why? Or could he have altered the watch before smashing it? Could Maybrick have been killed later?''

The Chief Constable was indulgent to this fancy: "A bit far-fetched, my boy. I think we've established the time of death pretty accurately. Bywaters puts it at between ten and eleven, judging by the degree of rigor. And we can't be sure in what order the killer struck. He could have hit the hand and shoulder first, and then the head. Or he could have gone for the head, then hit out wildly in panic. Pity you didn't hear anything, though."

Paul said: "We had the gramophone on pretty loudly and the doors and walls are very solid. And I'm afraid that by eleven thirty I wasn't in a state to notice much."

As Sir Rouse rose to go, Paul asked: "I'll be glad to have the use of the library if you've finished with it, or do you want to seal the door?"

"No, my boy, that's not necessary. We've done all we need to do. No prints, of course, but then we didn't expect to find them. They'll be on the weapon, no doubt, unless he wore gloves. But he's taken the weapon away with him."

The house seemed very quiet after the police had left. My grandmother, still in her room, had dinner on a tray and Paul and I, perhaps unwilling to face that empty chair in the dining room, made do with soup and sandwiches in the sitting room. I was restless, physically exhausted; I was also a little frightened. It would have helped if I could have spoken about the murder, but Paul said wearily: "Let's give it a rest. We've had enough of death for one day."

So we sat in silence. From seven forty we listened to Radio Vaudeville on the Home Service. Billy Cotton and his Band, the BBC Symphony Orchestra with Adrian Boult. After the nine o'clock news and the nine twenty War Commentary, Paul murmured that he'd better check with Seddon that he'd locked up.

It was then that, partly on impulse, I made my way across the hall to the library. I turned the door-handle gently as if I feared to see Rowland still sitting at the desk sorting through the coins with avaricious fingers. The black-out was drawn, the room smelled of old books, not blood. The desk, its top clear, was an ordinary unfrightening piece of furniture, the chair neatly in place. I stood at the door convinced that this room held a clue to the mystery. Then, partly from curiosity, I moved over to the desk and pulled out the drawers. On either side was a deep drawer with two shallower ones above it. The left was so crammed with papers and files that I had difficulty in opening it. The right-hand deep drawer was clear. I opened the smaller drawer above it. It contained a collection of bills and receipts. Riffling among them I found a receipt for £3,200 from a London coin dealer listing the purchase and dated five weeks previously.

There was nothing else of interest. I closed the drawer and began pacing and measuring the distance from the desk to the French windows. It was then that the door opened almost soundlessly and I saw my cousin.

Coming up quietly beside me, he said lightly: "What are you doing? Trying to exorcize the horror?"

I replied: "Something like that."

For a moment we stood in silence. Then he took my hand in his, drawing it through his arm. He said: "I'm sorry, cousin, it's been a beastly day for you. And all we wanted was to give you a peaceful Christmas."

I didn't reply. I was aware of his nearness, the warmth of his body, his strength. As we moved together to the door I thought, but did not say: Was that really what you wanted, to give me a peaceful Christmas? Was that all?

I had found it difficult to sleep since my husband had been killed, and now I lay rigid under the canopy of the four-poster reliving the extraordinary day, piecing together the anomalies, the small incidents, the clues, to form a satisfying pattern, trying to impose order on disorder. I think that is what I've been wanting to do all my life. It was that night at Stutleigh which decided my whole career.

Rowland had been killed at half-past ten by a single blow delivered across the width of a three foot six desk. But at half-past ten my cousin had been with me, had indeed been hardly out of my sight all day. I had provided an incontro-

vertible alibi. But wasn't that precisely why I had been
invited, cajoled to the house by the promise of peace, quiet,
good food and wine, exactly what a young widow, recently
recruited into the forces, would yearn for?

The victim, too, had been enticed to Stutleigh. His bait
was the prospect of getting his hands on valuable coins and
negotiating their sale. But the coins which I had been told
must of necessity be valued and sold, had in fact been pur-
chased only five weeks earlier, almost immediately after my
acceptance of my grandmother's invitation. For a moment
I wondered why the receipt hadn't been destroyed, but the
answer came quickly. The receipt was necessary so that the
coins, their purpose now served, could be sold and the
£3,200 recouped. And if I had been used, so had other
people. Christmas was the one day when the two servants
could be certain to be absent all night. The police, too,
could be relied upon to play their appointed part. The Inspector, honest and conscientious but not particularly intelligent, inhibited by respect for an old-established family
and by the presence of his Chief Constable. The Chief Constable, past retirement age but kept on because of the war,
inexperienced in dealing with murder, a friend of the family
and the last person to suspect the local squire of a brutal
murder. A pattern was taking shape, was forming into a
picture, a picture with a face. In imagination I walked in
the footsteps of a murderer. As is proper in a Christie-type
crime, I called him X.

Sometime during Christmas Eve the right-hand drawer
of the study desk was cleared, the papers stuffed into the
left-hand drawer, the wellington boots placed ready. The
weapon was hidden, perhaps in the drawer with the boots.
No, I reasoned, that wasn't possible; it would need to have
been longer than that to reach across the desk. I decided to
leave the question of the weapon until later.

And so to the fatal Christmas Day. At a quarter to ten
my grandmother goes up to bed telling Rowland that she
will get the coins out of the library safe so that he can
examine them before he leaves next day. X can be certain
that he will be there at half-past ten, sitting at the desk. He

enters quietly, taking the key with him and locking the door quietly behind him. The weapon is in his hands, or hidden somewhere within reach in the room.

X kills his victim, smashes the watch to establish the time, exchanges his shoes for the wellington boots, unlocks the door to the patio and opens it wide. Then he takes the longest possible run across the library and leaps into the darkness. He would have to be young, healthy and athletic in order to clear the six feet of snow and land on the gravel path; but then he is young, healthy and athletic. He need have no fear of footprints on the gravel. The snow has been scuffled by our afternoon snowballing. He makes the first set of footsteps to the library door, closes it, then makes the second set, being careful partly to cover the first. No need not worry about fingerprints on the door knob; his have every right to be there. And then he re-enters the house by a side-door left unbolted, puts on his own shoes and returns the wellington boots to their place in the front porch. It is while he is crossing the hall that a piece of snow falls from the boots and melts into a puddle on the wooden floor. How else could that small pool of water have got there? Certainly my cousin had lied in suggesting that it came from the water-carafe. The water-carafe, half-full, had been by my grandmother's bed with the glass over the rim. Water could not have been spilled from it unless the carrier had stumbled and fallen.

And now, at last, I gave the murderer a name. But if my cousin had killed Rowland, how had it been done in the time? He had left me for no more than three minutes to say goodnight to our grandmother. Could there have been time to fetch the weapon, go to the library, kill Rowland, make the footprints, dispose of the weapon, cleaning from it any blood, and return to me so calmly to tell me that I was needed upstairs? But suppose Dr. Bywater was wrong, seduced into an overhasty diagnosis by the watch. Suppose Paul had altered the watch before smashing it and the murder had taken place later than ten thirty. But the medical evidence was surely conclusive; it couldn't have been as late as half-past one. And even if it were, Paul had been too drunk to deliver that calculated blow. But had he in fact been drunk? Had that, too, been a ploy. He had inquired whether I liked whiskey before bringing in the bottle and I remembered how faint was the smell of the spirit on his breath. But no; the timing was incontrovertible. It was impossible that Paul could have killed Rowland. But suppose he'd merely been an accomplice; that someone else had done the actual deed, perhaps a fellow-officer whom he had secretly let into the house and concealed in one of its many rooms, someone who had stolen down at ten thirty and killed Maybrick while I gave Paul his alibi and the surging music of Wagner drowned the sound of the blows. Then, the deed done, he left the room with the weapon, hiding the key among the holly and mistletoe above the door, dislodging the bunch as he did so, so that the berries fell. Paul had then come, taking the key from the ledge, being careful to tread over the fallen berries, locked the library door behind him leaving the key in place, then fabricated the footprints just as I'd earlier imagined.

Paul as the accomplice not the actual murderer raised a number of unanswered questions, but it was by no means impossible. An army accomplice would have had the necessary skill and the nerve. Perhaps, I thought bitterly, they'd seen it as a training exercise. By the time I tried to compose myself to sleep I had come to a decision. Tomorrow I would do more thoroughly what the police had done perfunctorily. I would search for the weapon.

Looking back it seems to me that I felt no particular revulsion at the deed and certainly no compulsion to confide in the police. It wasn't just that I liked my cousin and had disliked Maybrick. I think the war had something to do with it. Good people were dying all over the world and the fact that one unlikeable one had been killed seemed somehow less important. I know now that I was wrong. Murder should never be excused or condoned. But I don't regret what I later did; no human being should die at the end of a rope.

I woke very early before it was light. I possessed myself in patience; there was no use in searching by artificial light and I didn't want to draw attention to myself. So I waited until Mrs. Seddon had brought up my early morning tea, bathed and dressed, and went down to breakfast just before nine. My cousin wasn't there. Mrs. Seddon said that he had driven to the village to get the car serviced. This was the opportunity I needed.

My search ended in a small lumber room at the top of the house. It was so full that I had to climb over trunks, tin boxes and old chests in order to search. There was a wooden chest containing rather battered cricket bats and balls, dusty, obviously unused since the grandsons last played in village matches. I touched a magnificent but shabby-looking horse and set it in vigorous creaking motion, got tangled in the piled tin track of a Hornby train set, cracked my ankle against a large Noah's Ark. Under the single window was a long wooden box which I opened. Dust rose from a sheet of brown paper covering six croquet mallets with balls and hoops. It struck me that a mallet, with its long handle, would have been an appropriate weapon, but these had obviously lain undisturbed for years. I replaced the lid and searched further. In a corner were two golf-bags and it was here I found what I was looking for. One of the clubs, the kind with a large wooden head, was different from its fellows. The head was shining-clean.

It was then I heard a footstep and, looking round, saw my cousin. I know that guilt must have been plain on my face but he seemed completely unworried. He asked: "Can I help you?"

"No," I said. "No. I was just looking for something."

"And have you found it?"

"Yes," I said. "I think I have."

He came into the room and shut the door, leaned across it and said casually: "Did you like Rowland Maybrick?"

"No," I said. "No, I didn't like him. But not liking him isn't a reason for killing him."

He said easily: "No, it isn't, is it? But there's something I think you should know about him. He was responsible for the death of my elder brother."

"You mean he murdered him?"

"Nothing as straightforward as that. He blackmailed him. Charles was a homosexual. Maybrick got to know and made him pay. Charles killed himself because he couldn't face a life of deceit, of being in Maybrick's power, of losing this place. He preferred the dignity of death."

Looking back on it I have to remind myself how different public attitudes were in the 1940s. Now it would seem extraordinary that anyone would kill himself for such a motive. Then I knew with desolate certainty that what he said was true.

I asked: "Does my grandmother know about the homosexuality?"

"Oh yes. There isn't much that her generation don't know, or guess. Grandmama adored Charles."

"I see. Thank you for telling me." After a moment I said: "I suppose if you'd gone on your first mission knowing Rowland Maybrick was alive and well, you'd have felt there was unfinished business."

He said: "How clever you are, cousin. And how well you put things. That's exactly what I should have felt, that I'd left unfinished business." Then he added: "So what were you doing here?"

I took out my handkerchief and looked him in the face, the face so disconcertingly like my own. I said:

"I was just dusting the tops of the golf-clubs."

I left the house two days later. We never spoke of it again. The investigation continued its fruitless course. I could have asked my cousin how he had done it, but I didn't. For years I thought I should never really know. My cousin died in France, not, thank God, under Gestapo interrogation, but shot in an ambush. I wondered whether his army accomplice had survived the war or had died with him. My grandmother lived on alone in the house, not dying until she was ninety-one when she left the property to a charity for indigent gentlewomen, either to maintain as a home or to sell. It was the last charity I would have expected her to chose. The charity sold.

My grandmother's one bequest to me was the books in the library. Most of these I, too, sold, but I went down to the house to look them over and decide which volumes I wished to keep. Among them I found a photograph album wedged between two rather dull tomes of nineteenth-century sermons. I sat at the same desk where Rowland had been murdered and turned the pages, smiling at the sepia photographs of high-bosomed ladies with their clinched waists and immense flowered hats. And then, suddenly, turning its stiff pages, I saw my grandmother as a young woman. She was wearing what seemed a ridiculous little cap like a jockey's and holding a golf-club as confidently as if it were a parasol. Beside the photograph was her name in careful script and underneath was written: "Ladies County Golf Champion 1898."

P. D. James was born in 1920 and educated at the Cambridge High School for Girls. She is the widow of a doctor and has two children and five grandchildren. For thirty years she was engaged in public service, first as an administrator in the National Health Service and then in the Home Office, from which she retired in 1979. Since then she has been a Governor of the BBC and on the Board of the British Council. She has also served on the Board of the Arts Council and been Chairman of its Literature Advisory Panel. In 1987 she was Chairman of the Booker Prize panel of judges. She was awarded an OBE in 1983 and a life peerage as Baroness James of Holland Park in 1991. She has written thirteen crime novels, nine of them featuring the poet-detective, Commander Adam Dalgliesh. The most recent, *Original Sin,* was published in 1994.

Operation Christmas

◆

TIM HEALD

He had been reaching for the top of the tree when he fell. Not so much a fall, more of a lurch. It was a three-legged stool and inherently unstable, though he had to concede the office party mulled wines hadn't helped. Nor had the bloody fairy whose hook had got bent, thus making her tricky to attach to her position on top of the ultimate twig.

At first he had thought it was a large Scotch job. Then, finding it wasn't, he rang his GP who advised wrapping his leg in a pack of frozen peas and maintaining the afflicted limb in an elevated position. By the following morning he knew that the injury needed more than alcohol or vegetables, so he took it into morning surgery and thence to St. Oswald's, where the consultant made him remove his trousers and exhibited him to a couple of trainee doctors with a knowing expression and a depressing verdict.

"Worse than a broken leg. Ruptured Achilles tendon. We'll operate ASAP, tie it together again, and put you in plaster. Crutches for two months; loads of physiotherapy; oh, and we'll keep you in over Christmas, just to be sure."

An affable smile and a firm handshake, and on into an

alarming session of blood tests and ECGs as well as disturbing questions about alcohol and tobacco followed by induction into an orthopaedic ward decked out with holly, mistletoe, paper chains and primitive daubs by local primary schoolchildren. The nurses were firm and smiling, his fellow patients mainly bed-bound and the principal activity an interplay between the two groups involving plastic urine bottles and bed-pans. "Give us a wee, Mr. Perkins," was the first sentence he heard as he was getting into his pajamas. But he was oddly content. He had brought *War and Peace* to read, and before long he was lulled with a jab of morphine and wheeled by trolley to total anaesthetic and a surprisingly unpainful operation. It was, on the whole, a welcome escape from the bloated bickering of a traditional family Christmas.

His two immediate neighbors were a permanently comatose individual on a variety of drips which, in effect, poured liquid in one end and out the other and a gentle octogenarian numismatist coming to terms with his new and highly sophisticated artificial knee. He smiled at Simon from time to time and wished him "Good morning" but otherwise left him alone.

Simon had not encouraged visitors. A bad hospital visitor himself, he recognized the fact that he would make an equally bad visitee. None of his friends knew of his mishap and all branches of his family were congregated at Granny's baronial mansion in darkest Ayrshire.

If he had expected no visitors at all, however, he had expected wrong. At all times of year there is a professional class of hospital visitor, but during festive and religious seasons they emerge in packs like weevils from an ancient biscuit.

Simon had not realized this until, gently coming out of his operational unconsciousness, he was aware of a small, eager woman with a light mustache talking avidly to his neighbor the numismatist. How nice, he thought, vaguely, that the old man and his wife were on such smiling talkative terms. It was only when the small woman turned her attentions to him and began to talk in a similarly animated manner that he realized his mistake—and it was only when he noticed the crucifix at her neck that the penny finally dropped.

"Oh my God!" he exclaimed silently. "It's a nun."

Not that he had anything against nuns. It was just that he hadn't been expecting one. She wasn't a heavy duty proselytiser, didn't try to sell him the Bible, didn't bless him, nor pardon him for his sins, just asked how his leg was, wanted to know how he'd done it and laughed when he told her. "Putting the fairy on the tree!" she said, "I'll be in again tomorrow. You take care now." An Irish voice. Tomorrow was Christmas Day. Rather a nice nun, he thought.

Half an hour later a new patient made an entrance. Most incoming men and women (this was notionally a mixed ward, though men far outnumbered women) arrived nervously, apprehensively, even furtively like eight-year-olds on their first day at boarding school, but this man came through the swing doors with aggression and truculence. He was in a wheelchair pushed by a wide-shouldered, short-haired, second-row forward type with a pencil mustache and tattoos on his fingers. The man in the chair had a small mustache too and the same sort of anonymous dark suit, but whereas his pusher was burly and bulky, he had a weedy, etiolated appearance. Indeed he seemed to the wheelchair born except that he was also manifestly in charge and used to getting his own way. Not only was he being pushed by a tame gorilla, he also had a further two apes in close attendance, like pedestrianized police outriders.

Simon recognized the man at once. He was Alfredo White, President of the Hitler League, and Britain's leading neo-Fascist. Not a significant political figure in the sense that he had only once managed to save his deposit in a parliamentary election, but a nasty piece of work and one perfectly capable of fomenting enough racial, sexual, social or even animal-rightist hatred to cause serious nuisance and grievous bodily harm. Hatred in any shape or form was his *raison d'être,* and he was the last form of life one would wish to see entering one's ward on Christmas Eve.

He was closely followed by the young doctor who had performed the stringent examination of Simon's body when he had first arrived. The doctor's name tag said "Dr. Stanislaus Zamoyski" but everyone called him "Dr. Stan." He was usually cheerful and smiling, but bobbing along in the wake of the Alfredo White invasion fleet he seemed uncharacteristically morose. Bothered even.

Simon smiled as Dr. Stan came alongside the foot of his bed and raised an enquiring eyebrow.

Dr. Stan paused.

"Problem?" asked Simon.

"This man is a racist," said the doctor. "He called me an effing Polack."

Simon shrugged. "That's mild beer by his standards," he said. "What's he in for?"

"I was born in Ealing," said the doctor. "The bastard broke his leg. He fell off his soap-box at a rally. I'm happy to say it's an extremely bad break."

"Oh come on, Dr. Stan," he said. "He can't help being a jerk. Season of peace and goodwill to all men."

"I've been on call for twenty-four hours and I shall probably do another forty-eight before I have serious sleep. I don't have goodwill to anyone very much. Certainly not to a fascist shit like that man."

Simon sympathized but told the doctor not to let it get him down. Life, in his experience, was too short for the indulgence of rising to the provocations of men like White. He was about to say, "Don't give him the satisfaction," when they heard shouting from the desk at the center of the ward from which Sister and her staff nurses controlled operations. The Sister on duty was a doughty, unflappable, Regimental Sergeant Major type with a bellow of a voice, tart turn of phrase and a heart more marshmallow than gold, though you could make a case for both.

Simon caught the words "Effing bloody boggo!" as Dr. Stan turned away and sped toward the disturbance.

It wasn't going to help that Sister O'Brien's two deputies were a diminutive Sri Lankan and a Bajan girl who could have packed down in the second row with White's pusher.

"The Leader's not going to be messed about by a load of Boggoes and Nig-Nogs," said the head supporter—not the chair-pusher but another similarly constructed suit with matching mustache and stencilled digits.

"Your friend," said Sister, with irony, "has broken his leg on Christmas Eve. He is very lucky indeed to have found a hospital bed of any kind and still more so to have doctors prepared to operate on him and nurses to care for him. He should count his blessings, so help me God."

"If you wasn't a woman I'd break your effing leg!" said the big suit.

"This is a hospital, not the House of Commons," said Dr. Stan, surprisingly, "and the sooner we get Mr. White into bed the happier we're all going to be."

This was incontestable, and after a moment of heavy glowering from both sides it seemed that truce had broken out. From Simon's bed the armistice looked fragile. Unwelcome too, for Alfredo White was clearly being directed toward the bed lately occupied by the numismatist with the new knee. He was moving in next door. Simon's heart sank.

Matters were made worse by the fact that external evidence suggested that Simon was a white Caucasian male of roughly the kind approved by the Hitler League. Not, perhaps of the blond sinuous variety celebrated in the photography of Leni Riefenstahl, but nevertheless a pink-grey in middle age.

As he was wheeled alongside the Leader favored him with a thin, tortured smile, and said, "Big book, eh, Brother?"

He had forgotten that he was still clutching *War and Peace* and wondered if Alfredo White was aware that it was written by a foreigner.

"Yes," he agreed, nervously and feebly, thinking to himself that it was cowardly to agree with such a person on anything, but having to accept that in this instance at least the Leader had right on his side. "Yes," he repeated, "in every sense."

The Leader abruptly stopped undressing.

"Yer what?" he wanted to know.

"A big book. It's a big book in every sense."

"I can see that." Mr. White's suspicions were obviously aroused. "I'm not stupid, yer know. You think I'm stupid, do you? Think I can't see it's an effing big book?"

"Yes," said Simon, alarmed and confused, "I mean no."

"You some sort of inter-bloody-lectual?"

"Absolutely not," said Simon, "I'm as English as you or . . . er . . . the next man."

Alfredo White and his three minions gave him a suspicious, old-fashioned look and the Leader continued preparing for bed. Sister strode Amazoniacally to his overhead light and slapped on a yellow sticker.

"They'll have you in the theater tomorrow as soon as they possibly can, Mr. White," she said. "You should be out in time for Christmas dinner. If you're feeling up to it that is." She bared her teeth and departed before the team could insist on her addressing their boss as "Leader." Simon knew what the sign said without having to look. The message was "Nil by mouth." Serve White right. Although the last meal of the day was long served a nurse came around shortly before lights out with all manner of long forgotten nursery bedtime drinks. There was Ovaltine; there was Hot Chocolate; there was Horlicks. These were precisely the evocative milky libations to delight the heart of a reactionary Little Englander, and tonight at least the man would go without.

When Simon's neighbor was tucked up in bed, still snarling in his old-fashioned flannelled and striped Chilprufe jim-jams, Sister reappeared with Dr. Zamoyski in purposeful tow.

"It's long past visiting hours," she said, "so I'm afraid I must ask you gentlemen to leave."

She didn't seem in the least afraid, though the doctor looked less than confident.

"Sorry missus," said the gang leader. "Not possible. The Leader's life is under constant threat and it's our duty to guard him day and night."

The words had a rehearsed air, as if learned from the autocue and recited with a mechanical absence of stress or tone which almost deprived them of meaning.

"It's true." Alfredo White's eyes gleamed. His voice had the high nasal whine of South London tinged with manic gripe. "The Forces of Darkness are pledged to extinguish the Torch of Truth. I am the Light."

The psychiatric ward was almost next door. Simon wondered if his friend shouldn't be put on the transfer list. On the other hand if you stripped away the barmy persiflage about Torches and Darkness there was no denying that Mr. White had a valid point. There had been many threats reported in the press; a couple of petrol bomb attempts at the very least; crazed gunmen and a would-be assassin with a knife. When the President of the Hitler League described himself as Public Enemy Number One, he spoke, for almost the only time in his life, the truth.

"Shut that bleeding noise, you effers!" came a strangled cry from a far corner of the ward where the ever cranky Mr. Moriarty lay in traction behind a wall of greetings cards and vivid red poinsettia.

"What the hell is that geezer mouthing off about?!" asked the Leader.

In raw phonetics it sounded as if he said "Wot the 'ell 'zat geezer mahfin off abaht."

"You heard!" Mr. Moriarty shouted. "Shut yer mouth! Some of us are trying to get some kip."

Sister O'Brien was flanked by her own followers now: the Polish doctor from Ealing, the big black nurse from Barbados and Kennington, and the small black nurse from Sri Lanka.

"You want me to sort him out, boss?" asked one of the Hitlerites—not the pusher this time.

"Nah," said the Leader, "sounds as if he'll be dead by the morning anyway. Leave him be."

"If your men don't leave the ward," said Dr. Stan, "I shall have no option but to call the police."

As he said it another visitor came through the doors

beaming broadly, rubbing his hands and waggling a dark bearded head which was perhaps half a size too large for a vertically threatened pear-shaped body.

"Good Evening, Sister! Good Evening, Doctor! Good Evening All of You!"

It was the rabbi. By rights, thought Simon, he shouldn't have been here, it not really being his festival, but on the other hand he was obviously a Reform rabbi of ecumenical bent and benign disposition who wanted to give and take of the goodwill which was supposed to be abroad.

"Get that Yiddish runt out of here!" said Alfredo White, pleasantly.

The rabbi, who had begun a sentence involving his grandmother and something funny that happened to her while cooking salt beef or gefilte fish, ground to a mid-sentence halt.

"I won't have you speaking to Rabbi Schlom in that blasphemous fashion," said Sister O'Brien, "and if your men aren't out of here in double quick time I'll have you out with them, broken leg or no broken leg, Christmas or no Christmas."

"I didn't come here to be gloated over by an effing rabbi," said Mr. White, part of whose belief, vociferously held, was that the holocaust was a Zionist invention.

"If your men aren't out of here PDQ," said Dr. Stan, "I'm calling the police."

"I wish you *would* call the police," said the Leader. "They owe me. Twenty-four hour protection I should have. That arty farty Paki Rushdie gets a twenty-four hour job but a decent Englishman pure born and bred what never hurts no one gets nothing but threats from a load of left-handed wanking foreign riff-raff."

The rabbi turned away grimacing and caught Simon's sympathetic gaze.

"If I were not a man of God," said the rabbi, "I would cut down this uncircumcised unbeliever and set his head on a spike at the hospital gates."

Simon smiled.

"No you wouldn't," he said.

"No I wouldn't," said the rabbi, "but I would be sorely tempted."

Meanwhile the matter of the Leader's bodyguard appeared to be settled in far from amicable compromise. Provided none of the goons were actually inside the ward neither Sister nor Doctor would object if they remained outside in the corridor. If the hospital security guards tried to move them on from this sentry-go position then that was another matter altogether. The hospital security guards were flimsy, incompetent and, tonight of all nights, almost certainly drunk, so such an eventuality was unlikely to occur.

The three gorillas moved out, muttering; the rabbi moved on, also muttering, though less unpleasantly; the hot drink trolley moved in, and Simon sipped his first Horlicks in thirty years while Alfredo White took nil by mouth and swore repetitively in a hoarse whisper like a demented baglady railing against the shoppers in a suburban High Street.

Presently the lights were turned out and the only illumination was of the three nurses at their desk leaning over plastic mugs of coffee and sundry documents. Occasionally they glanced up from the work-top in order to scan the ward for signs of anything untoward. They reminded Simon of the night watch on the bridge of a destroyer in the Battle of the Atlantic, scanning the ocean for enemy U-boats. Two miniature Christmas trees, all tinsel and twinkling fairy lights, flanked their command station like Disneyland wireless aerials. "All quiet on the Western front," he thought, for no very good reason, and wondered if he was suffering from post-operational shock or whether someone had slipped a Mickey Finn into his Horlicks.

Alongside him the neo-Fascist was restless and noisy, continuing a semi-coherent, hoarsely whispered, Horseley Wesselled diatribe against the human race. Perhaps it was, in part, a product of pain. At one point a nurse, the little Sri Lankan, handed him two pain-killers and a plastic cup of water which he swallowed with a bilious remark halfway between a curse and an imprecation. For a while after this he slept and was silent save for sudden spasms and muffled shrieks.

Snug in his hospital-cornered, crisp-sheeted bed, Simon pondered some paradoxes as Christmas approached. He remembered midnight masses in the past, thought of congregations, many of them unbelieving like himself, pouring into frosty churches, often literally, from pub to priest. Looking around him at the three nurses in silhouette he thought of the three wise men and of shepherds watching flocks by night. Did his fellow inmates qualify as sheep? If so, next door was a black one. And was there some macabre analogy involving this bitter Fascist creature, slouching but supplicant, not being turned away by the innkeeper like Joseph and Mary but invited in, even by those he vilified and abused? If there was a message, what was it? He did not know, for as so often, particularly in these, his middle years, he was bothered and confused.

He supposed also that the President of the Hitler League was under permanent threat of death and that the threat was of his own making. It was almost as if White was daring the world to do him in, and there were probably extremists—some would call them fanatics—who might come bursting through the doors of St. Oswald's, even on Christmas Day, brandishing automatic weapons, knives, cudgels or other instruments of death. Yet those he insulted most— the doctors, nurses, friendly visitors—were those most dedicated to keeping him alive.

Simon wondered how far the man would have to go in order to provoke an overworked hospital doctor to an uncharacteristic action, even if it was only a sin of omission, or perhaps a little over enthusiasm. The slip of a hand-held scalpel; an overdose of pre-med morphine. These things happened, didn't they? And if they did, would they, in the circumstances, be so very wrong, even on Christmas Day? Such were the imponderables with which Simon grappled before early morning tea, nursely greetings to salute the happy morn, and a return to Tolstoy. Alfredo White did not appreciate his lack of morning tea. He swore horribly.

A choir of child carol singers shrilled into the ward just before breakfast and sang "God Rest You Merry Gentlemen!," which made Simon smile and Alfredo scowl. He scowled even more as the trolley passed him by with its cargo of toast and hard-boiled eggs and shouted angrily when the nurse in charge (colored of course) wagged a finger at him, smiled seraphically, and said "Nil by mouth, Alfredo!"

Presently an anaesthetist, clad entirely in green from slippers to surgical hat, came to the White bed with a clipboard and questions relating to allergies, dietary habits, height, weight and other matters which, naturally, Alfredo White regarded as none of anybody else's business. This he told the anaesthetist, who shrugged with relative disinterest though expressively for, as luck would have it, he was an Italian, Tristano from Padua, and very good at his job. He had indeed anaesthetized Simon earlier. Mr. White called him a "Wop" and an "Eyetie" and made reference to the North African Campaign in the Second World War as well as to hanging the Duce and his mistress upside down from a lamp post—a reference which seemed ill advised given the similarity between the politics of Mussolini and Mr. White. Tristano remarked, mildly, that Alfredo was such an interesting name for such an English Englishman. But Simon, who thought the same, found out no more because the remark only reduced the patient to further incoherence. How simple it would be, thought Simon, for Tristano to mix his potion in proportions just that little bit more lethal than required. It seemed foolish for the Leader to be quite so truculent when he was so absolutely at the mercy of the National Health.

The padre was next, a limp earnest curate of mildly happy clappy disposition from the Archbishop of Canterbury's wing of the divided of C. of E. Mr. White, predictably, zoned in immediately on the man's sexuality.

"We'd be better off with bleeding women priests if you ask me," he said. "At least they're the genuine article, not limp-wristed woofters like you. Effing queer!"

"Happy Christmas," said the reverend.

"Up yours, matey!" said the Leader, who seemed to be in good spirits. He obviously relished so many sitting targets, particularly on a day like this.

The curate turned despairingly to Simon, who told him not to worry. "He's in a lot of pain, padre, and he's going in for major surgery any moment."

"I shall pray for him," said the curate, with a grim twitch of the mouth.

"You do that, you little wanker, and I'll have you outed and exposed and all over the effing *Sun*."

The wretched visitor had all the marks of a serious celibate whose sexuality was a decorously gray area, but the Leader clearly had him marked down as Militant Gay Tendency. For a moment he looked as if he might be about to proclaim his innocent gray celibacy but instead, inspired, he made the sign of the cross and said, "Bless you, my son."

"Eff off, poof!" replied Mr. White.

Simon sighed but was relieved to see two nurses approach with a tray, syringes and a white hospital robe.

"Time for your pre-med, Mr. White. Off with your pajamas and put this on, then we'll give you a nice little jab in your botty and you'll be ever so peaceful and happy . . ."

The rest of these words were drowned in a prolonged snarl of racist outrage. The nurses drew the curtains around the bed and went about their business. Simon, half listening to the Morning Service on his headset, half immersed in the great Russian novel, still found time to marvel at their cheerfulness, optimism, equanimity and skill. Rather them than him.

Presently a trolley arrived and Mr. White was lifted onto it and wheeled away to be cut open and mended. He was still mouthing off, but the morphine had taken hold, so that the voice had lost something of its cutting edge and become more of a babble. As he disappeared through the swing doors, horizontal and at speed, the ward seemed to exhale a collective gasp of relief.

Extraordinary how a single unpleasant person can so easily dominate whereas benign influences have to struggle.

Quite apart from the staff there were seventeen patients in the ward, none noticeably evil or malevolent. Yet the whole place had become infected by the personality of Alfredo White. It was the school bully syndrome. Frightening. It was obvious that he was a man of no worth and yet he had imposed himself effectively, insidiously and inexplicably. Now that he was away for his operation, the spell was, just as mysteriously, lifted.

His was not supposed to be complicated surgery, yet he was away a long while. A series of visitors, mainly religious, all of whom would have been *persona non grata* to the Hitler League, busied their way through. A group representing the Friends of St. Oswald's sang more carols, slightly off-key, and handed out token presents to all the patients.

Shortly before noon a Christmas lunch appeared with turkey and trimmings and plum pudding. There was even a nut-roast for vegetarians. Crackers were pulled. Simon pulled his with a pretty nurse—a New Zealand blonde as it happened, of whom even Mr. White might not have disapproved. Everyone donned paper hats.

In the middle of this Bacchanalia of the halt and the lame, the Leader returned on his trolley.

He did not look good.

He was breathing but not, apparently, conscious. There were tubes in his arms; tubes protruding from under the bedclothes; a tube up his nose. For a moment the ward missed a beat. Simon himself ran through a gamut of immediate emotion ranging from guilty satisfaction to "there but for the grace of God go I," and guessed that many of the others were thinking the same. Dr. Stan, gray with fatigue, appeared seconds later, eating a mince pie. Simon raised an enquiring eyebrow.

"He'll live," said Dr. Stan, "but it was more complicated than we expected. His bodyguard didn't help. We had to call the police."

"I'm sorry," said Simon, enigmatically.

"Yes," said the doctor, seeming just as ambiguous.

What happened next was almost like a conscious act of exorcism. The nurses began to sing, and they sang stunningly well. Dr. Stan joined in and turned out to have a rather fine tenor voice. The small Irish nun suddenly materialized, and she too could sing. Another doctor arrived with a fiddle, and he could play. The basis of their music was the Christmas carol canon but was only a platform for a strange, inspired Christmas jam session: Improvisations on a Yuletide theme.

For a few moments Simon listened and watched and was mildly moved.

Then he went back to Tolstoy, where Pierre and Prince Andrei were discussing, more or less, the meaning of life.

Pierre was telling his friend the story of his duel.

"The one thing which I thank God for is that I didn't kill the man," said Pierre.

"Why so?" asked Prince Andrei. "To kill a vicious dog is a very good thing really."

Simon glanced across at his neighbor and thought he saw a tremor of an eyelid, a curl of the lip.

At the far end of the ward the big black nurse and the little black nurse were doing things to "The First Noel" which would have impressed Lena Horne or Miriam Makeeba.

Simon's leg was painful but he could hop. All eyes were on the impromptu choir. Awkwardly he swung himself out of bed and half hopped, half fell toward Alfredo. The man's eyes opened briefly and seemed to recognize him. Simon smiled. "Happy Christmas," he said, and gently removed two of the most crucial looking tubes. The eyes closed. Simon managed to fall back into bed and return to his book. Prince Andrei was saying, "It is not given to man to judge of what is right or wrong."

He saw that Alfredo White's color was very poor and his breathing becoming worse.

In the distance "The First Noel" slid seamlessly into "In the Bleak Midwinter." Simon shivered slightly and read on. Prince Andrei was speaking again.

"As to what's right and what's good—you must leave that to Him Who knows all things: it is not for us to decide."

Simon smiled. He was sure Bolkonsky was wrong. But he was glad he had chosen Tolstoy for Christmas.

Tim Heald was born just over a month after Christmas 1943. He has written a dozen or so crime novels, a handful of non-fiction books and is a former Chairman of the Crime Writers Association. He invented the Cartier Diamond Dagger while reporting elephant polo in Nepal and always puts cloves in his bread-sauce. Shortly after Christmas 1994 he ruptured his Achilles tendon playing Real Tennis at Hampton Court.

A Card or a Kitten

LIZA CODY

"She's just a gold-digging tramp," Elaine says. She coughs—a dry nervous cough. " 'Scuse me, Liza, but that's what she is. Everyone knows it. All my friends say so."

I am a friend. I was saying nothing. Elaine didn't leave me any space to speak in. She coughed and talked, talked and coughed.

"Lew's thinking with his dick. 'Scuse me, Liza, but even his accountant says that. She flies in from Carolina, screws his brains out and flies away again. She does stuff to him nice women don't do. But, see, Liza, she ain't a nice woman: she says her family's from Venezuela but I bet she's Cuban."

Cough, cough, cough. Elaine sips iced Coke. Highway 41 growls under her condo window.

I say, "I'm really sorry, Elaine. I had no idea."

I think, "Get me out of here." I know the way Elaine talks when she's over-excited. This could go on for hours. At her best, Elaine is a good talker, a great story-teller. But at her worst she is obsessive and repetitive. She is not at her best right now, and I can't blame her. Betrayal brings out the worst in everyone.

"He said he was going fishing up on Lake Kissimee. I coulda went with him, Liza. But I thought, nah, he's safe fishing. It was a pro-am tournament, see. He always goes. Every year. I went one time, Liza, but it was just fish, fish, fish and no fun. I shoulda went this time, Liza, 'cos it was fun, fun, fun and no fish."

Elaine tells and retells every incident. Endlessly, she picks at her emotional scabs. Endlessly, I watch them bleed. Nothing more is required than my body on her couch, my ears at her disposal. I can't help. She won't let me talk. She just wants me to listen. I hope it is enough, but of course it isn't. When you lose your husband to a gold-digging tramp nothing anyone can do or say will make it better.

Cough, cough, cough and around we go again.

"I've always said to him, Lew, I said, when a tennis pro tries to live like his clients that's when you *know* he's gonna die a poor man. I said that to him I don't know how many times, Liza. So what does he do? He's bought her a house on the island, where the rich folk live. He's bought her diamonds. Diamonds, Liza."

She fingers the diamond tennis bracelet Lew gave her three years ago. She's still wearing it.

"She's a gold-digging tramp, Liza. 'Scuse me, but she is. She's making him spend money he doesn't have. She screws his brains out, Liza, she's screwed him brain-dead. I was brought up a Catholic and I never even heard of the stuff she does. I'd never of allowed stuff like that. So he buys her a house on the island. And diamonds, Liza. Whachoo think of that?"

Phrases like, "virtue is its own reward" do not strike me as appropriate, and besides I am not given time to utter them.

"She's a whore, Liza," Elaine says. "Even his accountant said so. All his friends are laughing at him."

Trouble in paradise. Lew is one of the best-respected tennis pros on Manattee Key. He runs the program at the

Manattee Tennis Club. Elaine used to run the pro shop. Now she is living in a small condo right next to Highway 41 and working for Budget Cars at Sarasota Airport.

I was truly sorry for her. But, I have to admit it, I was also a little sorry for myself. I go to Manattee Key nearly every year at Christmas for a few weeks' rest and sun. One of my great pleasures was to lean against Elaine's counter at the pro shop and gas with her. From there, between the racks of skirts, shorts, shirts, I could see Lew giving a lesson out on Court 1. I would listen to Elaine's stories and at the same time take note of Lew's grace. The way he bent his knees to take a low shot, how still his head was when he hit the ball. Sunshine, grace, great stories: that was my idea of a good Christmas. You can keep your sleigh bells and roasting chestnuts—they only mean chilblains to me.

I was very fond of Elaine, but I was very fond of Lew too. It's the great conundrum facing anyone who knows a divorced couple. How do you stay loyal to two people who hate each other? The answer is that you can't. You can only pick your way stealthily between the rock and the hard place and hope neither of them notices.

I didn't tell Elaine, but I had already been to see Lew and he had told me quite a different story.

The one I had not yet seen was the gold-digging tramp, Bianca, the love of Lew's middle age. But I certainly saw her handiwork: Lew was looking ten years younger. To be fair, so was Elaine: she'd had her hair frosted and bought a whole new wardrobe. She'd never looked better. It was amazing to me, a mere tourist in their lives, how things changed between one Christmas and the next.

It was amazing, too, how Elaine, living out by Highway 41, knew every detail of Lew and Bianca's lives. But Elaine's stories always came from a complicated network of informers. I would have to tread carefully.

Lew knew all this better than I did, and the next day, after my four o'clock game he called over to me from Court 1. He said, "Liza, stick around. You want a beer? We'll have a beer."

So I had a shower and stuck around. And all that the
other club members and maintenance staff knew was that
I was going for a beer with the head pro. That was Lew,
being discreet. If he had secrets to keep he'd have to do a
bit better than that.

We left in his Bronco and as soon as we'd left the club,
Lew said, "I need a chaperone."

"So I'm told," I couldn't resist saying.

He started laughing. "Been talking to Elaine?" he said.
"Yes."

He didn't mind. He said, "She hates my guts at the moment."

I said nothing. I thought it might be for more than just
a moment.

Lew drove in silence for a minute. Then he said, "You
takin' sides?"

"Not if I can help it," I said.

" 'Cos I need a chaperone and I don't want it to get back
to Elaine. She's been talking to my accountant and he
thinks she wants to take me for every cent I've got."

Lew started life as a poor, simple Australian boy with
nothing on his side but wonderful hand-eye co-ordination
and an equally wonderful capacity for hard work. He was
uneducated. He had more faith in hard currency that in
checks or plastic. He had more hard currency than he ever
admitted to any Revenue official or Elaine. He thought he
was shrewd.

Shrewd Lew said, "So Liza, will you help?"

I say, "What do you need a chaperone for?" Lew's
weakness is shrewdness. Mine is curiosity.

"I'm meeting a woman at the Main Street Diner," Lew
says.

"What? Another?" I say.

But he ignores me. "I never seen her before. I don't trust
her. She don't trust me."

"Makes sense," I say before I can stop myself. Unlike
Elaine, Lew leaves me plenty of space for inappropriate
comments.

"Well, Liza, it's Christmas in a coupla days," Lew says.

"This woman, she put an ad in the *Sarasota Tribune*. She's got a Rolex diamond watch she wants to sell and I want to look at it."

"Oh," I say.

"For Bianca," he says. "I din't have time to buy her a present yet. This watch goes for thirty-two new."

"Thirty-two?"

"Thirty-two thousand bucks," Lew says, as if to a subnormal child. "Thirty-two new. This woman, see, she'll let me have it for ten. Cash."

"Ten?" says the subnormal child. I have, once in a blue moon, met the kind of man who gives that sort of Christmas present—to other women—but none of them was a simple Aussie tennis pro. It puts Lew's tax and alimony problems into perspective.

"It's a snip," says shrewd Lew. "If the Rolex . . ."

"Is kosher," I say, "if the woman is kosher . . ."

"Exactly," Lew says. "That's what I need you for, Liza."

"But . . ." I say, quite unable to put my objections in sequence.

"All you have to do is sit with the woman and the money while I get the watch valued."

It is beginning to make a little, demented sense to me. The Main Street Diner is on the same block as Farfell's Fine Jewelry. The fact that it's beginning to make sense worries me considerably. We are driving down the road which runs through the middle of Manattee Key. On either side are blocks of condominiums interspersed with yacht clubs and golf clubs. The sun is making its evening dive into the glassy blue sea, and already the horizon is turning turquoise and gold. Soon we'll be on the causeway which joins the island to mainland Florida, which joins paradise to the real world: where palm trees give way to high-rise finance companies, where fine restaurants turn into pawn shops, where Highway 41 groans and grinds its way past Elaine's window.

I am unprepared for the transition.

"Cash?" I say weakly.

Lew jerks his thumb toward the floor. His Bronco is as neat and clean as he is. The only thing out of place is a brown supermarket bag which I had thought might hold what was left over from his lunch. Brown bag cash.

"Count it," offers Lew.

I do not. I don't want to touch it.

"Funny thing is," Lew says, "if I gave Bianca a card or a kitten she'd love it just as much."

"Yes?" I say.

"I really have to fight to give her something worth keepin'." Lew smiles. "She's just a kid, Liza. You'll love her."

"A card or a kitten," I say.

We park outside the Court House and walk back to the Main Street Diner.

Lew says, "This woman, she says she'll be wearing a red jacket. We got to meet in a public place. She doesn't trust me with the Rolex anymore than I trust her with the money. She's afraid I might roll her."

"But Lew," I say, "what if *she* is planning to roll *you*? What if she hands you some worthless Taiwan fake to take to Farfell's and then does a runner? What do you expect me to do about it?"

He grins. Hours teaching tennis in the sun have given him a skin which looks like creased leather when he smiles. He says, "You're a big girl. Knock her down and sit on her till I get back."

Clearly, he isn't expecting trouble, but if he calls me a big girl again, the trouble might come from his chaperone. I give him my wolf look.

"That's the ticket," he says, misunderstanding completely.

There are three women in red jackets inside the Main Street Diner. It is a long thin café, dark brown and old-fashioned. We walk slowly between the booths and photographs signed long ago by Ringling Circus performers.

The two red jackets closest to the street take no notice, but the one right at the back eyes us nervously, the attitude of someone waiting for a stranger. I suppose we are similarly obvious for she gets awkwardly to her feet.

"Terri?" Lew says. "I'm Lew. I brought my friend, Liza."

"That's okay," Terri says. "I brought my friend Frank."

"Hi," says Frank. "I'm Frank."

As far as I can see, in the gloomy back of the Main Street Diner, Frank is a serious body-builder. Although he is not much taller than I am he could wrap himself twice around Lew and still have enough left over to fill a meat sandwich. If Lew is not beginning to have doubts about this transaction, I have enough for both of us.

Terri, on the other hand, is all curly-girly. I would never go to a party with her unless I wanted a very thin time indeed. She'd wear a dress which wouldn't even fit my arm and say "I don't know what everyone's getting so excited about: it's only little old me."

We sit—two utterly mismatched couples—facing each other across the small brown table. I can tell that Lew thinks Terri is cute, and suddenly I feel very blue. Elaine wasn't like Terri. Elaine was bustling, bossy, full of stories. I am blue because I'm afraid that Bianca, the gold-digging tramp, will be more like Terri than Elaine. I'm afraid that if she is, my friendship with Lew is coming to an end. I'm afraid that Frank will beat Lew up and rip off his brown bag full of cash.

They get down to business with alarming speed—the way it often happens in the States. "Let's have a look at the Rolex," Lew says.

Terri fishes in an alligator skin bag and hooks a black leather box. She hands it to Frank and looks expectantly at Lew. Lew passes the brown bag to me. Frank gives me a quick flash at the watch. I give him a glimpse of ten thousand bucks. I feel like a prat.

Then Frank hands the watch to Lew, so I hand the brown bag to Terri. I still feel like a prat.

Shrewd Lew examines the watch. He says, "Whaddya think, Liza?"

I hold the watch. I stare at the little white face. I would not be able to tell the time accurately without reading

glasses, so I stare at the gold and glittering stones instead.
The watch is hideous.

"Whaddya think?"

I turn the watch over. It says Rolex on the back. "It
looks alright to me," I say judiciously.

Lew leans closer and whispers, "It's fuckin' gorgeous. I
can't wait to see Bianca's face."

"*If* it's the business," I warn. "Anyway, if it's dodgy,
remember a card or a kitten would do just as well."

"No *way*!" Lew hisses. His eyes are alight with diamonds. He's in love and not, therefore, open to reason.

And now, having started, he can't wait. He practically
drags bulky Frank out of the diner and off to Farfell's down
the block.

I tried to slow him down. "Why don't we all go?" I
asked. But it isn't part of the plan. Lew and Frank disap-
pear, leaving me alone with Terri and a brown bag full of
paper money.

"I can't go to Farfell's," Terri informs me. "My boyfriend bought the watch there. I don't want them to know
how I gotta let it go."

I worry about shrewd Lew some more: if there is a chi-
cane in this deal, maybe Farfell's is in on it too.

Terri says, "Your boyfriend seems like a real cute guy—
d'you think he'd like to buy you a ring to go with the
watch? I gotta let my ring go too."

I say, "Lew's buying a Christmas present for his fiancée.
I'm just a friend."

"My boyfriend married his other fiancée," Terri says,
"that's why I need to get liquid real fast. I wouldn't sell
if'n I didn't gotta pay the rent. I never paid the rent before
neither. I got a cute little apartment too. But maybe I'll
have to find some place not so cute now."

"So Frank isn't your boyfriend," I say.

"You gotta be kiddin," Terri says. "He's the janitor in
my apartment building, and that's *not* my kind of guy. I
never spoke to him before my boyfriend walked out, but
we got to talking in the lobby one time and I was tellin'
him how I gotta sell some things and he tells me how I

need some protection. He said I shouldn't meet some strange guy alone with a valuable watch. He's lookin' after me. But now I've met your, er, friend I think maybe he was wrong. Your friend's kinda sexy.''

All this is making me more relaxed. Compared with Terri Lew is very shrewd indeed.

"I'll show you the ring anyways," she says. "It's so neat. I just hate to let it go. But maybe you'll love it like I do and tell your friend.''

The ring is a diamond egg in a nest of sapphires. I swear privately that if I ever tell Lew about it I will urge Elaine to cut my tongue out slowly, with a rusty scalpel.

Terri puts it on. It looks like hell. Her hands are small and her nails are the color of bruised apricots. She gazes sadly at her hand.

"If I can find a buyer for the ring," she says, "I figure maybe I can keep the car. My boyfriend din't finish paying for that before he walked out.''

Lew comes back, quick and graceful. He has the eager competitive look he gets when coming in to the net for an easy volley.

"Well, Terri," he says. "It looks like you got yourself a deal.''

"I don't know," she says, suddenly hesitant. "Maybe I shoulda' asked for more.''

Frank blunders up to the table, blowing hard.

"You think maybe I should ask for more?" Terri asks him.

"Quick sale," Lew says. "Cash down.''

"You couldn't do better," Frank says.

Terri bites her lip and looks at me. I say nothing. I am hoping Lew won't notice the ring she's still wearing.

Frank says, "You'd have to put another ad in the paper. You'd have to take more calls. It's more trouble, more risk.''

I lean over and whisper in Lew's ear, "Is Farfell's reputable?''

"Don't worry," he whispers back. "They know me in there, and I know them." Shrewd Lew.

Terri is still biting her lip. She says, "I guess maybe Frank's right—who knows—the next lot of people mightn't be as nice as you guys."

She looks at Lew while she says this. I have been worrying about the wrong person: I can't understand how anyone as dumb as Terri has lived so long and collected so much hardware.

Lew and I drive back to Manattee Key in the dark. "I'm surprised at Frank," I say over the Bronco's hum. "I thought he was supposed to be helping Terri."

"Why should he care?" Lew says. "It wasn't his watch." He is so pleased with himself he might have just won the US Open. We stop on the way so that he can buy wrapping paper for the watch and a cassette for his camcorder.

"I'm going to video Bianca when she opens her present," he says. "I'll show you later. I just can't wait to see her face when she sees what's inside that box."

I hope he forgets. I don't want to see Bianca putting on Terri's watch.

Christmas came and went almost unnoticeably, the way it does on the Island: one moment everyone is preparing for it, and the next it is gone and forgotten. The only way you know it happened is that for a few days afterwards everyone is wearing new outfits, new jewelry, skating on new roller blades. Then the gloss wears off.

It was Lew who told me the news. We met at the water fountain between Courts 1 and 2.

"You remember those two at the Main Street Diner?" Lew begins, as if it were years ago instead of days. "Well I heard he beat up on her in the garage under where she lives."

"What?" I say. "Frank beat up Terri?" I am shocked but not surprised.

"That's them," Lew says, "Frank and Terri. He kinda mugged her. Took the ten grand and a big ring she was wearing. Some women coming home from a party found her in a heap and called the paramedics. The cops caught Frank somewhere in downtown Tampa trying to sell the ring. They never found the ten grand but at least she got her ring back.''

I wipe the sweat out of my eyes. I say, ''Poor Terri. Frank was the one who persuaded her she needed a minder in the first place.''

''No kidding?'' Lew says. ''That's tough.''

''How is she?''

''Dunno,'' Lew says. '' 'Recovering in hospital' is all I heard.''

I hope the ex-boyfriend bought her some health insurance to go with the car and the cute apartment. I doubt it though: he didn't sound like that sort of boyfriend.

''Maybe I should go look at the ring,'' Lew muses, shading his eyes against the golden sun. ''Maybe she'll have to sell that. She was cute, though, wasn't she, Liza? Din't you think she was cute?''

''I thought she was a bit sad, Lew,'' I say. ''Down on her luck.''

''Yeah, but Liza, a cute kid like that don't have to wait long to get lucky again,'' Lew says. ''What goes around comes around. Which reminds me—are you going to see Elaine?''

As a matter of fact, I was going to have dinner with her that very night. She was off to Pittsburgh in the morning to spend New Year with her family. I tell Lew this.

He says, ''Oh right. I hope she has a great time. But the thing of it is—you won't tell her, will you? About the watch and the money.''

I give him my ''what do you take me for'' look. We grin warily at each other. We are still friends.

Of course, Lew and I were being ridiculously naïve. Elaine already knew about the watch. Elaine and Bianca shared the same manicurist. Fortunately the manicurist didn't know about me.

''You hear what Lew went and gave that tramp for Christmas?'' Elaine says. She swallows a spoonful of key-lime pie and coughs nervously. ''He gave her a thirty grand Rolex watch. Thirty grand, Liza. Whachoo think of that? He doesn't want me to know, but how can he keep it quiet when she shows it off all the time? She'd sooner go around butt-naked than take that watch off. Probably does, Liza, if half of what I hear about her's true. The accountant says ·she's going to take him for every cent he's got.''

She coughs, and I take the opportunity to say, ''Elaine, I've never met her, but maybe she isn't as bad as you think. Maybe it's what Lew *thinks* she wants. He said himself she'd be as happy with a card or a kitten.''

Elaine coughs so hard she almost chokes. She says, ''Don't take this the wrong way—but you are so dumb. 'Scuse me, Liza, but you are. I mean, think about it. Where's the card? Where's the kitten?''

I can't answer.

''See what I mean?'' Elaine says. ''You should listen to me. Lew never did, but I told him, I said, 'You'll die a poor man, Lew,' I said. But what can you do when a man thinks with his . . . and the woman's a gold-digging tramp? 'Scuse me, Liza, but that's how it is.''

Liza Cody won the John Creasey Award in 1980 for her first novel, *Dupe*. Although best known as the author of the Anna Lee series of private investigator novels, in *Bucket Nut* and *Monkey Wrench* she has taken a female wrestler as her new heroine. She has an absent-minded disposition and tends to forget about Christmas until she trips over it on the bathroom landing.

Political Corrections

◆

SIMON BRETT

There was a large and, to the minds of many observers, unconventional house party assembled for Christmas at Stebbings. The Dowager Duchess of Haslemere had never had any inhibitions about mixing her guests, though the composition of the assembly would have been unthinkable had her husband, the Duke, still been alive.

Apart from her two children, Hubert—who had inherited the title—and his sister Lady Cynthia, none of the Dowager Duchess's guests was quite the goods. There was Adolphus Weinburg, the well-to-do Hebrew financier, whose—

"I'm sorry. We can't have this."

Tilson Gutteridge did not lift the nicotine-yellowed finger that was following the lines of faded typescript, but raised his eyes to the young woman beside him. She was undeniable pretty, but in a way that didn't appeal. The dark red hair was too geometrically cut, the pale blue eyes behind the dark-rimmed round glasses were too pale and humorless to accord with his, perhaps old-fashioned, taste.

"What's the problem?" he asked ingenuously.

"This is anti-semitic," said Juanita Rainbird. "We can't say 'Hebrew financier.' "

"Why not? It just means that he's Jewish."

"We can't say that nowadays. It's discriminatory."

"But look, that's what Eunice Brock wrote. It was the kind of thing they all wrote in the Thirties. You'll find the same in Agatha Christie, Dorothy L. Sayers, the lot of them."

"We still can't say it. Not in something we're publishing for the first time in the nineteen-nineties." Her accent became more American as her assertiveness grew.

"But all Eunice Brock's other books have been reprinted as she wrote them."

"Some of the titles have been changed. Like *The Company of Ishmaels* became *The Company of Fraudsters*."

"That amendment can hardly have been considered very flattering to the Jews, can it?"

"It has made for an acceptable title," Juanita Rainbird replied evenly. "And think how many changes Agatha Christie's *Ten Little Niggers* has been through. First it became *Ten Little Indians*—"

"Then *Ten Little Native Americans* . . . ?" Tilson Gutteridge suggested mischievously.

The editor was unamused. "No. Now it's known as *Then There Were None* . . . And I'm sure if its manuscript arrived today on the desk of any editor in the country, it would be re-edited for publication.

"Hm. Shall we press on?"

His finger hadn't moved from the line of text. As his eyes reverted to the typescript, Juanita Rainbird looked at her visitor without enthusiasm. Tilson Gutteridge was a man in his sixties, wearing the shapeless tweeds and knitted tie of another generation. A whiff of cherrywood tobacco, whiskey, and something else less wholesome hung around him. It was only with difficulty that Juanita had convinced him there were no exceptions to Krieper & Thoday's no smoking policy and persuaded him to put the noisesome pipe back into his bulging pocket.

There was something over-the-top, almost operatic, about

the man's appearance. The pebble glasses seemed too thick, the eyebrows too bushy, the ill-fitting false teeth too yellowed. Tilson Gutteridge looked a parodic archetype of a literary figure who had never succeeded and was now long past any possible sell-by-date.

Still, Juanita knew she had to humor him. He still hadn't revealed how he'd come by the manuscript, but it was undoubtedly a valuable commodity. Krieper & Thoday were still doing very well from the sales stimulated by the continuing Wenceslas Potter television series. The discovery of a new Eunice Brock would be just the sort of publishing coup to endear Juanita Rainbird to her new Australian Managing Director, Keith Chappick.

The Publicity Department could get a lot of mileage out of a long-lost manuscript. Regardless of the quality of the book, after some judicious editing it would sell well on curiosity value alone.

And with a bit of luck there wouldn't be any royalties to pay. Eunice Brock had died in 1939. For the fifty years after her death, the royalties on the Wenceslas Potter books had gone to her niece, Dierdre Townley, who had conveniently passed on in 1990, leaving no heirs. Dierdre hadn't made much out of her inheritance. Though the books had remained more or less in print, the real revival of interest in Eunice Brock had started in 1992 with the first Wenceslas Potter television series. That was when the estate had started to be worth something, and by then of course all the profits went direct to Krieper & Thoday.

Increasingly Juanita Rainbird wondered where Tilson Gutteridge had found the manuscript they were perusing, and whether or not he had any rights in it. If he could prove ownership, he'd have to be paid something for the typescript. If he could prove he also owned the copyright, he and his heirs would receive royalties for fifty years after the book's publication.

Juanita knew she must move cautiously, suppress her instinctive curiosity and play the scene at her guest's pace. The information she needed would come in time.

"Could I offer you something to drink . . . ?" she suggested, to thaw the developing atmosphere between them. "Coffee . . . or something from the fridge . . . ?"

Tilson Gutteridge's eye gleamed. "Something from the fridge, please."

She reached to the side of her desk and swung the door open to reveal the fridge's packed interior. "Orange juice or Perrier?"

The man's face fell. "I'll have a black coffee, thanks."

Before she filled a cup for him from the machine, Juanita Rainbird explained severely, "I should just point out that my getting coffee for you is not an expression of any subservient gender role-play. I would be equally ready to get coffee for a guest of my own sex."

Tilson Gutteridge looked bewildered. "Fine," he murmured.

Juanita Rainbird placed the cup of coffee on the desk in front of him. "Right, let's get back to the text, shall we?"

His finger moved along under the lines as they both silently read on.

. . . the well-to-do Hebrew financier . . .

Without comment, Juanita Rainbird stuck a yellow Post-it sticker in the margin beside these words, and scribbled a pencil note on her clipboard.

. . . whose hair, black, thick and naturally curly, exuded the fragrance of some violet-scented pomade. He had fleshy, prominent features, his long nose curving down almost in mirror image of his jutting chin . . .

"That's unacceptable too."

"She's just saying what the bloke looked like," Tilson Gutteridge protested wearily.

"Yes, but couched in those terms it becomes a racist slur."

"Oh, come on, that's how everyone talked in the Thirties. For heaven's sake, don't make such a meal of it, darling."

Juanita's eyes beamed blue fire at her visitor. "I am sorry, Mr. Gutteridge, but I must ask you to refrain from the use of diminishing sexist endearments."

"Er . . . ?"

She took no notice of his puzzlement, but returned to the typescript.

Another of the Dowager Duchess's guests also aspired to, but failed to meet, the qualification of an English gentleman. Though not of the Semitic brotherhood, he too was an oily cog in the machinery of finance . . .

Juanita Rainbird's pencil, once again offended, raced across her pad.

Ras Gupta was an oriental gentleman, who had made a killing from firms about to go smash, scooping up their shares at cat's meat prices . . .

Tilson Gutteridge's finger stopped and he looked up solicitously to Juanita. "Any worries about complaints from the cat protection lobby?"

The editor pursed her lips. "Let's just press on, shall we?"

This dark-complexioned aspirant's attempts to pass himself off as the genuine article were let down by the flashiness of the loud attire he favored, not to mention a native predilection for shoddy jewelry. The ridiculousness of his appearance was accentuated by his dwarfish stature, which qualified him better for a circus ring than the drawing room of a Dowager Duchess.

Juanita Rainbird could restrain herself no longer. "That'll have to be changed," she blurted out.

"Why?"

"It's sizeist."

"Eh?"

"The emphasis on the man's non-average altitudinal endowment could cause offense to readers similarly afflicted." She realized her mistake and moved quickly to limit the damage. "That is, I don't use the word 'afflicted' in any pejorative sense. In no way do I wish to imply that someone vertically challenged has less validity or viability as a human being than someone of more traditional anatomical configuration."

"Er . . . ?" Tilson Gutteridge looked at her blankly. "So what are you saying—Ras Gupta can't be described as short . . . ?"

"No."

". . . even though the plot hinges on the fact that he is the only one of the house guests small enough to have crawled out of the scullery window on Christmas night after the Dowager Duchess had been murdered?"

"Well . . ." Juanita Rainbird was momentarily checked. Then her pencil dashed down another note. "I'm sure we'll be able to find an alternative formula of words to deal with that problem."

Tilson Gutteridge shrugged and readdressed his attention to the typescript.

Another of the guests at the Stebbings gloried in the name of the Vicomte de Fleurie-Rizeau. An effeminate Gallic lounge lizard, whose fractured English was uttered in an affected lisp and whose movements were almost ladylike in their dainty—

"This won't do," said Juanita Rainbird. But before she could launch into her homophobia lecture, she caught sight of the watch on her wrist. "Oh, goodness, I didn't realize it was so late. It's lunchtime."

Tilson Gutteridge grinned. "Splendid. Where are we going? Needn't be too lavish. Just an Italian or something. So long as they serve a decent red wine, eh?"

Juanita Rainbird looked at him primly. "I'm sorry, Mr. Gutteridge. That was not an invitation. I'm already committed to sharing a working sandwich with my Managing Director."

"Oh well, have to do it another time, won't we?"

"I should also point out that Krieper & Thoday have recently instituted an across-the-board no-lunching policy. The only exception to that rule being the lunching on publication day of authors whose previous works have made the *Sunday Times* bestseller lists."

"Oh. I thought lunch was one of the main activities of publishers."

"You have a rather dated image of our industry, I'm afraid, Mr. Gutteridge," said Juanita Rainbird austerely. "Anyway, it's not as if you're even an author, are you?"

"No," he agreed. "So . . . what? We'll continue going through the manuscript another time?"

"Yes. Unless you'd like to leave it with me and I'd—"

His hands were instantly out to snatch up the typescript and clutch it protectively to his chest. "I'm not letting this out of my sight."

"Well, maybe you'd like to stay here while one of my assistants—" She quickly corrected herself "—one of my *co-workers* photocopies—"

Tilson Gutteridge shook his head firmly. "This stays with me and is not reproduced until we've sorted out a deal."

"Yes . . ." Juanita Rainbird paused, selecting her next words with care. "This does of course bring us onto the question of ownership . . . more specifically perhaps, how you came to be in possession of the manuscript . . . ?"

The man grinned complacently.

". . . and indeed what rights—if any—you might have in the property . . . ?"

"Oh, it's mine all right," he assured her.

"It may be yours in the sense that you physically have the typescript in your possession, but the issue of copyright is a totally different—"

"The copyright is mine too."

Juanita Rainbird allowed herself a little laugh. "I don't see how that could be possible, Mr. Gutteridge."

"It's possible," he told her, "because I have recently discovered something of my family history."

"Oh?"

"I have always known myself to be illegitimate. I was adopted as a baby. It was only last month that I found out the identity of my real mother."

He played the silence for a little more than it was worth.

"My real mother was Eunice Brock."

Juanita Rainbird said nothing, but her mind was racing.

"So I am not only the owner of the physical manifestation of this manuscript, but also of its copyright."

The editor did the sums quickly in her head. It wasn't a

disaster. So they'd have to pay royalties on the one book; their profits on the rest of the Eunice Brock *œuvre* would remain intact.

"Not only that," Tilson Gutteridge went on gleefully. "I am also the copyright-holder on the rest of my mother's published work."

Juanita Rainbird gave a confident smile as, politely but deftly, she dashed his aspirations.

"I'm sorry, Mr. Gutteridge, but I'm afraid your mother's published works went out of copyright in 1989."

"I know that, Juanita sweetie." He didn't give her time to object to the sexist diminutive as he went on. "But I'm sure I don't have to tell someone in publishing that, as of summer 1995, the period of copyright is to be extended from fifty to seventy years after an author's death . . ."

Juanita Rainbird gaped.

". . . so my mother's works are about to come back into copyright, where they will remain until the year 2009."

Keith Chappick didn't know much about books, but he was good at sacking people, so he was doing very well in publishing. In his native Australia he'd started by sacking people in newspapers, then moved on to sacking people in television. It was as a television executive that he'd arrived in England, and the move to sacking people in publishing had been a logical one. He had been through two other publishing houses before taking up the appointment at Krieper & Thoday. In each one he'd sacked more people and been given a higher-profile job with more money.

The Keith Chappick management style had been quickly imposed on Krieper & Thoday. On his first day he'd sacked the Publishing Director and two Senior Editors; thereafter he ruled by simple terror. The staff, secure in nothing save the knowledge that their jobs were permanently on the line, spread themselves ever thinner, taking on more and more work, putting in longer and longer hours. Uncomplaining, they annexed the responsibilities of sacked colleagues, knowing that refusal of any additional burden was a one-way ticket to the dole queue. Within six months of the new

Managing Director's arrival, the same amount of work was being done by a third of the previous staff. Krieper & Thoday's shareholders were delighted.

Complaints about Keith Chappick's idiosyncratic management techniques became as improbable as complaints about work-load. No one demurred when the nine o'clock half-hour of Aikido was made mandatory for all staff. They trotted off like lambs to the slaughter of paint-ball combat weekends. Even the no-lunching diktat was accepted without a murmur by people who had hitherto been among the most dedicated contributors to the profits of Orso, Nico Ladenis and the Groucho Club.

Nor would any member of staff contemplate refusing the Managing Director's summons to "share a working sandwich" in the half-hour before he went off to lunch at the Connaught.

The invitation—"subpoena" might be a better word—was literal. The sandwich was singular, and it was shared. That day Juanita Rainbird got half a tuna and cucumber, while Keith Chappick probed her working record for reasons that might allow him to sack her.

Juanita gave him the good news and the bad news. Coming across a new Eunice Brock manuscript was undoubtedly good news; coming across an accompanying copyright-holder with a claim to the whole estate undoubtedly bad.

"What proof do we have that he's who he says he is?" asked Keith Chappick once the full story was out.

"None yet, but he's assured me he can produce documentation to authenticate his claim."

"Hm . . ." The Managing Director looked thoughtfully out of his top-floor aquarium of an office at the slate-grey winter sky. "And from what you say, he seems to have an accurate knowledge of copyright law . . . ?"

"An unhealthily accurate knowledge. He reckons, when the extension to seventy years comes in, he'll be due royalties on all Eunice Brock sales since the old girl's niece died."

"Shit. That's the period when the television series has

been on. That's when the books have been really coining it.''

''I know.''

''Could make a nasty big hole in the company's profits—particularly as it'd be retrospective.''

''Yes.''

''Well, there's no way we're going to pay him. We've got to get around it somehow.'' He looked blandly at his employee. ''Any ideas?''

This was another typical Keith Chappick management technique. Sacking was really all he did. He didn't regard it as part of his job to have ideas; that's what the staff were there for. Whatever the problem, they had to come up with the solution to it. If they didn't, they got sacked.

''The best thing would be . . .'' Juanita Rainbird began cautiously, ''. . . if we could prove that his claim was false, that he actually isn't who he says he is . . .''

''Is it known that Eunice Brock did have an illegitimate child?''

''There were strong rumors. That muck-raking biography of her that came out a couple of years back stated it as an acknowledged fact.''

''Hm.'' Keith Chappick scratched his chin as he looked out over the London skyline.

''And Tilson Gutteridge'd be about the right age.'' Juanita shook her head ruefully. ''The best thing'd be if we could prove someone else was really Eunice Brock's illegitimate child . . . and that that someone was either dead or totally unaware of their true identity.''

''Yes . . .'' said the Managing Director; then, with increasing enthusiasm as the idea took hold, ''Yes. That's what you'd better do, Juanita.''

''What?''

''Find a rival claimant.''

''But supposing there isn't one . . . ?''

Keith Chappick shrugged. ''That's your problem. Incidentally . . . did this old geezer say whether he'd got family . . . you know, heirs of his own . . . ?''

''He's got no one. Not married, no relatives.''

"So, if he were to die . . ." The Managing Director grinned, letting the idea float for a moment in the air-conditioned air, ". . . our problem would be at an end."

"Yes."

Keith Chappick looked briskly at his watch. The audience was over. "Leave it with you, Juanita. I'm relying on you to get it sorted . . . or . . ."

He didn't need to finish the sentence. The threat had been implicit from the beginning of the interview.

"This is man's work," averred Wenceslas Potter. "Don't you bother your pretty little nut about it."

"But I want to know who murdered Mummy," Lady Cynthia insisted. "It'd be a pretty shabby sort of daughter who wasn't interested."

"You're absolutely right!" the detective ejaculated. "And let it never be said that I could entertain the idea of anyone as pretty as you ever doing anything shabby. But believe me, I have your best interests at heart. I'm afraid the conscienceless cove who did for your mother might strike again."

"Oh!" Lady Cynthia's soft hand leapt in alarm to her ruby lips, and beneath the fine silk of her evening gown her bosom heaved. "How beyond words ghastly if that should happen! Wenceslas," she interrogated in a hushed voice, "are you suggesting that I myself am at risk from this bounder?"

"Not while I am here to protect you, milady," he responded with a gallant bow. "You may be no more than a feeble woman but—"

"This is horribly sexist," said Juanita Rainbird, her objections no longer satisfied by the continuous notes she was scribbling.

"Is it?" asked Tilson Gutteridge innocently. "I actually thought it was rather sexy."

The editor looked at him with distaste. Tilson Gutteridge seemed to have taken up squatting rights in her office. His tweed jacket was spread untidily across the back of his chair. The braces over his checked shirt were not trendy nineties braces; their perished elastic was reminiscent rather of the truss industry. The tobacco staleness that hung around him seemed to intensify the longer he spent in the room.

Juanita Rainbird wished she had never got into her current situation, having to spend long hours closeted with a man every detail of whose character she loathed. But there was no alternative. She needed to play for time, stretch out the line-by-line copy-editing of Eunice Brock's manuscript until she could see the way out of her dilemma. Because, if she wanted to keep her job, a way out had to be found.

She had made some headway in her investigations. Long hours of research at St. Catherine's House in Kingsway had finally yielded the undeniable fact of a birth certificate. Eunice Brock, under her real name of Phyllis Townley, had given birth to a male child in September 1927. No father's name was recorded.

Unearthing that information, though in one way satisfying, had at the same time been dispiriting, because it strengthened the possibility that Tilson Gutteridge was telling the truth. Proof that Eunice Brock had never had a son would have provided much more comfort.

Finding records of the baby's adoption was proving considerably more difficult, and Juanita Rainbird was beginning to suspect deliberate obfuscation. At the time of her son's birth Eunice Brock was already a published author and something of a celebrity, so it was possible that she had intentionally clouded the waters to prevent any successful probing into her shameful lapse.

Juanita could not at that moment see what the next step of her investigation should be. Her eye strayed to the shelf of hardbacks on the wall and the thought she had been trying half-heartedly to suppress for some days bubbled back to the surface of her mind.

"If he were to die . . ." Keith Chappick had said, ". . . our problem would be at an end."

As a crime editor, Juanita Rainbird was extremely well versed in the means of murder. The fantasy methods of crime fiction's Golden Age—injecting air bubbles into veins, high musical notes shattering glass containers of poisonous gases—had given way to greater realism in contemporary examples of the genre. If Juanita ever did decide to murder someone, the works she had edited offered a rich variety of ways to achieve that end.

"So . . . are you suggesting it should be rewritten?"

Tilson Gutteridge's words brought her out of her reverie and back to the typescript. "Well, I don't like it."

"That's not the point."

"All its attitudes are very demeaning and diminishing to women."

"That's not the point either. And I would draw your attention to the fact that it was written by a woman—my mother, as it happens."

"Yes, but she was simply conforming to the phallocentric norms of the period. She didn't dare write Lady Cynthia as an assured, assertive woman, so she made her a pathetic little bit of fluff."

"Actually, it's rather important for the plot that Lady Cynthia's a pathetic little bit of fluff. For God's sake, why shouldn't Eunice Brock write about a stupid woman? Stupid women do exist, you know."

Tilson Gutteridge looked at Juanita Rainbird very directly as he said this last sentence; there was an edge of insolence in his expression. She turned away, as if suddenly interested in the one Christmas card on her desk. Its message was "Happy Holidays." (Juanita had thrown all cards with specifically Christian messages straight into the bin; she did not believe in prescriptive religion and had no wish to offend people of other faiths.)

Once again it was borne in on her what an utterly hateful man Tilson Gutteridge was. At times she didn't think she'd have any problem with her conscience if she did have to end up murdering him.

And, if she couldn't get another lead in her investigation, she probably would have to end up murdering him.

"Shall we press on?" he said rather tetchily, and once again his nicotine-stained finger traced along the lines of typescript.

"You may be no more than a feeble woman, but with me by your side you'd be safe in a jungle full of man-eating fuzzy-wuzzies."

"We can't have that!" Juanita Rainbird objected instinctively.

"Offend vegetarians, will it?" Tilson Gutteridge baited her.

"It will offend people of alternative—though no less viable—pigmentation."

"Oh, for God's sake! You can't pretend black people aren't black. When I was at school, there was a black chap in my class and his nickname was 'Fuzzy-Wuzzy,' Everyone called him that. He didn't mind—or at least he never said he minded."

Juanita prepared to embark on her lecture about how sensibilities had changed, but thought better of it. Instead, she asked casually, "Where were you at school, actually, Mr. Gutteridge?"

"Public school called Whittinghams. South London. You heard of it?"

"No."

"Not surprising. It closed during the war. Never reopened."

"Oh, right," said Juanita Rainbird, carefully salting away the information.

"Now excuse me . . . just got to see a man about a dog."

Tilson Gutteridge's trips to the Gents were becoming ever more frequent, and each time he used the same odious, arch euphemism. Prostate trouble, Juanita surmised without great interest.

Only when he was out of the room did she realize it was the first time he'd not taken his jacket with him. While this confounded her conjecture that he kept a half-bottle of Scotch in the pocket, it did also open up new investigative possibilities.

She had no conscience about going through Tilson Gutteridge's pockets. Moral qualms prompted by such a minor offense would be pretty specious from someone who was contemplating the option of murder.

The jacket pockets, as she could have predicted, were full of unpleasantness. A handkerchief stained with snot and the nicotine dottle from his pipe. The pipe itself, which would probably be banned in any civilized country on environmental grounds. Some half-sucked peppermints, and other bits of fluff whose precise provenance she did not wish to know.

And an old diary. A 1989 diary, which had clearly been kept because its owner had been too lazy to transfer the telephone numbers in the January of 1990 and of every other year since.

It was to this section that Juanita Rainbird hastily flicked the pages. Few of the addresses and phone numbers had any relevance for her.

The one she did note down, however, belonged to "BREEN, Horace Old Whittinghamians Association."

By the time Tilson Gutteridge returned from the Gents, trying once again to wheedle an Italian lunch "with a decent bottle of red wine" out of Krieper & Thoday, the diary was innocently back in his jacket pocket.

The voice on the answerphone at Horace Breen's number sounded incredibly old, and when Juanita Rainbird met him at a pub in Dulwich, the reality of the man matched. He must have been well into his eighties, probably once as tall as Tilson Gutteridge, but now bent and shrunken. His face and hands were blotched and freckled; his pale milky eyes peered through thick glasses; and the flat mat of a toupee perched on top of his head seemed to accentuate rather than disguise his age. A shiny pinstriped suit hung off his wire-coat-hanger shoulders. He wore a blue and yellow striped tie, which in his first sentence he identified as "the Old Whittinghamians."

He offered the tiresome resistance of his generation to Juanita Rainbird's offer of a drink. "No, surely it's down to us chaps to buy drinks for the pretty little ladies, not the other way—" But she had no difficulty in cutting through all that. Walking from the door to their table seemed to

have consumed his limited stock of energy; the journey to
the bar and back would have crippled him.

As she ordered the requested half of bitter and her own
habitual Perrier, she looked covertly back at the wizened
figure and congratulated herself on her luck. If Horace
Breen did hold the key to Tilson Gutteridge's past, she'd
been fortunate to catch the old man before he enrolled in
that great Old Boys' Club in the sky.

Horace Breen thanked her with excessive gallantry for
the drink, taking one sip and then ignoring it for the rest
of their conversation.

"I'm delighted to find someone of your generation interested in the history of Whittinghams. You see, I devoted
my whole life to the school. I was there as a pupil, then I
taught Latin and Greek for many years, and finally acted
as Bursar. No, splendid to know that a young person is
drawn to the history of Whittinghams. Particularly someone
in publishing. You say you think there might be a book in
it?"

"Yes," Juanita Rainbird replied, confirming the lie she
had used to engineer their meeting.

"Well, I suppose there wouldn't be that many people
still around who'd be interested, but I can assure you that
those who do survive would appreciate the book enormously." He let out a wheezy chuckle. "I wouldn't hold
out hopes for a 'bestseller.' " He separated the word out
with racy daring "but I think I can guarantee you a *succès
d'estime*."

"Excellent. Now could we—?"

"Of course the foundation of the school goes back to
the seventeenth century. In 1692, Thomas Wooltrap, merchant of the City of London, made an endowment for the
education of twelve impoverished young scholars, 'that
they might enjoy the benefits bestowed by a knowledge of
the classical authors.' And for the first hundred and seventy
years of the school's existence . . ."

Juanita Rainbird had to endure getting on for an hour of
this before she could divert the conversation in her desired
direction. Why, she wondered bitterly, had it become her

fate to spend long hours closeted with boring old men?

All too readily the answer supplied itself. Because she wanted to keep her job. And because, if she didn't solve the Tilson Gutteridge problem, Keith Chappick would have not the tiniest qualm about sacking another editor.

This thought spurred her to interruption. "When you were Bursar, Mr. Breen, were you in charge of the collection of fees?"

He looked somewhat taken aback and disappointed by her brusqueness, but replied meekly that such had indeed been his duties.

"And presumably the fees would be paid in a variety of different ways? From a variety of different sources?"

"Yes."

"I mean some directly from parents, from grandparents, from family trusts, solicitors and so on . . . ?"

"Indeed."

"Mr. Breen, did it ever happen that a boy's fees were paid secretly?"

"How exactly do you mean—'secretly,' " Miss Rainbird?"

"I mean, say, in the case of an illegitimate child . . . Did it ever happen that you were asked to be discreet about the actual source of the fees?"

Horace Breen's old-world values were deeply offended. "If that is the sort of book Krieper & Thoday are planning to publish about Whittinghams, I'm afraid I would feel honor bound to dissociate myself from—"

"No, Mr. Breen. My question is relevant, I promise, and nothing to do with muck-raking. Specifically," she moved speedily on, "I'm interested in a boy who would have started at the school around 1939, 1940 . . . Do you remember individual pupils?"

This question was a challenge to his professional pride. Drawing himself up—or at least as much as it was possible for someone so shriveled to draw himself up—he asserted that he remembered every boy in precise detail.

"The one I wanted to ask about was called Gutteridge."

The old man looked blank.

"Tilson Gutteridge."

"Tilson Gutteridge?" he echoed.

The total lack of recognition in his voice brought a flutter of hope to Juanita Rainbird. "Yes," she confirmed breathlessly.

"I'm sorry. There was no pupil at Whittinghams of that name in all the time I was at the school."

"Are you sure?"

Once again she'd offended him. "Of course. I'm sure, Miss Rainbird! Was this imagined Gutteridge boy the one on whose legitimacy you were casting doubt?"

"Yes."

"Well, since he didn't exist, the details of his parentage becomes rather irrelevant, so far as I can see."

"Mm . . ."

"Of course, in the period we're talking about, illegitimacy was a rather more serious matter than it is in these benighted days. And yes, as you suggested, a parent in such unfortunate circumstances might have obscured the issue of who was actually paying the fees."

"Did that happen often, Mr. Breen?"

"At Whittinghams? Good heavens, no. It certainly wasn't that sort of school. In fact, I can only recall one instance of illegitimacy in all the time I was there."

"When was that?"

"Round the period we are talking about. During the War. Just before the school so sadly closed. There was one pupil called Crabbett. Crabbett, P. J. Nice lad. Very successful in the school plays—gave a lovely Titania, I recall, and then went on, I gather, to take up the theater as a profession— one would have hoped for rather better from an Old Whittinghamian. Still, maybe blood will out. He was illegitimate, you see, having been adopted soon after birth, but, er . . ."

His undecided pause was agony for Juanita. "Oh, well," he said eventually, "I suppose it's too long ago now for my telling you to do any harm . . . The boy's fees at Whittinghams were paid by his natural mother."

"You don't happen to remember what the mother's name was, do you, Mr. Breen?"

"Oh yes," the old man said with self-righteous pride. "I remember everything about Whittinghams."

Juanita Rainbird gazed at him eagerly through her little around glasses.

"The mother's name was Phyllis Townley."

"I baint abaht to tell you no lies," the booking-clerk confided. " 'Taint my hoccupation to tell lies, no way, guv'nor. I done hissued eight tickets for the 3:27 to Lancaster—three third singles, two third returns, and three first returns."

"So if our birds did catch that train," Wenceslas Potter mused, "they'd have been in time to catch the 4:03 from Preston, joining up at Godlings Halt with the 5:17 fast from Wolverhampton, which should have passed the 3:02 Glasgow Pullman Express going in the other direction in the Fairgrave Cutting at 6:13, though the unscheduled stop to take on water at Hulkiston Yard would have made it 6:21 before—"

"No objections to this bit?" asked Tilson Gutteridge.

"No." Juanita Rainbird looked at him curiously. "Why? There's nothing wrong with it."

A silence.

"What do you think's wrong with it?"

"Just a bit boring, that's all."

"Boring's all right. That's not unacceptable." She hastily qualified this generalization. "That is—it could be unacceptable if a person were described as 'boring.' It could be offensive to say that a person is attentiveness-challenging—particularly in a case where you were discussing a person of alternative, but nonetheless viable, ethnicity."

She spoke the words automatically. Her mind was elsewhere, full of her forthcoming meeting with Peter Crabbett. On the off chance, she'd rung Equity, the British Actors' Union, to see if they had a "P. Crabbett" registered as a member, and she had struck gold. They had been unwilling to release his address and phone number until she fabricated the line that she was a Hollywood casting director. With the rare prospect of potential work for one of its members, the Union became suddenly more forthcoming.

Pete—he insisted on "Pete"—Crabbett had sounded mild and amiable on the phone, and readily agreed to meet up with her. By coincidence, he too lived in the Dulwich area, and their rendezvous had been fixed for that evening at the same pub.

Juanita Rainbird's feverish anticipation made the line-by-line editing with Tilson Gutteridge more tedious that ever. Now she knew for certain the man was an imposter, she could hardly wait till she had the solid evidence with which she would be able to denounce him.

Her frustration mounting, Juanita returned to Eunice Brock's manuscript.

"*. . . would have made it 6:21 before the trains passed each other, so it was then that the poisoned dart from the blowpipe must have been projected into the Vicomte de Fleurie-Rizeau's first-class compartment.*"

The booking-clerk was lost in admiration. "Blimey, Mr. Potter, guv'nor, you're a whale on detection, and no mistake. How come you can work out difficult hinvestigations so easy while the likes of me's in a real pea-souper of a fog about 'em?"

The aristocratic sleuth laughed lightly. "Sorry, old chap," he commiserated. "Simple matter of breeding."

Juanita Rainbird ground her teeth.

Pete Crabbett was probably about the same age as Tilson Gutteridge, but whereas Tilson was revolting the actor was all charm. Not aggressive, sexist charm, just a laid-back quiet integrity, and an engaging honesty.

He made no demur about accepting a drink from Juanita. "Never refuse a free drink," he said with a rueful grin. "Never in a position to, I'm afraid."

"Not much acting work around?"

"Not for me, it seems. Not much writing work either."

"You're a writer too?"

"Well, I try. Without marked success."

From the bar Juanita Rainbird looked back at the table, as she had done the previous week. Pete Crabbett wore jeans and a floppy navy jumper. He had thick gray hair. Not unattractive. The pub was evidently his local; he kept smiling and nodding at people.

In the time since Juanita had met Horace Breen, the bar had been decorated for Christmas. Every surface was tin-selled and frosted. For the first time, Juanita began to think she might even enjoy Christmas. The Tilson Gutteridge nightmare was about to end.

Pete Crabbett raised the pint of Guinness gratefully to his lips. "Wonderful," he said after a long swallow. "Now what can I do for you?"

Juanita Rainbird took a prim sip of Perrier before launching into her latest prepared falsehood. "Well, Mr. Crab-bett—"

"Pete, please."

"Pete. As I mentioned on the phone, I'm an editor for Krieper & Thoday, the publishers, and I'm exploring the possibility of commissioning a book on changing attitudes to illegitimacy in the twentieth century."

"Uhuh."

"And this is . . . I hope you don't mind my asking you about this, Mr. Crabbett . . . ?"

"No problem." He grinned ingenuously. "I knew I was a little bastard from the moment I could understand any-thing. I don't have any problems with it."

"Good. In fact, I was put onto you by a Mr. Horace Breen . . . from Whittinghams School . . . ?"

"Good God, 'Sniffer' Breen! I'm surprised to hear the old boy hasn't popped his clogs yet."

"I don't think it'll be long. He looks pretty decrepit. I actually met him last week in this very pub, and he men-tioned that you were one of the few, er . . ."

"Bastards?" he offered hopefully.

Juanita Rainbird smiled. It was comforting to find that all men in their sixties were not as repellent as Tilson Gut-teridge.

"Exactly, . . . that you were one of the few, er, bastards at Whittinghams."

"Hm. I'm actually surprised the school knew."

"Oh?"

"Well, I was adopted at a very early age. The Crabbetts always treated me as their own."

"But they didn't pretend to you that you were theirs?"

"No. As I said, I knew I was a bastard. Just lucky they took pity on me."

"But you did know who your birth mother was . . . ?"

"What?" Pete Crabbett grinned again and shook his head.

A surge like an electrical current ran through Juanita Rainbird as he said, "Good heavens, no. It never really interested me. If she'd showed such a lack of taste as not to want me, why should I want her?"

"So you've never been curious?"

He gave another life-affirming shake of his head. "Never once."

"And your adoptive parents—the Crabbetts—paid your fees at Whittinghams?"

He looked a little puzzled by the change of direction. "Well, I assume so. I wasn't chucked out, so I guess they must have done."

Oh, it was marvelous. He was so innocent, so ingenuous. It was only with restraint that Juanita Rainbird could stop hugging herself. Everything had turned out better than she'd dared hope.

It was the dream scenario. Tilson Gutteridge could be exposed as an imposter. The genuine claimant to Eunice Brock's estate was totally unaware of his good fortune. He could be kept forever in blissful ignorance. Krieper & Thoday could continue to rake in the profits on the Eunice Brock books without paying any royalties. Keith Chappick would be pleased, and Juanita Rainbird would keep her job.

Just one more thing to check, then she could just relax and enjoy chatting to this rather amiable actor. "Tell me, Pete, have you ever met anyone called Tilson Gutteridge?"

He looked surprised. "Well, yes, I have actually. But what connection do you have with him?"

"He wasn't at school with you, was he?"

"Good heavens, no. I've only met him once."

"When was that?"

"Three or four months ago, I suppose."

"How did you meet him?"

"He just came and knocked on my door. Said he was a collector of old books and manuscripts—had I got anything around? Well, there was some stuff in the loft that I'd inherited when my father—that's Mr. Crabbett—died. I said he could have a look at it if he liked. He seemed to see something there that interested him, so he made me an offer."

"How much?"

"Fifty quid. I was dead chuffed, I can tell you."

I bet Tilson Gutteridge was too, thought Juanita grimly.

"Well, it can't have been worth that much. Just some old typescripts, no doubt way out of copyright."

Juanita Rainbird once again curbed her excitement. Could he really be as naïve as he appeared? "What do you mean—'out of copyright'?"

"Well, doesn't copyright go on for fifty years after something's written ... ?" he said vaguely and without much interest.

Better and better. Not only did he not know he had any connection with Eunice Brock, he also had no understanding of copyright law. And he certainly didn't know that the fifty-year limit from an author's death or a posthumous publication was about to be extended to seventy.

"Yes," said Juanita Rainbird calmly. "That's right."

"The unutterable sweep who did this has forgotten every decent thing," opined Wenceslas Potter, as he gazed down at the body on the floor of the ice-house.

"But how *did he do it?"* queried Lady Cynthia, from whose cheeks the roses had fled to leave a snowy pallor. *"Mr. Weinberg looks as though he has been* frozen *to death."*

"He has," the aristocratic sleuth confirmed grimly. *"But, if we had not come in here by chance, nobody would ever have known that."*

"Elucidate, Wenceslas," Lady Cynthia begged. *"I'm a simpleton when it comes to deduction. My feminine mind does not proceed as speedily as yours."*

Even in the presence of death, the noble detective could not let by an opportunity for a compliment. "When a lady is as beautiful as you are," *he offered gallantly,* "let her feminine mind move at whatsoever speed it chooses."

Juanita Rainbird sucked her teeth, but still deferred the inevitable confrontation. She felt nervous, knowing she could not put it off forever. Downstairs the office Christmas party that Keith Chappick had decreed would be coming to its end, the Perrier by now flowing like water. Soon Juanita would be alone in the building with the odious Tilson Gutteridge.

"No," Wenceslas Potter continued, *"our murderer did not wish the body to be discovered like this."* He knelt down and sniffed at the Hebrew financier's thick, frozen lips. *"As I thought."*

Lady Cynthia's eyes engaged his interrogatively.

"You see," the sleuth expatiated, *"our homicidal friend required the sturdy Semite to die of natural causes—so far as the world was concerned. I recognize on Mr. Weinberg's lips the smell of a nerve-deadening drug—almost unknown in Harley Street—whose paralyzing properties last exactly an hour and then cease, leaving no trace in the victim's bloodstream. Having immobilized the Israelite with that and dragged him out here, our murderer then filled the man's insensiate, gaping mouth with water which, in the cold of the ice-house, froze solid and clogged the poor fellow's windpipe."*

"How ghastly," murmured Lady Cynthia. *"How beyond everything ghastly."*

"His intention then was to take the defunct Ishmael to his bedroom where, the paralytic drug having worn off and the water melted, he would have appeared to have died of natural—"

Juanita Rainbird could stand it no longer. "God, I hate this stuff! It's so unrealistic! It treats the readers like complete idiots. A murder could never happen like that."

"No?" asked Tilson Gutteridge.

"No. And, since we've stopped, I think the moment has come for me to say what I've been putting off saying to you all day."

"Oh yes?"

"You're an imposter, Tilson Gutteridge!"

"What?"

"You are not who you claim to be. I have absolute proof of that." Juanita Rainbird reached suddenly into her desk drawer and pulled out a bound sheaf of typewritten pages. "It's all in here. My boss has a copy. Your little game is up, Mr. Gutteridge."

Meekly, with apparent puzzlement, the elderly man took the dossier and started to read. He showed no reaction as, with great concentration, he devoured every word. At the end, he placed it down on Juanita's desk.

"So . . . you've found out the truth?"

"Yes."

"This document proves, beyond any shadow of a doubt, that the rightful heir to Eunice Brock's estate—and to all royalties deriving from it until the new copyright expiry date of 2009—is Peter Crabbett."

"Exactly." Juanita Rainbird looked defiantly at Tilson Gutteridge, glad that at last the pretenses were over and she could let her hatred for him show. "And what do you propose to do about that?"

He moved so quickly, she had no chance to protect herself. In an instant the syringe was out of his jacket pocket and stabbed into her upper arm. The plunger was deftly pressed home.

Juanita Rainbird's eyes widened, and her mouth twitched, but the paralyzing drug took effect before any words could emerge.

"Thank God for that," said Tilson Gutteridge, with feeling. "For once you'll keep your bloody mouth shut!"

She was still conscious as he opened the fridge. Still

conscious, but unable to resist, as he crammed the contents of the ice-tray into her mouth. There was awareness in her eyes as he laid her down with her head on the floor of the fridge. She seemed aware too of his turning the dial to its lowest setting, of his closing the door against her neck, and of the gradual, drop-by-drop way he poured the Perrier to congeal with the ice cubes in her throat.

Then the awareness faded from Juanita Rainbird's eyes.

Tilson Gutteridge waited until the drug—still almost unknown in Harley Street—released its hold and the girl's body slumped in death. Then he sat Juanita Rainbird in the swivel chair behind her desk.

By the time she was found after the Christmas holiday, the building's central heating had melted the obstruction in her throat. Except for a small needle puncture in her upper arm and the symptoms of asphyxiation, there seemed no obvious explanation for Juanita Rainbird's death. Many of her colleagues put it down to overwork. Keith Chappick was happy to go along with this diagnosis; it made the rest of his staff even more paranoid.

The Managing Director did not mind about the death. Once Juanita had sorted out the Eunice Brock copyright trouble, he'd been intending to sack her anyway. Thwarted in this ambition, on New Year's Eve he sacked the Publicity Director instead. That cheered him up enormously.

And Keith Chappick remained cheerful, until he got a call from Pete Crabbett's solicitor, staking his client's claim to the estate of Eunice Brock.

In the event the case didn't go to court, but if it had, Juanita Rainbird's meticulously detailed dossier would certainly have ensured that the verdict went in Pete Crabbett's favor. Realizing this and unwilling to add legal costs to the amount they already owed him in back royalties, Krieper & Thoday grudgingly accepted the actor's claim.

With his rights thus established, Pete Crabbett settled down to enjoy his good fortune. He could afford as many pints of Guinness as he wanted now. He even had enough to pay an upmarket nursing home to look after his beloved ninety-year-old natural mother.

And of course he'd long since destroyed the costumes and make-up he'd worn as Tilson Gutteridge and Horace Breen.

He couldn't help feeling rather pleased with himself for how well it'd all worked. The invention of the public school "Whittinghams" was one of the details that gave him most satisfaction.

And he couldn't really feel much regret for the fact that Phyllis Townley's illegitimate son Terence had been killed in the Blitz.

Peter Crabbett might, at some point, be moved to "discover" more Eunice Brocks. But he decided, at the risk of anachronism, he'd make any subsequent typescripts a bit more politically correct than the first one. It'd probably save time in the long run.

Simon Brett is a novelist and playwright whose detective novels, featuring the seedy but likeable actor Charles Paris, include wicked depictions of different aspects of British showbusiness. His first job out of Oxford University was as Father Christmas in a department store.

Boxing Unclever

◆

ROBERT BARNARD

"The true spirit of Christmas," said Sir Adrian Tremayne, fingering the stem of the small glass of port which was all he was allowed, "is not to be found in the gluttony and ostentation which that charlatan and sentimentalist Charles Dickens encouraged." He looked disparagingly around at the remains of the dinner still encumbering the long table. "Not in turkey and plum pudding, still less in crackers and expensive gifts. No—a thousand times!" His voice was thrilling, but was then lowered to a whisper, and it carried as it once had carried through the theaters of the nation. "The true spirit of Christmas lies of course in reconciliation."

"Reconciliation—very true," said the Reverend Sykes.

"Why else, in the Christmas story, do we find simple shepherds and rich kings worshipping together in the stable?"

"I don't think they actually—" began the Reverend Fortescue, but he was waved aside.

"To show that man is one, of one nature, in the eyes of God. This reconciliation of opposites is the one true heart

of the Christmas message. That was the plan that, at every
Christmastide, was acted upon by myself and my dear wife
Alice, now no longer with us. Or indeed with anyone.
Christmas Day we would spend quietly and simply, with
just ourselves for company once the children had grown up
and made their own lives. On Boxing Day we would invite
a lot of people around to Herriton Hall, and in particular
people with whom there had been some breech, with whom
we needed to be reconciled.'' He paused, reaching for re-
serves in that treacle and molasses voice that had thrilled
audiences up and down the country.

"That was what we did that memorable Christmas of
1936. Ten . . . years . . . ago.''

There were many nods around the table, both from those
who had heard the story before, and from those who were
hearing it for the first time.

"Christmas Day was quiet—even, it must be confessed,
a little dull,'' Sir Adrian resumed. "We listened to the new
King's broadcast, and wondered at his conquest of his unfortunate speech impediment. It is always good to reflect
on those who do not have one's own natural advantages. I
confess the day was for me mainly notable for a sense of
anticipation. I thought with joy of the beautiful work of
reconciliation that was to be undertaken on the next day.
And of the other work . . .''

There was a regrettable snigger from one or two quarters
of the table.

"Reconciliation has its limits,'' suggested Martin Lovejoy.

"Regrettably it does,'' acknowledged Sir Adrian, with a
courteous bow in Martin's direction. "We are but human,
after all. I could only hope that the Christian work of reconciliation in all cases but one would plead for me at the
Judgement Seat against that one where . . . Ah well, who
knows? Does not the Bible speak of there being only one
unforgivable sin?''

The three reverend gentlemen present all seemed to want
to talk at once, which enabled Sir Adrian to sweep ahead
with his story. "The first to arrive that Boxing morning

was Angela Montfort, closely followed by Daniel West, the critic. Indeed, I think it probable that they in fact arrived *together*, because there was no sign of transport for Angela. West's reviews of her recent performances had made me wonder—so mindlessly enthusiastic were they—whether Something was going on. Something usually was, with Angela, and the idea that the English critic is incorruptible is pure stardust. My quarrel with Angela, however, had nothing to do with sex. It was her ludicrous and constant upstaging of me during the national tour of *Private Lives*, for which I had taken over the Coward role, and gave a performance which many thought—but, no matter. Old triumphs, old triumphs.''

It was given a weary intonation worthy of Prospero's farewell to his art.

"And West's offense?" asked Martin Lovejoy innocently. He was the most theatrically sophisticated of them, and he knew.

"A review in his provincial newspaper of my Malvolio," said Sir Adrian shortly, "which was hurtful in the extreme."

"Was that the one which spoke of your 'shrunken shanks'?" asked Peter Carbury, who was the only person present who read the *Manchester Guardian*.

"A deliberate effect of costuming!" said Sir Adrian fiercely. "A very clever design by my dear friend Binkie Mather. Typical of a critic's ignorance and malice that he could not see that."

He took a sip of port to restore his equanimity, and while he did so Peter winked at Martin and Martin winked at Peter.

"Angela gushed, of course," resumed Sir Adrian, "as I led her into the drawing room. 'So wonderful to be back at dear old Herriton again'—that kind of thing. West looked around with a cynical expression on his face. He had been there before, when I had been under the illusion that he was one of the more perceptive of the up-and-coming critics, and I knew he coveted the house, with its magnificent views over the Sussex Downs. I suspected that he found the idea of the gentleman actor rather ridiculous, but the idea of the gentleman critic not ridiculous at all. The gentleman's code allows dabbling. West had a large independent income, which is no guarantee of sound judgement. His cynical expression was assumed, but I was relentlessly courteous to them both, and it was while I was mixing them cocktails that Alice—dear Alice—led in Frank Mandeville.''

"Her lover," said Peter Carbury.

"My dear boy, do not show your provinciality and vulgarity," said Sir Adrian severely. "In the theater we take such things in our stride. Let us say merely that in the past he had been her *cavalier servente*."

"Her *what*?" demanded Stephen Coates in an aggrieved voice. He had an oft-proclaimed and very British hatred of pretension.

"An Italian term," explained Sir Adrian kindly, "for a man who serves a lady as a sort of additional husband. There is a long tradition of such people in Italy."

"They are usually a lot younger," said Peter Carbury. "And in this case."

"Younger," conceded Sir Adrian. "Though hardly a *lot* younger. Frank Mandeville had been playing juvenile leads for so long he could have taken a Ph.D. in juvenility. Alice's . . . patronage of him was short and long over, and when she led him in it was clear to me from the expression on her face that she was mystified as to what had once attracted her. When I saw his hair, slicked back with so much oil that it must have felt like being pleasured by a garage mechanic, I felt similarly mystified."

"It must have been a jolly party," commented Stephen Coates. Sir Adrian smiled at him, to signify to all that Stephen was not the sort of young man who could be expected to understand the ways of polite, still less theatrical society.

"I must confess that when Frank bounced in Angela did say, 'What is this?' and looked suspiciously from Alice to me and back. But we had taken—I had taken—the precaution of inviting a number of local nonentities—the headmaster of a good school, an impoverished squire and his

dreary wife, at least two vicars, and other such good people—and as they now began arriving they, so to speak,
defused suspicion."

"Suspicion?" asked Mike, who had never heard the
story before and was far from bright. Sir Adrian waved his
hand with an airy grandness gained playing aristocrats of
the old school.

"It was not until things were well under way that Richard Mallatrat and his wife arrived,"

"The greatest Hamlet of his generation," put in Peter
Carbury, with malicious intent.

"I cannot think of fainter praise," responded Sir Adrian
loftily. "The art of Shakespearean acting is dead. If the
newspapers are to be believed the theatre today is domi-
nated by young Olivier, who can no more speak the Bard
than he can underplay a role."

"You and Mallatrat were rivals for the part, weren't
you?" Carbury asked. Sir Adrian, after a pause, allowed
the point.

"At the Old Vic. No money to speak of, but a great deal
of prestige. I certainly wanted the part badly."

"To revive your career?" suggested the Reverend Sykes.
He received a look of concentrated hatred.

"My career has never needed revival! To show the
younger generation how it should be done! To set standards
for people who had lost the true art of acting. Instead of
which Mallatrat was given the role and had in it a showy success, lacking totally the quality of *thought*, which is essen-
tial to the role, and quite without too the *music* which . . .
another more experienced actor would have brought to it."
He bent forward malevolently, eyes glinting, *"And I was
offered the role of Polonius."*

"It's a good role," said the Reverend Fortescue, probably to rub salt in the wound. He was ignored.

"That was his malice, of course. He organized that, put
the management up to it, then told the story to all his
friends. I never played the Old Vic again. I had to disap-
point my legion of fans, but there are some insults not to
be brooked."

"You did try to get even through his wife, didn't you?" asked Martin Lovejoy, who was all too well informed in that sort of area.

"A mere newspaper story. Gloria Davere was not then his wife, though as good as, and she was not the trumpery Hollywood 'star' she has since become. Certainly we had—what is this new film called?—a brief encounter. I have told you the morality of the theater is not the morality of Leamington Spa or Catford. We happened to meet on Crewe Station one Saturday night, after theater engagements elsewhere. I confess—sordid though it may sound—that for me it was no more than a means of passing the time, stranded as we were by the vagaries of the London, Midland and Scottish Railway. But the thought did occur to me that I would be teaching this gauche young thing more gracious ways—introducing her to the lovemaking of an earlier generation, when romance still reigned, and a lady was treated with chivalry and respect."

"I believe she told the *News of the World* it was like fucking Old Father Time," said Carbury to Martin Lovejoy, but so *sotto* was his *voce* that Sir Adrian was able to roll on regardless.

"She later, of course, talked, and spitefully, but the idea that our encounter had anything in it of revenge on my part is sheer moonshine. On her part, perhaps, in view of the talk she put around, but as to myself, I plead innocent of any such sordid emotion."

"So that was the cast-list assembled, was it?" asked the Reverend Sykes.

"Nearly, nearly," said Sir Adrian, with the unhurried stance of the habitual narrator, which in the case of this story he certainly was. "Thus far the party seemed to be going well. The attractions of Richard Mallatrat and his flashy wife to the nonentities was something I had anticipated: they crowded around them, larding them with gushing compliments and expressions of admiration for this or that trumpery performance on stage or screen. Everyone, it seemed, had seen a Gloria Davere talkie or Richard Mallatrat as Hamlet, or Romeo, or Richard II. I knew it would be nauseating, and nauseating it was. Angela Montfort, for one, was immensely put out, with no knot of admirers to feed her self-love. She contented herself with swapping barbs with Frank Mandeville, who was of course enraged by the attention paid to Richard Mallatrat.''

"Hardly a Shakespearean actor, though, this Frank Mandeville,'' commented Peter Carbury.

"Hardly an actor at all,'' amended Sir Adrian. "But logic does not come into theatrical feuds and jealousies. Mandeville playing Hamlet would hardly have passed muster on a wet Tuesday in Bolton, but that did not stop him grinding his teeth at the popularity of Richard Mallatrat.''

"He wasn't the only one,'' whispered Stephen Coates.

"And so it was time for a second round of drinks. I decided on that as I saw toiling up the drive the figure of my dear old dresser Jack Roden. My once-dear old dresser. I poured out a variety of drinks including some already-mixed cocktails, two kinds of sherry, some gins and tonic, and two glasses of neat whiskey. There was only one person in the room with the appalling taste to drink neat whiskey before luncheon. Pouring two glasses gave that person a fifty-fifty chance of survival. Depending on how the tray was presented. With my back to the guests I dropped the hyoscine into one of the whiskey glasses.''

"Who was the whiskey-drinker?'' asked Roland, knowing the question would not be answered.

"The one with the worst taste,'' said Sir Adrian dismissively. "Then I went off to open the front door. Jack shuffled in, muttering something about the dreadful train and bus service you got over Christmas. He was a pathetic sight. The man who had been seduced away from me by Richard Mallatrat, and then dumped because he was not up to the contemporary demands of the job, could hardly any longer keep himself clean and neat, let alone anyone else. I threw the bottle of hyoscine as far as I could manage into the shrubbery, then ushered him with conspicuous kindness into the drawing-room, solicitously introducing him to people he didn't know and people he did. 'But you two are old friends,' I remember saying when I led him up the scoundrel Mallatrat. Even that bounder had the grace to smile a mite queasily. Out of the corner of my eye I was pleased to see that some of the guests had already helped themselves from the tray."

"Why were you pleased?"

"It meant that others than myself had been up the tray. And it would obviously be theatrical people—the nonentities wouldn't dare."

"It doesn't sound the happiest of parties," commented Lovejoy.

"Doesn't it? Oh, but theater people can relax anywhere, particularly if there are admirers present. Once some of the nonentities felt they should tear themselves away from the star duo of Mallatrat and Davere, then Angela got her share of attention, and Alice as hostess had her little knot—she had left the stage long before, of course, though she was still by nature a stage person. No it was far from an unhappy party."

"Until the fatality," suggested the Reverend Fortescue.

"Until the fatality," agreed Sir Adrian. "Though even that . . ."

"Did not dampen spirits?"

"Not entirely. Poison is slow, of course. You can have a quick, dramatic effect with cyanide—even I have acted on occasion in thrillers, and know that—but most of them take their time. People thought at first it was an upset tummy. Alice said she hoped that was all it was. She of course was not in on my plans. I've never found women entirely reliable, have you?"

He looked around the table. None of his listeners had found women entirely reliable.

"So it wasn't she who took the tray round?" asked Simon. "Was it one of your servants?"

"No, indeed. The servants had been set to preparing lunch, and that was *all* they did. As a gentleman I had an instinctive aversion to involving faithful retainers in . . . a matter of this kind."

"I assume you didn't take it around yourself, though?"

"I did not. I tapped poor old Jack Roden on the shoulder—he was deep in rambling reminiscence with Daniel West (viewpoints from well away from the footlights)—and I asked him if he could help by taking around fresh drinks. That had always been my plan, though I confess that when I saw how doddering and uncertain he had become I very nearly changed it, fearing he would drop everything on the floor. But I placed the tray in his hands exactly as I wanted it, so that the poisoned whiskey would be closest to hand when he got to the victim.''

"And—to state the obvious—the victim took it," suggested the Reverend Fortescue.

"He took it. That was the signal for the toast. I cleared my throat and all fell silent. I flatter myself I know how to enforce silence. I had thought hard about the toast, and even today I think it rather beautiful. 'My friends,' I said. 'To friends old and new, to renewal and reconciliation, to the true spirit of Christmas.' There was much warm assent to my words, and glasses were raised. We all drank to Christmas, and the victim drank his down.''

"He wasn't a sipper?" inquired Stephen.

"No. The victim was the sort who drank down and then had an interval before the next. I rather think myself that sipping is more social.''

"How long was it before the effects were felt?''

"Oh, twenty minutes or more," said Sir Adrian, his face set in a reminiscent smile. "First just the look of queasiness, then some time later confessions of feeling ill. Alice was all solicitude. She took the victim to my study, plied him with glasses of water, nostrums from our medicine cupboard. He was sweating badly, and his vision was impaired. Finally she came in and suggested that I ring Dr. Cameron from the village. He was *not* happy at being fetched out on Boxing Day, particularly as he had not been invited to the party.''

"Because he might have spotted what was wrong with him and saved him in time?''

"Precisely. Fortunately Dr. Cameron was the old-fashioned type of doctor, now rare, who went everywhere on foot. By the time he arrived, all Scottish tetchiness and wounded self-esteem, there was nothing to be done. Then it was questions, suspicions, and eventually demands that the police be called in. It made for an exciting if somewhat uneasy atmosphere—not a Boxing Day, I fancy, that anyone present will forget.''

"And the police were quick to fix the blame, were they?'' asked Mike. Sir Adrian sighed a Chekhovian sigh.

"Faster, I confess, than even I could have feared. The village bobby was an unknown quantity to me, being new to the district. I had counted on a thick-headed rural flatfoot of the usual kind, but even my first impression told me that he was unusually bright. He telephoned at once for a superior from Mordwick, the nearest town, but before he arrived with the usual team so familiar to us from detective fiction, the local man had established the main sequence of events, and could set out clearly for the investigating inspector's benefit all the relevant facts.''

"But those facts would have left many people open to suspicion,'' suggested Peter Carbury.

"Oh, of course. Practically all the theater people had been near the tray, except the victim, and all of them might be thought to bear malice to the victim. It was, alas, my wife Alice who narrowed things down so disastrously— quite inadvertently, of course.'' Sir Adrian was unaware that the foot of the Reverend Sykes touched the foot of the Reverend Fortescue at this point. They knew a thing or two about human nature, those clerics. And not just their own sins of the flesh. "Yes, Alice was apparently already on friendly terms with our new constable.'' The feet touched again. "And when she was chatting to him quite informally after a somewhat fraught lunch, she happened to mention at some point that she had been standing near the window and imagined she saw something flying through the air.''

"The bottle?''

"The bottle. That did it. The grounds were searched, the bottle was found, and its content analyzed. Then there could be no doubt.''

"No doubt?'' asked Mike, not the brightest person there.

"Because the hyoscine had been put in the second

round of drinks, and the only person who had left the room to go to the door had been myself—to let in Jack Roden. Roden could not have done it because the bottle was empty and thrown away by the time he got into the drawing-room. It could only be me. I was arrested and charged, and theatre was the poorer.''

They all shook their heads, conscious they had reached the penultimate point in Sir Adrian's narrative.

''Come along all,'' said Archie by the door, on cue and jangling his keys. ''Time you were making a move. We've got Christmas dinner to go to as well, you know.''

''But tell us,'' said Mike who, apart from being stupid, hadn't heard the story before, ''who the victim was.''

Sir Adrian turned and surveyed them, standing around the table and the debris of their meal. He was now well into the run of this particular performance: there had been ten Christmases since a concerted chorus of thespians had persuaded the new King not to celebrate his coronation with a theatrical knight on the scaffold. His head came forward and his stance came to resemble his long-ago performance as Richard III.

''You have to ask?'' he rasped. ''Who else could it be but the *critic*?'' How he spat it out! ''Who else could it be but the man who had libelled my legs?''

As he turned and led the shuffle back to the cells all eyes were fixed on the shrunken thighs and calves of one who had once been to tights what Betty Grable now was to silk stockings.

Robert Barnard was born an Essex Man, but has spent his adult life expiating the fact in Australia, Norway and Yorkshire. Before becoming a full-time writer he was Professor of English at the University of Tromso, the most northerly university in the world. In addition to thirty-odd crime novels, he has published books on Dickens, Agatha Christie and a *Short History of English Literature*. His attitude to Christmas is that Charles Dickens and Prince Albert have a lot to answer for.

Gold, Frankincense

and Murder

◆

CATHERINE AIRD

"Christmas!" said Henry Tyler. "Bah!"

"And we're expecting you on Christmas Eve as usual," went on his sister Wendy placidly.

"But . . ." He was speaking down the telephone from London, "but, Wen . . ."

"Now it's no use your pretending to be Ebenezer Scrooge in disguise, Henry."

"Humbug," exclaimed Henry more firmly.

"Nonsense," declared his sister, quite unmoved. "You enjoy Christmas just as much as the children. You know you do."

"Ah, but this year I may just have to stay on in London over the holiday . . ." Henry Tyler spent his working days—and, in these troubled times, quite a lot of his working nights as well—at the Foreign Office in Whitehall.

What he was doing now to his sister would have been immediately recognized in ambassadorial circles as "testing the reaction." In the lower echelons of his department it was known more simply as "flying a kite." Whatever you called it, Henry Tyler was an expert.

"And it's no use your saying there's trouble in the Baltic either," countered Wendy Witherington warmly.

"Actually," said Henry, "it's the Balkans which are giving us a bit of a headache just now."

"The children would never forgive you if you weren't there," said Wendy, playing a trump card; although it wasn't really necessary. She knew that nothing short of an international crisis would keep Henry away from her home in the little market town of Berebury in the heart of rural Calleshire at Christmastime. The trouble was that these days international crises were not nearly so rare as they used to be.

"Ah, the children," said their doting uncle. "And what is it that they want Father Christmas to bring this year?"

"Edward wants a model railway engine for his set."

"Does he indeed?"

"A Hornby LMS red engine called 'Princess Elizabeth,' " said Wendy Witherington readily. "It's a 4–6–2."

Henry made a note, marveling that his sister, who seemed totally unable to differentiate between the Baltic and the Balkans—and quite probably the Balearics as well—had the details of a child's model train absolutely at her fingertips.

"And Jennifer?" he asked.

Wendy sighed. "The Good Ship Lollipop. Oh, and when you come, Henry, you'd better be able to explain to her how it is that while she could see Shirley Temple at the pictures—we took her last week—Shirley Temple couldn't see her."

Henry, who had devoted a great deal of time in the last ten days trying to explain to a Minister in His Majesty's Government exactly what Monsieur Pierre Laval might have in mind for the best future of France, said he would do his best.

"Who else will be staying, Wen?"

"Our old friends Peter and Dora Watkins—you remember them, don't you?"

"He's something in the bank, isn't he?" said Henry.

"Nearly a manager," replied Wendy.

"Then there'll be Tom's old Uncle George."

"I hope," groaned Henry, "that your barometer's up to it. It had a hard time last year." Tom's Uncle George had been a renowned maker of scientific instruments in his day. "He's nearly tapped it to death."

Wendy's mind was still on her house guests. "Oh, and there'll be two refugees."

"Two refugees?" Henry frowned, even though he was alone in his room at the Foreign Office. They were beginning to be very careful about some refugees.

"Yes, the rector has asked us each to invite two refugees from the camp on the Calleford Road to stay for Christmas this year. You remember our Mr. Wallis, don't you, Henry?"

"Long sermons?" hazarded Henry.

"Then you do remember him," said Wendy without irony. "Well, he's arranged it all through some church organization. We've got to be very kind to them because they've lost everything."

"Give them useful presents, you mean," said Henry, decoding this last without difficulty.

"Warm socks and scarves and things," agreed Wendy Witherington vaguely. "And then we've got some people coming to dinner here on Christmas Eve."

"Oh, yes?"

"Our doctor and his wife. Friar's their name. She's a bit heavy in the hand but he's quite good company. And," said Wendy drawing breath, "our new next-door neighbors—they're called Steele—are coming too. He bought the pharmacy in the square last summer. We don't know them very well—I think he married one of his assistants—but it seemed the right thing to invite them at Christmas."

"Quite so," said Henry. "That all?"

"Oh, and little Miss Hooper."

"Sent her measurements, did she?"

"You know what I mean," said his sister, unperturbed. "She always comes then. Besides, I expect she'll know the refugees. She does a lot of church work."

"What sort of refugees are they?" asked Henry cautiously.

But that Wendy did not know.

Henry himself wasn't sure even after he'd first met them, and his brother-in-law was no help.

"Sorry, old man," said that worthy as they foregathered in the drawing-room, awaiting the arrival of the rest of the dinner guests on Christmas Eve. "All I know is that this pair arrived from somewhere in Mitteleuropa last month with only what they stood up in."

"Better out than in," contributed Gordon Friar, the doctor, adding an old medical aphorism, "like laudable pus."

"I understand," said Tom Witherington, "that they only just got out, too. Skin of their teeth and all that."

"As the poet so wisely said," murmured Henry, " 'The only certain freedom's in departure.' "

"If you ask me," said old Uncle George, a veteran of the Boer War, "they did well to go while the going was good."

"It's the sort of thing you can leave too late," pronounced Dr. Friar weightily. Leaving things too late was every doctor's nightmare.

"I don't envy 'em being where they are now," said Tom. "That camp they're in is pretty bleak, especially in the winter."

This was immediately confirmed by Mrs. Godiesky the moment she entered the room. She regarded the Witheringtons' glowing fire with deep appreciation. "We 'ave been so cooald, so cooaald," she said as she stared hungrily at the logs stacked by the open fireside. "So very cooald . . ."

Her husband's English was slightly better, although also heavily accented. "If we had not left when we did, then," he opened his hands expressively, "then who knows what would have become of us?"

"Who, indeed?" echoed Henry, who actually had a very much better idea than anyone else present of what might have become of the Godieskys had they not left their native heath when they did. Reports reaching the Foreign Office were very, very discouraging.

"They closed my university department down overnight," explained Professor Hans Godiesky. "Without any warning at all."

"It was terrrrrible," said Mrs. Godiesky, holding her hands out to the fire as if she could never be warm again.

"What sort of a department was it, sir?" inquired Henry casually of the Professor.

"Chemistry," said the refugee, just as the two Watkins came in and the hanging mistletoe was put to good use. They were followed fairly quickly by Robert and Lorraine Steele from next door. The introductions in their case were more formal. Robert Steele was a good bit older than his wife, who was dressed in a very becoming mixture of red and dark green, though with a skirt that was rather shorter than either Wendy's or Dora's and even more noticeably so than that of Marjorie Friar, who was clearly no dresser.

"We're so glad you could get away in time," exclaimed Wendy, while Tom busied himself with furnishing everyone with sherry. "It must be difficult if there's late dispensing to be done."

"No trouble these days," boomed Robert Steele. "I've got a young assistant now. He's a great help."

Then Miss Hooper, whose skirt was longest of all, was shown in. She was out of breath and full of apology for being so late. "Wendy, dear, I am so very sorry," she fluttered. "I'm afraid the Waits will be here in no time at all . . ."

"And they won't wait," said Henry guilelessly, "will they?"

"If you ask me," opined Tom Witherington, "they won't get past the 'Royal Oak' in a hurry."

"The children are coming down in their dressing-gowns to listen to the carols," said Wendy, rightly ignoring both remarks. "And I don't mind how tired they get tonight."

"Who's playing Father Christmas?" asked Robert Steele jovially. He was a plump fellow, whose gaze rested fondly on his young wife most of the time.

"Not me," said Tom Witherington.

"I am," declared Henry. "For my sins."

"Then, when I am tackled on the matter," said the children's father piously, "I can put my hand on my heart and swear total innocence."

"And how will you get out of giving an honest answer, Henry?" inquired Dora Watkins playfully.

"I shall hope," replied Henry, "to remain true to the

traditions of the Foreign Service and give an answer that is at one and the same time absolutely correct and totally meaningless . . .''

At which moment the sound of the dinner gong being struck came from the hall and presently the whole party moved through to the dining-room, Uncle George giving the barometer a surreptitious tap on the way.

Henry Tyler studied the members of the party under cover of a certain amount of merry chat. It was part and parcel of his training that he could at one and the same time discuss Christmas festivities in England with poor Mrs. Godiesky while covertly observing the other guests. Lorraine Steele was clearly the apple of her husband's eye, but he wasn't sure that the same could be said for Marjorie Friar, who emerged as a complainer and sounded—and looked—quite aggrieved with life.

Lorraine Steele though, was anything but dowdy. Henry decided her choice of red and green—Christmas colors— was a sign of a new outfit for yuletide.

He was also listening for useful clues about their homeland in the Professor's conversation, while becoming aware that Tom's old Uncle George really was getting quite senile now and learning that the latest of Mrs. Friar's succession of housemaids had given in her notice.

"And at Christmas, too," she complained. "So inconsiderate."

Peter Watkins was displaying a modest pride in his Christmas present to his wife.

"Well," he said in the measured tones of his profession of banking, "personally, I'm sure that refrigerators are going to be the thing of the future."

"There's nothing wrong with a good old-fashioned larder," said Wendy stoutly, like the good wife she was. There was little chance of Tom Witherington being able to afford a refrigerator for a very long time. "Besides, I don't think Cook would want to change her ways now. She's quite set in them, you know."

"But think of the food we'll save," said Dora. "It'll never go bad now."

" 'Use it up, wear it out.' " Something had stirred in old Uncle George's memory.

" 'Make it do, do without or we'll send it to Belgium.' "

"And you'll be more likely to avoid food poisoning, too," said Robert Steele earnestly. "Won't they, Dr. Friar?"

"Yes, indeed," the medical man agreed at once. "There's always too much of that about and it can be very dangerous."

The pharmacist looked at both the Watkins and said gallantly, "I can't think of a better present."

"But you did, darling," chipped in Lorraine Steele brightly, "didn't you?"

Henry was aware of an unspoken communication passing between the two Steeles; and then Lorraine Steele allowed her left hand casually to appear above the table. Her fourth finger was adorned with both a broad gold wedding ring and a ring on which was set a beautiful solitaire diamond.

"Robert's present," she said rather complacently, patting her blond Marcel waved hair and twisting the diamond ring round. "Isn't it lovely?"

"I wanted her to wear it on her right hand," put in Robert Steele, "because she's left-handed, but she won't hear of it."

"I should think not," said Dora Watkins at once. "The gold wedding ring sets it off so nicely."

"That's what I say, too," said Mrs. Steele prettily, lowering her beringed hand out of sight again.

"Listen!" cried Wendy suddenly. "It's the Waits. I can hear them now. Come along, everyone . . . it's mince pies and coffee all around in the hall afterwards."

The Berebury carol-singers parked their lanterns outside the front door and crowded around the Christmas tree in the Witheringtons' entrance hall, their sheets of music held at the ready.

"Right," called out their leader, a young man with a rather prominent Adam's apple. He began waving a little baton. "All together now . . ."

The familiar words of "Once in Royal David's City"

soon rang out through the house, filling it with joyous
sound. Henry caught a glimpse of a tear in Mrs. Godiesky's
eye; and noted a look of great nostalgia in little Miss
Hooper's earnest expression. There must have been ghosts
of Christmases Past in the scene for her, too.

Afterwards, when it became important to recreate the
scene in his mind for the police, Henry could only place
the Steeles at the back of the entrance hall with Dr. Friar
and Uncle George beside them. Peter and Dora Watkins
had opted to stand a few steps up the stairs to the first-floor
landing, slightly out of the press of people but giving them
a good view. Mrs. Friar was standing awkwardly in front
of the leader of the choir. Of Professor Hans Godiesky there
was no sign whatsoever while the carols were being sung.

Henry remembered noticing suppressed excitement in the
faces of his niece and nephew perched at the top of the stairs
and hoping it was the music that they had found entrancing
and not the piles of mince pies awaiting them among the decorative smilax on the credenza at the back of the hall.

They—and everyone else—fell upon them nonetheless
as soon as the last carol had been sung. There was a hot
punch, too, carefully mulled to just the right temperature
by Tom Witherington, for those old enough to partake of
it, and home-made lemonade for the young.

Almost before the last choirboy had scoffed the last
mince pie the party at the Witheringtons' broke up.

The pharmacist and his wife were the first to leave. They
shook hands all round.

"I know it's early," said Lorraine Steele apologetically,
"but I'm afraid Robert's poor old tummy's been playing
him up again." Henry, who had been expecting a rather
limp paw, was surprised to find how firm her handshake
was.

"If you'll forgive us," said Lorraine's husband to
Wendy, "I think we'd better be on our way now." Robert
Steele essayed a glassy, strained smile, but to Henry's eye
he looked more than a little white at the gills. Perhaps he,
too, had spotted that the ring that was his Christmas present
to his wife had got a nasty stain on the inner side of it.

The pair hurried off together in a flurry of farewells. Then the wispy Miss Hooper declared the evening a great success but said she wanted to check everything at St. Faith's before the midnight service, and she, too, slipped away.

"What I want to know," said Dora Watkins provocatively when the rest of the guests had reassembled in the drawing-room and Edward and Jennifer had been sent back—very unwillingly—to bed, "is whether it's better to be an old man's darling or a young man's slave?"

A frown crossed Wendy's face. "I'm not sure," she said seriously.

"I reckon our Mrs. Steele's got her husband where she wants him, all right," said Peter Watkins, "don't you?"

"Come back, William Wilberforce, there's more work on slavery still to be done," said Tom Witherington lightly. "What about a night-cap, anyone?"

But there were no takers, and in a few moments the Friars, too, had left.

Wendy suddenly said she had decided against going to the Midnight Service after all and would see everyone in the morning. The rest of the household also opted for an early night and in the event Henry Tyler was the only one of the party to attend the Midnight Service at St. Faith's church that night.

The words of the last carol, "We Three Kings of Orient Are . . ." were still ringing in his ears as he crossed the Market Square to the church. Henry wished that the Foreign Office had only kings to deal with: life would be simpler then. Dictators and Presidents—particularly one President not so very many miles from "perfidious Albion"—were much more unpredictable.

He hummed the words of the last verse of the carol as he climbed the church steps:

> Myrrh is mine; it's bitter perfume
> Breathes a life of gathering gloom;
> Sorrowing, sighing, bleeding, dying,
> Sealed in the stone-cold tomb.

Perhaps, he thought, as he sought a back pew and his nostrils caught the inimical odor of a mixture of burning candles and church flowers, he should have been thinking of frankincense or even—when he saw the burnished candlesticks and altar cross—Melchior's gold . . .

His private orisons were interrupted a few minutes later by a sudden flurry of activity near the front of the church, and he looked up in time to see little Miss Hooper being helped out by the two churchwardens.

"If I might just have a drink of water," he heard her say before she was borne off to the vestry. "I'll be all right in a minute. So sorry to make a fuss. So very sorry . . ."

The rector's sermon was its usual interminable length and he was able to wish his congregation a happy Christmas as they left the church. As Henry walked back across the square he met Dr. Friar coming out of the Steeles' house.

"Chap's collapsed," he murmured. "Severe epigastric pain and vomiting. Mrs. Steele came around to ask me if I would go and see him. There was blood in the vomit and that frightened her."

"It would," said Henry. "He's pretty ill," said the doctor.

"I'm getting him into hospital as soon as possible."

"Could it have been something he ate here?" said Henry, telling him about little Miss Hooper.

"Too soon to tell but quite possible," said the doctor gruffly. "You'd better check how the others are when you get in. I rather think Wendy might be ill, too, from the look of her when we left, and I must say my wife wasn't feeling too grand when I went out. Ring me if you need me."

Henry came back to a very disturbed house indeed, with several bedroom lights on. No one was very ill but Wendy and Mrs. Godiesky were distinctly unwell. Dora Watkins was perfectly all right and was busy ministering to those that weren't.

Happily, there was no sound from the children's room and he crept in there to place a full stocking beside each of their beds. As he came back downstairs to the hall, he thought he heard an ambulance bell next door.

"The position will be clearer in the morning," he said to himself, a Foreign Office man to the end of his fingertips.

It was.

Half the Witherington household had had a severe gastro-intestinal upset during the night, and Robert Steele had died in the Berebury Royal Infirmary at about two o'clock in the morning.

When Henry met his sister on Christmas morning she had a very wan face indeed.

"Oh, Henry," she cried, "isn't it terrible about Robert Steele? And the rector says half the young Waits were ill in the night, too, and poor little Miss Hooper as well!"

"That lets the punch out, doesn't it?" said Henry thoughtfully, "seeing as the youngsters weren't supposed to have any."

"Cook says . . ."

"Is she all right?" inquired Henry curiously.

"She hasn't been ill, if that's what you mean, but she's very upset." Wendy sounded quite nervous. "Cook says nothing like this has ever happened to her before."

"It hasn't happened to her now," pointed out Henry unkindly but Wendy wasn't listening.

"And Edward and Jennifer are all right, thank goodness," said Wendy a little tearfully. "Tom's beginning to feel better but I hear Mrs. Friar's pretty ill still and poor Mrs. Godiesky is feeling terrible. And as for Robert Steele . . . I just don't know what to think. Oh, Henry, I feel it's all my fault."

"Well, it wasn't the lemonade," deduced Henry. "Both children had lots. I saw them drinking it."

"They had a mince pie each, too," said their mother. "I noticed. But some people who had them have been very ill since . . ."

"Exactly, my dear. Some, but not all."

"But what could it have been, then?" quavered Wendy. "Cook is quite sure she only used the best of everything. And it stands to reason it was something that they ate here." She struggled to put her fears into words. "Here was the only place they all were."

"It stands to reason that it was something they were given here," agreed Henry, whom more than one ambassador had accused of pedantry, "which is not quite the same thing."

She stared at him. "Henry, what do you mean?"

Inspector Milson knew what he meant.

It was the evening of Boxing Day when he and Constable Bewman came to the Witheringtons' house.

"A number of people would appear to have suffered from the effects of ingesting a small quantity of a dangerous substance at this address," Milsom announced to the company assembled at his behest. "One with fatal results."

Mrs. Godiesky shuddered. "Me, I suffer a lot."

"Me, too," Peter Watkins chimed in.

"But not, I think, sir, your wife?" Inspector Milsom looked interrogatively at Dora Watkins.

"No, Inspector," said Dora. "I was quite all right."

"Just as well," said Tom Witherington. He still looked pale. "We needed her to look after us."

"Quite so," said the Inspector.

"It wasn't food poisoning, then?" said Wendy eagerly. "Cook will be very pleased . . ."

"It would be more accurate, madam," said Inspector Milsom, who didn't have a cook to be in awe of, "to say that there was poison in the food."

Wendy paled. "Oh . . ."

"This dangerous substance of which you speak," inquired Professor Godiesky with interest, "is its nature known?"

"In England," said the Inspector, "we call it corrosive sublimate . . ."

"Mercury? Ah," the refugee nodded sagely, "that would explain everything."

"Not quite everything, sir," said the inspector mildly. "Now, if we might see you one at a time, please."

"This poison, Inspector," said Henry after he had given his account of the carol-singing to the two policemen, "I take it that it is not easily available?"

"That is correct, sir. But specific groups of people can obtain it."

"Doctors and pharmacists?" hazarded Henry.

"And certain manufacturers . . . "

"Certain . . . Oh, Uncle George?" said Henry. "Of course. There's plenty of mercury in thermometers."

"The old gentleman is definitely a little confused, sir."

"And Professors of Chemistry?" said Henry.

"In his position," said the Inspector judiciously, "I should myself have considered having something with me just in case."

"There being a fate worse than death," agreed Henry swiftly, "such as life in some places in Europe today. Inspector, might I ask what form this poison takes?"

"It's a white crystalline substance."

"Easily confused with sugar?"

"It would seem easily enough," said the policeman dryly.

"And what you don't know, Inspector," deduced Henry intelligently, "is whether it was scattered on the mince pies . . . I take it it was on the mince pies?"

"They were the most likely vehicle," conceded the policeman.

"By accident or whether it was meant to make a number of people slightly ill or . . ."

"Or," put in Detective Constable Bewman keenly, "one person very ill indeed?"

"Or," persisted Henry quietly, "both."

"That is so." He gave a dry cough. "As it happens it did both make several people ill and one fatally so."

"Which also might have been intended?" Nobody had ever called Henry slow.

"From all accounts," said Milsom obliquely, "Mr. Steele had a weak tummy before he ingested the corrosive sublimate of mercury."

"Uncle George wasn't ill, was he?"

"No, sir, nor Dr. Friar." He gave his dry cough. "I am told that Dr. Friar never partakes of pastry."

"Mrs. Steele?"

"Slightly ill. She says she just had one mince pie. Mrs. Watkins didn't have any. Nor did the Professor."

"The one without the parsley," quoted Henry, "is the one without the poison."

"Just so, sir. It would appear at first sight from our immediate calculations quite possible that . . ."

"Inspector, if you can hedge your bets as well as that before you say anything, we could find you a job in the Foreign Office."

"Thank you, sir. As I was saying, sir, it is possible that the poison was only in the mince pies furthest from the staircase. Bewman here has done a chart of where the victims took their pies from."

"Which would explain why some people were unaffected," said Henry.

"Which might explain it, sir." The Inspector clearly rivalled Henry in his precision. "The Professor just wasn't there to take one at all. He says he went to his room to finish his wife's Christmas present. He was carving something for her out of a piece of old wood."

"Needs must when the devil drives," responded Henry absently. He was still thinking. "It's a pretty little problem, as they say."

"Means and opportunity would seem to be present," murmured Milsom.

"That leaves motive, doesn't it?" said Henry.

"The old gentleman mightn't have had one, seeing he's as he is, sir, if you take my meaning and of course we don't know anything about the Professor and his wife, do we, sir? Not yet."

"Not a thing."

"That leaves the doctor . . ."

"I'd've murdered Mrs. Friar years ago," announced Henry cheerfully, "if she had been my wife."

"And Mrs. Steele." There was a little pause and then Inspector Milsom said, "I understand the new young assistant at the pharmacy is more what you might call a contemporary of Mrs. Steele."

"Ah, so that's the way the wind's blowing, is it?"

"And then, sir," said the policeman, "after motive there's still what we always call down at the station the fourth dimension of crime . . ."

"And what might that be, Inspector?"

"Proof." He got up to go. "Thank you for your help, sir."

Henry sat quite still after the two policemen had gone, his memory teasing him. Someone he knew had been poisoned with corrosive sublimate of mercury, served to him in tarts. By a tart, too, if history was to be believed.

No, not someone he knew.

Someone he knew of.

Someone they knew about at the Foreign Office because it had been a political murder, a famous political murder set around an eternal triangle . . .

Henry Tyler sought out Professor Godiesky and explained.

"It was recorded by contemporary authors," Henry said, "that when the tarts poisoned with mercury were delivered to the Tower of London for Sir Thomas Overbury, the fingernail of the woman delivering them had accidentally been poked through the pastry . . ."

The professor nodded sapiently. "And it was stained black?"

"That's right," said Henry. History did have some lessons to teach, in spite of what Henry Ford had said. "But it would wash off?"

"Yes," said Hans Godiesky simply.

"So I'm afraid that doesn't get us anywhere, does it?"

The academic leaned forward slightly, as if addressing a tutorial. "There is, however, one substance on which mercury always leaves its mark."

"There is?" said Henry.

"Its—how do you say it in English?—its ineradicable mark."

"That's how we say it," said Henry slowly. "And which substance, sir, would that be?"

"Gold, Mr. Tyler. Mercury stains gold."

"For ever?"

"For ever." He waved a hand. "An amalgam is created."

"And I," Henry gave a faint smile, "I was foolish enough to think it was diamonds that were forever."

"Pardon?"

"Nothing, Professor. Nothing at all. Forgive me, but I think I may be able to catch the Inspector and tell him to look to the lady. And her gold wedding ring."

"Look to the lady?" The refugee was now totally bewildered. "I do not understand . . ."

"It's a quotation."

"Ach, sir, I fear I am only a scientist."

"There's a better quotation," said Henry, "about looking to science for the righting of wrongs. I rather think Mrs. Steele may have looked to science, too, to—er—improve her lot. And if she carefully scattered the corrosive sublimate over some mince pieces and not others it would have been with her left hand . . ."

"Because she was left-handed," said the Professor immediately. "That I remember. And you think one mince pie would have had—I know the English think this important—more than its fair share?"

"I do. Then all she had to do was to give her husband that one and Bob's your uncle. Clever of her to do it in someone else's house."

Hans Godiesky looked totally mystified. "And who was Bob?"

"Don't worry about Bob," said Henry from the door. "Think about Melchior and his gold instead."

Catherine Aird is the author of seventeen detective stories and a volume of crime short stories. She is a former Chairman of the Crime Writers Association and is one of the editors of the forthcoming Oxford University Press of New York *Companion to Crime and Mystery Writing*. She is thankful that Christmas comes but once a year.